LAS VEGAS NOIR

LAS VEGAS NOIR

EDITED BY
JARRET KEENE & TODD JAMES PIERCE

AKASHIC BOOKS
NEW YORK

Published by Akashic Books
©2008 Akashic Books

Series concept by Tim McLoughlin and Johnny Temple
Las Vegas map by Sohrab Habibion

ISBN-13: 978-1-933354-49-1
Library of Congress Control Number: 2007939596
All rights reserved

Printed in Canada
First printing

Akashic Books
PO Box 1456
New York, NY 10009
info@akashicbooks.com
www.akashicbooks.com

Also in the Akashic Noir Series:

Forthcoming:

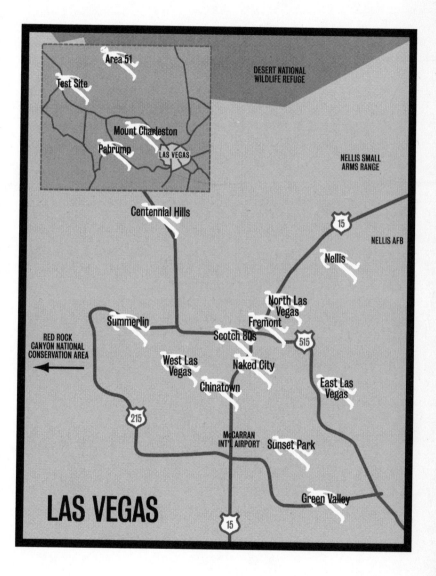

To John O'Brien and his sister Erin O'Brien

TABLE OF CONTENTS

PART III: TALES FROM THE OUTSKIRTS

INTRODUCTION
The Most Dangerous City in America

O*oh, Las Vegas,*" sang the pioneering country-rocker Gram Parsons. "*Every time I hit your Crystal City, you know you're gonna make a wreck out of me.*" As Las Vegans, we regularly read about these wrecked lives in newspapers and magazines. We routinely observe people going about their wildly destructive antics on mainstream TV. Often we can't believe these stories are unfolding in our city. They almost seem like put-ons, elaborate pranks borrowed from atrocious cut-rate screenplays. But there they are, these inhabitants of our city, their mug shots staring us down, making us wonder if what Parsons said is really true—that in Las Vegas your only real friend is the queen of spades.

How crazy does crime get in Las Vegas? Well, consider these tales taken from local papers:

Husband-and-wife champion bodybuilders strangle their personal assistant, torching her body in a red Jaguar in the Vegas desert. Eventually police apprehend the couple in a shopping center, where the killers are drinking root beer and getting manicures.

Failing in his effort to sexually assault a female parishioner, a Catholic priest clobbers his intended victim with a wine bottle before going on the lam. According to a police report, he tells the church worker, her consciousness fading, "I am over the edge."

And then there's this: O.J. Simpson, who years ago was found "not guilty" of decapitating his wife and her lover, storms into a hotel room with armed accomplices to "retrieve items that belonged to him," sports memorabilia like his Hall of Fame certificate and photos of him standing beside J. Edgar Hoover.

On it goes, a litany of wicked behavior and stupid folly. People come from all over the world to do dumb, dangerous things in Sin City, whether it's someone locking himself in a Fremont Street motel to kick a nasty heroin habit, hooking up to an oxygen tank in a last-ditch scheme to double his nest egg at the downtown slots, or shooting a weekend porn flick that goes disastrously wrong once a rabid pit bull is introduced. In these true-life narratives, no one shows up in Las Vegas to do anything smart, tactful, or even kind. Instead, they come here to fuck up. Big time.

The sheer range of true Las Vegas crime—no doubt spurred on by the city's explosive growth (which recently passed the two million mark)—can be intimidating to crime writers and readers alike. How can literary fiction surpass the strangeness of this place? Indeed, it takes a lot to top the gaudy spectacle that is Las Vegas, and we're happy to report that the writers who contributed to this volume have done just that. They've beaten the odds to conjure characters and stories that transcend any of the lurid dramas of Vegas you'll read about in newspapers or watch on the tube.

The stories gathered in *Las Vegas Noir* are written by long-time residents and avid chroniclers of Sin City, authors who take you far beyond the neon of Caesars Palace and into neighborhoods too dangerous for *CSI*. Absolutely cliché-free, these stories are full of flesh-and-blood characters trapped in dire circumstances that only real Las Vegas neighborhoods can spring.

The late John O'Brien, author of *Leaving Las Vegas*, gives us the story "The Tik," in which a junkie hooked on a mysterious drug reunites with his wealthy ex-lover to embark on a thrill-killing expedition. In David Corbett's mystifying "Pretty

Little Parasite," a Fremont Street cocktail waitress plagued by Holocaust nightmares believes coke dealing is the best way to become a stay-at-home mom. In Lori Kozlowski's "Three Times a Night, Every Other Night," an Irish pub singer banished to North Las Vegas and at the end of his professional rope is destined for a mobbed-up fate. Jaq Greenspon's "Disappear" centers on a down-and-out magician whose former assistant steals money—and may be fingering him to the bad guys. And in Celeste Starr's chilling "Dirty Blood," a simple pickup in a gay bar takes an unusual twist when the protagonist finds more than lubricant in his date's sock drawer.

There is plenty of heartbreak and humor (albeit of the blackest order) too. In Tod Goldberg's "Mitzvah," for instance, a con man masquerading as a rabbi feels trapped in the suburbs until he plans a brutal means of escape. In Scott Phillips's "Babs," an ex-stripper turned bar owner drags along a visiting Midwestern cartoon aficionado to reclaim some meth for a mutual friend. And Vu Tran's devastating "This or Any Desert" explores the fractured psyche of a renegade cop looking to avenge his Asian ex-wife's physical abuse at the hands of her new husband, a Chinatown businessman, with searing emotional and psychological insight.

Like we said, as fantastic and diverse as the Strip can be at night, it's got nothing on the vast array of stories collected here. Indeed, *Las Vegas Noir*, as you will soon discover, brings you into the gaudy bosom of our fair city—that is, the gaudy, lethal bosom that eventually presents itself once you wander far away from the Strip.

Jarret Keene & Todd James Pierce
Las Vegas, Nevada
March 2008

PART I

Sin City

THE TIK

BY JOHN O'BRIEN

Scotch 80s

Part of me wished that I had asked the cab to wait. I hadn't. I stared up at the big double doors, weathered from the desert sun, yes, but still so imposing that you half expected to see a muscled bodyguard when they opened. The doorbell didn't work. It never had. I felt the familiar quiver begin in the back of my neck as twice I dropped the ornate knocker, an upside-down black iron cross. I peered over my back to see if the cab was still in sight. The long drive was empty.

Despite the impending nightfall, I noticed the German shepherd asleep on the grass, his white face a beacon in the otherwise black lawn. I knew this dog and wondered if he would remember me. I walked over to nudge him awake.

When I had last left this house over ten years ago, I was certain that I was through with this all-consuming part of my life, but as I bent over to pet the dog, it was clear this place was far from finished with me; rather, like the dog, it was merely lying in wait for some new awakening. The shepherd lifted his head and growled, but whether the snarl was for me or something else, I did not know. I followed his gaze and was startled to find that I was being watched by a tall slim figure, standing where only moments before the closed doors had been.

"Timmers, you're back," she said, not at all surprised to see me.

I cringed at her easy, reflexive use of my nickname; at her prosaic manner of observation, as if I'd just returned from a short walk—when in fact I had been gone for a decade. This meeting was nothing less than heart-stopping for me.

"Melinda, I . . . I didn't hear the door open. You startled me . . ." So much so, in fact, that I couldn't remember anything that I had planned to say. "You sound as if you've been expecting me." She ignored this.

"Come in," she said.

As I followed her through the foyer and into the heart of the house, I began to feel a sort of resignation; a feeling that, now that I had set things in motion, I could sit back and relax, free from the burden of decision making. It was not an unpleasant outlook.

"Christ," I said as we walked into the living room, its windowed ceiling a full twenty feet above me. "I'd forgotten how damn big this place is."

"I doubt that," she responded. "Still drink bourbon?"

"Finally a question. Apparently there is at least one thing that you're not sure of." I was starting to feel cocky. How else could I feel? I'd come this far into the house, into my past. The less I thought about it, the better it felt. I was comfortable here. Melinda understood me in a way that no one else could.

"Not really, Timmers." She reached into an antique Spanish sideboard and extracted a dusty bottle of Wild Turkey.

"My brand, even. I'm impressed." I narrowed my eyes and grinned at her. Her presence was making me giddy. I was excited—this was so easy. She knew why I was here. It was like being in a cathouse—no pretense. You ask for sex and they give it to you. But a cathouse would seem like a church compared to this place.

"Your bottle, actually," she said.

"Fuck it," I said. "We can drink all we want later."

Without missing a beat she set down the bottle, picked up my hand, and turned silently toward the staircase. I willingly followed her determined walk and flowing silk robe. This was the beginning of the end of ten years' anxiety. It seemed as if I'd barely been away. Right now nothing seemed less relevant than my time away from her.

But I did have that time, and I had to remember that. I had to remember the futile years of trying to ignore this hidden life, with Melinda and this extravagant house standing at the center. I had to remember why I was here.

Why was I here?

What if I did like it? Liking it—living it—had been the whole point. I was back now and it was time to unlearn compassion and let Melinda take me again.

We climbed the staircase to her bedroom; ten years since it had been *our* bedroom and yet it looked exactly the same to me. Perhaps it would always be our bedroom. Melinda dropped my hand and turned to face me. She stepped back and looked into my eyes as she untied her robe and let it fall to the floor. I was amazed at her perfection. Though life had left its many marks on my body, she was just as I remembered—flawless, still possessing all the curves and textures of a nineteen-year-old showgirl.

She unbuttoned my shirt and in a moment I, too, was naked. Melinda wrapped herself around me. I lifted her onto the bed, the raw heat rising inside of me. It was exactly as I remembered. I ran my hands along her thighs, stopping short of the cleft of her. Her nipples were hard and brown. I took one between my teeth, one between thumb and finger, and bit and pinched with exacting pressure. Melinda cried out, but did not move to stop me. She was open beneath me, ready. It was time. I licked and tasted her until her legs quivered on the brink. I stopped short of her orgasm and lay on top of her, breathing in the intermission. Finally, I pushed into her. She climaxed in waves, acute bursts of pleasure. I was close behind, teetering on that exquisite edge.

Melinda sensed this, as I knew she would, and stopped all her motion. At once my imminent climax was completely in her control. She slid from beneath me and sat up on the side of the bed. She opened the nightstand drawer. I waited, trembling, as she extracted a stainless steel tray and with slick efficiency prepared the injection. The glowing black fluid filled the syringe. My hardness raged. I swallowed against it all, my throat dry.

At that moment it was impossible for me to understand how I had stayed away from this drug—we called it "The Tik"—for all those years. I had never heard of it outside this room and had never looked for it elsewhere. Somehow I knew that it existed nowhere but here. This place was as much a part of The Tik as I, moments before, had been a part of Melinda. She lived here in a desert oasis with it, and the whole scene had always been one great, indivisible, seductive, eternal entity to me. I had once believed that I could escape it by running. Now I had run back, and was going to try to escape another way.

Melinda tapped the needle of the syringe with a long red fingernail. The sexual tension and my own anticipation had my heart nearly beating out of my chest. My bloodstream was primed to rush the drug to my brain. Melinda turned, ready with the needle. I closed my eyes and offered my arm.

The beautiful pinch.

As the hot fluid rushed through my veins, Melinda prepared another hypo and injected herself. Then she dropped the syringe onto the tray and kicked it, lunging into me. As the stainless steel and empty vial clattered to the floor, Melinda clutched my waist and took me into her mouth. The heat of The Tik inside of me and the heat of Melinda's tongue outside of me combined into that perfect euphoria I'd known only within these walls. She held me on the brink for as long as she could. Then I yelled out, pumping into her.

The feeling of being alive poured over me, elemental and singular. We were finally together again.

The Tik.

We blinked in the aftermath, verifying it was real. I lay on my back, Melinda's head on my stomach. Then she reared up and playfully bit me. I laughed and pushed her off. Full of new energy, I bounded out of the bed and down the stairs, returning with the bottle of bourbon. Melinda already had her panties on and was rolling up her fishnets. I sucked the bottle as I watched her dress. She grabbed it from me and took a big swallow.

"I have a surprise for you," she said. She shoved the bottle back into my hand and pulled open the door of what had been my closet. I was stunned. Before me hung all my old clothes, just as I had left them.

I laughed. "Unfuckingbelievable. Do you still have the Jag too?"

"In the garage," she said.

Nothing had changed.

Melinda and the drug were working in perfect harmony. My head spun with satisfaction and lust. I grinned wildly and shook on the leather jacket that had always fit me like a second skin. It still did. My boots, my jeans, everything was in place. I gulped some more bourbon and pounced on Melinda.

We fell onto the bed and I ripped off the black lace bra she had just put on. She laughed as the zipper on my jacket scratched her. We fucked again, more perfunctorily this time, then got dressed.

After finishing the bottle of bourbon we went down to the garage. Melinda's vintage Jag, a black 1967 XKE, was still in perfect shape, just as I, by now, expected everything to be. The car had also fit me. I slid into the driver's seat and palmed the bulb of the stick shift. Melinda's perfume blended with the smell of leather and night air. We squealed down the driveway and onto the moneyed side street. The ragtop was down and the wind blew Melinda's hair all around. I flew through a red light. We vanished into the night.

We headed for the Strip, battling traffic. I didn't mind. I basked in the stares this beautiful woman and car garnered beneath the streetlights and neon.

"Let's go to the Barbary Coast," I said.

"The Barbary Coast? You've got to be kidding," said Melinda. "Why?"

"Dunno," I said, shrugging my shoulders. "The $3.99 prime rib dinner?"

Melinda laughed, throwing her head back. "Oh, Timmers," she said. "I'd forgotten how you make me laugh."

We parked off the Strip and starting walking hand in hand through the crowd. The Tik pulsed inside me and mixed with the bourbon. Melinda was on my arm. I was ten feet tall.

Overweight Midwesterners stared at the two of us, wishing they could be us. We were the Las Vegas they came to see. A middle-aged man in Bermuda shorts eyed Melinda's long legs.

"Loosest slots on the Strip," I said to him with a conspiratorial nod as we passed. Completely stunned, he looked up at me, his mouth agape. Melinda and I folded with laughter, then broke into a run.

After a few minutes, Melinda stopped, breathless, and turned to me. She squeezed my hand. Her nails broke the skin.

"It feels so good to have you back, Tim," she said.

I pushed her against the cold brick wall and put my mouth on hers while pressing my thigh between her legs.

"I love you," I whispered. My hand was sticky with blood.

She returned my kiss, our tongues rolling together until Melinda pulled back.

"Why then," she said, "are you going to make me go in there?" She nodded toward the billowing entrance of the Coast.

"Come on," I said. "I feel so good. I feel like slumming. And if we don't find any action in there"—I indicated the space in front of me with a grandiose sweep of my arm—"the entire Strip awaits us." We stepped through the forced air plenum and into the clanging miasma of the casino.

A semi-attractive blonde with a very large chest caught my attention. She was sitting alone at a blackjack table.

"I'm going to the girls' room," Melinda shouted over the cacophony of bells and chimes that rang from the slot carousels. "I'll catch up to you in a couple of minutes."

I nodded and watched her meander off, as did most of the people she passed. The fishnet stockings had that effect.

I sat down next to the blonde and threw a hundred dollars on the table. The dealer set a short stack of chips in front of me as a cocktail waitress in a bad pirate costume appeared at my elbow.

"A double bullshot," I said, placing a chip on her tray.

"What's that?" said the blonde as she slurped at a frothy blender drink.

"It's beef bouillon and vodka," I said, peering at my cards.

She wrinkled her nose into a grimace. "*Ewww!* Why are you drinking *that*?" The end of her straw was coated in waxy orange lipstick.

"I'm hungry," I said. After all, I was. I nodded yes to a hit from the dealer.

"That's so gross," she said.

"Fuck you," I said. Maybe semi-attractive was too generous a description for her, stacked or not. The bad casino lighting wasn't shoring up her odds either. "Now shut up and finish your snow cone."

"Okay, I will," she said. "And then you can."

"I can what?" I said, rolling my eyes. The waitress set down my drink with exactly the speed a pre-tip buys. I placed another chip on her tray and turned back to the blonde.

"You can fuck me," she said as the dealer flipped over his jack and ace.

"Who the fuck are you?" With characteristically perfect timing and an equally perfect brunette, led by the hand, Melinda intervened. The blonde sized up the two women and picked up her drink. "I'm more than you could handle anyway," she said, then collected her remaining chips and walked away, flipping us off.

"Tim, this is Teena," said Melinda, not even looking after the blonde. "She's new in town. Just got a job as a waitress over at the Peppermill."

"After I finish the training course," said Teena. "Of course," she added, giggling at her own quip.

"Right," said Melinda. "After you finish the training course." She wrapped an arm around Teena's waist and turned to me. "She's coming home with us for a nightcap." One look at Teena and I could see that Melinda had bribed her with the coke she always kept in her purse.

"Hi, Tim. I saw you walk in and thought you were really cute. I'm really glad to meet you," said Teena. She seemed like a willing little lamb, naïve and very sexy. Exactly what I'd had in mind.

"With that perky attitude," I said, "my bet is you'll sail right through that training course." Teena gave me a prom queen smile. Perfect, just like everything else so far.

"So what do you say, Tim?" asked Melinda, though she already knew the answer. "Nightcaps at our place?"

Our place. "That sounds just fine," I said. "First let's have a drink for the road." I pushed a chip toward the dealer and steered the girls around to the bar. "Will you be riding with us, Teena, or do you have your own car?"

"Teena will follow us out to the house," said Melinda, lifting an eyebrow down the bar.

I smiled at Teena.

"What can I get for you?" said the bartender, one eye eclipsed by a fake black eye patch.

Melinda looked at me. "Make a wish," she said.

I motioned Teena to park next to the Jag in the garage. Melinda took Teena inside to show her around while I looked over Teena's Honda and then locked up the garage. I went in the back door of the house and found Melinda and Teena necking in the kitchen. I didn't seem to disturb them.

"Save some for me, Mel," I said. "Anyone want a drink?"

"Tequila," said Melinda.

"Got any champagne?" asked Teena.

I headed for the sideboard to crack open a new bottle of bourbon.

"Join us upstairs when you're ready, Timmers," Melinda shouted down the hall. She was anxious despite her cool veneer. It had been a long time for her too. I was eager to do a number on Teena, but something vague seemed to be holding me back. *Fuck that*, I thought, and took the longest drink of bourbon in my life.

By the time I got up to the bedroom, Melinda's face was buried between Teena's legs. Teena seemed a little dazed but was holding up her end quite well, no doubt aided by the small mountain of coke next to her on the nightstand. Melinda saw me and bolted upright. She was covered with sweat.

"Fuck her, Tim," she said. "Fuck her proper."

Teena rolled over and did another line, then she lay back on the bed. "Yeah, fuck me," she said.

I did. I was rough but she took it. When I got off her, bruises started to form on the insides of her thighs. I reached for the bourbon and watched her and Melinda work on each other. I felt strange. The Tik still moved through me, though now at an even keel. I drank more bourbon.

I drank for a long time.

Melinda screamed and dug her nails into Teena's skin. Teena threw her head back on the pillow. Melinda rolled over and beckoned me. My head was spinning. I placed my hands on Teena's knees and opened her as Melinda reached for the nightstand. I centered all my consciousness on Teena. I focused my whole body on my mouth, and my mouth on her. Melinda moved on the bed. I heard a whisper of rushing air. Teena stiffened and bucked under me. A hot spray rained across my back. Something clinked against the wall. I squeezed Teena's waist with all my strength. Tears came to my eyes. Teena's body went limp.

I lay hugging her, my breath so fast. The room was quiet.

After a time I looked up at Melinda. She smiled and wiped the blood from her eyes. She got off the bed and picked up the straight razor, which she had thrown against the wall. She dropped it in the nightstand drawer.

"You okay, Timmers?" she asked. "I know it's been awhile." She paused, then reached back into the drawer. "Maybe it's time for another shot."

"No," I said. "Not yet."

I picked up the bourbon and had a sip. Melinda closed the drawer and turned toward the bathroom.

"Suit yourself, but we shouldn't wait too long," she said. "I'm going to clean up. Will you take care of that?" She nodded at the blood-soaked bed and the still body, naked and staring wide-eyed at the ceiling.

"Of course I will," I said. "Don't I always?"

I finished the bourbon as Melinda closed the bathroom door behind her. Out the window, dawn announced itself quietly with a barely perceptible change of color in the east. A car started off in the distance and I reflexively glanced at the garage door. It was still locked. I really didn't worry. Melinda and I had always led a charmed existence. I sighed and put on my pants.

"Wash my back, Tim," Melinda called from the shower when she heard me enter the bathroom. I opened the curtain and soaped up my hands. I massaged her back as I washed it.

"Ahhh, that feels good," she said. "Get in here. I'm ready for a good fucking."

She put her cheek against the wall and closed her eyes. I pulled her razor from my back pocket. With one motion I grabbed her hair and drew the blade across her throat. For an instant she stretched her neck out, exposing it even more, and then she slumped quietly to the bottom of the tub. I turned off the water and went into the bedroom, dropped the razor into her nightstand.

I cleaned up and finished dressing in the clothes that I had arrived in the day before. I kissed Teena's forehead. I kissed Melinda's hand and held it to my mouth for a long time.

Downstairs I lit a small fire on the love seat in the living room, then went to the kitchen and turned on all the gas jets. On my way out to the garage I stopped and, as an after-thought, picked up my leather jacket.

I backed the Jag out of the drive and looked for but did not see the German shepherd. It suddenly occurred to me how very old he must have been. As I put the Jag into gear, my eyes paused at the mailbox, an unlikely witness. I pulled away and, driving down the road, watched it disappear in the rearview mirror. I thought about how badly I needed to sleep.

PRETTY LITTLE PARASITE

BY DAVID CORBETT

Fremont

One hand on her hip, the other lofting her cocktail tray, Sam Pitney scanned the gaming floor from the Roundup's mezzanine, dressed in her bright red cowgirl outfit and fresh from a bracing toot in the ladies'. Stream-of-nothingness mode, mid-shift, slow night, only the blow keeping her vertical—and she had this odd craving for some stir-fry—she stared out at the flagging crowd and manically finger-brushed the outcrop of blond bangs showing beneath her tipped-back hat.

Maybe it was seeing her own reflection fragmented in dozens of angled mirrors to the left and right and even overhead, or the sight of the usual trudge of losers wandering the noisy mazelike neon, clutching change buckets, chip trays, chain smoking (still legal, this was the '80s), hoping for one good score to recoup a little dignity—whatever the reason, she found herself revisiting a TV program from a few nights back, about Auschwitz, Dachau, one of those places. Men and women and children and even poor helpless babies cradled by their mothers, stripped naked then marched into giant shower rooms, only to notice too late—doors slamming, bolts thrown, gas soon hissing from the showerheads: a smell like almonds, the voice on the program said.

Sam found herself wondering—no particular reason—what it would be like if the doors to the casino suddenly rumbled shut, trapping everybody inside.

For a moment or two, she supposed, no one would even notice, gamblers being what they are. But soon enough word would ripple through the crowd, especially when the fire sprinklers in the ceiling started to mist. Even then, people would be puzzled and vaguely put out but not frightened, not until somebody nearby started gagging, buckled over, a barking cough, the scalding phlegm, a slime of blood in the palm.

Then panic, the rush for the doors. Animal screams. Blind terror.

Sam wondered where she'd get found when they finally reopened the doors to deal with the dead. Would she be one of those with bloody nails or, worse, fingers worn down to raw gory bone, having tried to claw her way past so many others to sniff at an air vent, a door crack, ready to kill for just one more breath? Or would she be one of the others, one of those they found alone, having caught on quick and then surrendered, figuring she was screwed, knowing it in the pit of her soul, curled up on the floor, waiting for God or Mommy or Satan or who-the-fuck-ever to put an end to the tedious phony bullshit, the nerves and the worry and the always being tired, the lonely winner-takes-all, the grand American nothing . . .

"Could I possibly have another whiskey and ginger, luv?"

Sam snapped to, turning toward the voice—the accent crisply British once, now blurred by years among the Vegas gypsies. It came from a face of singular unlucky pallor: high brow with a sickly froth of chestnut hair, flat bloodless lips, no chin to speak of. The Roundup sat just east of Las Vegas Boulevard on Fremont, closer to the LVMPD tower than the tonier downtown houses—the Four Queens, the Golden Nugget—catering to whoever showed up first and stayed longest, cheap tourists mostly, dopes who'd just stumbled out of the drunk tank and felt lucky (figure that one out), or, most inexplicably, locals, the transplant kind especially, the ones who went on and on about old Las Vegas, which meant goofs like this bird. What was his name? Harvey, Harold, something with an H. He taught at UNLV if she remembered right, came here three nights a week at least, often more, said it was for the nostalgia.

"You are on the clock, my dear, am I right?"

She gazed into his soupy green eyes. Centuries of inbreeding. Hail, Brittania.

"I'm pregnant," she said.

Come midnight she began looking for Mike and found him off by himself in the dollar slots, an odd little nook where there were fewer mirrors and the eye in the sky had a less than perfect angle (he thought of these things). He wore white linen slacks, a pastel tee, the sleeves of his sport jacket rolled up. All Sonny Crockett, the dick.

"Hey," she said, coming up.

He shot her a vaguely proprietary smile. His eyes looked wrecked but his hair was flawless. He said, "The usual?"

"No, weekend coming up. Make it two."

The smile thawed, till it seemed almost friendly. "Double your pleasure."

She clipped off to the bar, ordered a Stoli-rocks-twist, discreetly assembling the twelve twenties on her tray in a tight thin stack. The casino's monotonous racket jangled all around, same at midnight as happy hour—the eternal now, she thought, Vegas time. Returning to where he was sitting, she bowed at the waist, so he could reach the tray. He carefully set a five down, under which he'd tucked two wax-paper bindles. Then he collected the twelve twenties off her tray, as though they were his change, and she remembered the last time they were together, in her bed, the faraway look he got afterwards, not wanting to be touched, the kind of thing guys did when they'd had enough of you.

"Whoever you get this from," she said, "I want to meet him."

From the look on his face, you would've thought she'd asked for the money back. "Come again?"

"You heard me."

He cocked his head. The hair didn't budge. "I'm not sure I like your attitude."

She broke the news. In the span of only a second or so, his expression went from stunned to deflated to distinctly pissed, then: "You saying it's mine?"

She rolled her eyes. "No. An angel came to me."

"Don't get smart."

"Oh, smart's exactly what I'm going for, believe me."

"Okay then, take care of it."

With those few words, she got a picture of his ideal woman—a collie in heat, basically, but with fewer scruples. Lay out a few lines, bend her over the sofa, splay her ass— then a few weeks later, tell her to *take care of it.*

"Sorry," she said. "Not gonna happen."

He chuckled acidly. "Since when are you maternal?"

"Don't think you know me. We fucked, that's it."

"You're shaking me down."

"I'm filling you in. But yeah, I could make this a problem. Instead, I'm trying to do the right thing. For everybody. But I'm not gonna be able to work here much longer, understand? This ain't about you, it's about money. Introduce me to your guy."

He thought about it, and as he did his lips curled into a grin. The eyes were still scared though. "Who says it's a guy?"

A twinge lit up her lower back. Get used to it, she thought. "Don't push me, Mike. I'm a woman scorned, with a muffin in the oven." She did a quick pivot and headed off. Over her shoulder, she added, "I'm off at 2. Set it up."

It didn't happen that night, as it turned out, and that didn't surprise her. What did surprise her was that it happened only two nights later, and she didn't have to hound him half as bad as she'd expected—more surprising still, he hadn't been jiving: It really wasn't a guy.

Her name was Claudia, a Cuban, maybe fifty, could pass for forty, calm dark eyes that waxed and waned between cordial welcome and cold appraisal—a tiny woman, raven-black hair coiled tight into a long braid, body as sleek as a razor, sheathed in a simple black dress. She lived in one of the newer condos at the other end of Fremont, near Sahara, where it turned into Boulder Highway.

Claudia showed them in, dead-bolted the door, offered a cool muscular hand to Sam with a nod, then gestured everyone into the living room: suede furniture, Navajo rugs, ferns. Two fluffed and imperial Persian cats nestled near the window on matching cushions. Across the room, a mobile of tiny tin birds, dozens of them, all painted bright tropical colors, hung from the ceiling. Interesting, Sam thought, glancing up as she tucked her skirt against her thighs. Thing must torment the cats.

"Like I said before," Mike began, addressing Claudia, "I think this is a bad idea, but you said okay, so here we are."

Sam resisted an urge to storm over, take two fistfuls of that pampered hair, and rip it out by the roots. She turned to the woman. "Can we talk alone?"

"That doesn't work for me," Mike said.

With the grace of a model, Claudia slowly pivoted toward him. "I think it's for the best." For the sake of his pride, she added, "I'm sure I'll be fine."

That was that. He sulked off to the patio, the two women talked. It didn't take long for Sam to explain her situation, lay out her plan, make it clear she wasn't being flaky or impulsive. She'd thought it through—she didn't want to get even, pick off Mike's customers, nothing like that. "I don't want to hand my baby off to day care, some stranger. I want to be there. At home."

Claudia eyed her, saying nothing, for what seemed an eternity. Don't look away, Sam told herself. Accept the scrutiny, know your role. But don't act scared.

"There are those," Claudia said finally, "who would find what you just said very peculiar." Her smile seemed a kind of warning, and yet it wasn't without warmth. "I'm sure you realize that."

"I do. But I think you understand."

It turned out she understood only too well—she had a son, Marco, eleven years old, away at boarding school in Seville. "I miss him terribly." She made a sawing motion. "Like someone cut off my arm."

"Why don't you have him here, with you?"

For the first time, Claudia looked away. Her face darkened. "Mothers make sacrifices. It's not all about staying home with the baby."

Sam felt backward, foolish, hopelessly American. Behold the future, she thought, ten years down the road, doing this, and your kid is where? In the corner of her eye, she saw one of the cats rise sleepily and arch its back. Out on the patio, Mike sat in the moonlight, a sudden red glow as he dragged on his cigarette.

Claudia steered the conversation to terms: Sam would start off buying ounces at two thousand dollars each, which she would divide into grams and eightballs for sale. If things went well, she could move up to a QP—quarter pound—at $7,800, build her clientele. She might well plateau at that point, many did. If she was ambitious, though, she could move up to an elbow—for "lb," meaning a pound—with the tacit agreement she would not interfere with Claudia's wholesale trade.

"I want you to look me in the eye, Samantha. Good. Do not confuse my sympathy for weakness. I'm generous by nature. That doesn't mean I'm stupid. I have men who take care of certain matters for me, men not at all like our friend out there." She nodded toward Mike all alone on the moonlit patio. "These men, you will never meet them unless it comes to that. And if it does, the time will have passed for you to say or do anything to help yourself. I trust I'm clear."

The first and oddest thing? She lost five pounds. God, she thought, what have I done? She checked her sheets for blood, then ran to Valley Medical, no appointment, demanded to see her ob-gyn. The receptionist—sagging desert face, kinky gray perm—shot her one of those knowing, gallingly sympathetic looks you never really live down.

"Your body thinks you've got a parasite, dear," the woman said. "Just keep eating."

She did, and she stunned herself, how quickly her habits turned healthy. No more coke, ditto booze—instead a passion for bananas (craving potassium), an obsession with yogurt (good for bone mass, the immune system, the intestinal lining), a sudden interest in whole grains (to keep her regular), citrus (for iron absorption), even liver (prevent anemia). She took to grazing, little meals here and there, to keep the nausea at bay, and when her appetite craved more she turned to her newfound favorite: stir-fry.

She continued working for three months, time enough to groom a clientele—fellow casino rats (her old quitting-time buddies, basically, and their buddies), a few select customers from the Roundup (including, strangely enough, Harry the homely Brit, who came from Manchester, she learned, taught mechanical engineering, vacationed in Cabo most winters, not half the schmuck she'd pegged him for), plus a few locals she decided to trust (the girls at Diva's Hair-and-Nail, the boys at Monte Carlo Tanning Salon, a locksmith named Nick Perino, had a shop just up Fremont Street, total card, used to host a midnight movie show in town)—all of this happening in the shadow of the police tower on Stewart Avenue, all those cops just four blocks away.

Business was brisk. She got current on her bills, socked away a few grand. At sixteen weeks her stomach popped out, like she'd suddenly inflated, and that was the end of cocktail shift. Sam bid it goodbye with no regrets, the red pleated dress, the cowboy hat, the tasseled boots. From that point forward, she conducted business where she pleased, permitting a trustworthy inner circle to come to her place, the others she met out and about, merrily invisible in her maternity clothes.

The birth was strangely easy, two-hour labor, a snap by most standards, and Sam shed twenty pounds before heading home. The best thing about seeing it go was no longer having to endure strangers—older women especially, riding with her in elevators or standing in line at the store—who would notice the tight globe of her late-term belly and instinctively reach out, stroke the shuddering roundness, cooing in a helpless, mysterious, covetous way that almost rekindled Sam's child-hood fear of witches.

As for the last of the weight gain, it all seemed to settle in her chest—first time in her life, she had cleavage. This little girl's been good to you all over, Sam thought—her skin shone, her eyes glowed, she looked happy. Guys seemed to notice, clients especially, but she made sure to keep it all professional: So much as hint at sex with coke in the room, next thing you knew the guy'd be eyeing your muff like it was veal.

Besides, the interest on her end had vanished. Curiously, that didn't faze her. Whatever it was she'd once craved from her lovers she now got from Natalie, feeling it strongest when she nursed, enjoying something she'd secretly thought didn't exist—the kind of fierce unshakeable oneness she'd always thought was just Hollywood. Now she knew better. The crimped pink face, the curled doughy hands, the wispy black strands of impossibly fine hair: "Look at you," she'd whisper, over and over and over.

By the end of two months, she'd pitched all her old clothes, not just the maternity duds. Some bad habits got the heave-ho as well: the trashy attitude, slutty speech, negative turns of mind. Nor would the apartment do anymore—too dark, too small, too blah. The little one deserves better, she told herself, as does her mother. Besides, maybe someone had noticed all the in-and-out, the visitors night and day. Half paranoia, half healthy faith in who she'd become, she upscaled to a three-bedroom out on Boulder Highway, furnished it in suede, added ferns. She bought two cats.

Nick Perino sat alone in an interview room in the Stewart Avenue tower—dull yellow walls, scuffed black linoleum, humming fluorescent light—tapping his thumbs together and cracking his neck as he waited. Finally the door opened, and he tried to muster some advantage, assert control, by challenging the man who entered, blurting out, "I don't know you."

The newcomer ignored him, tossing a manila folder onto the table as he drew back his chair to sit. He was in his thirties, shaggy hair, wiry build, dressed in a Runnin' Rebels T-shirt and faded jeans. Something about him said one-time jock. Something else said unmitigated prick. Looking bored, he opened the file, began leafing through the pages, sipping from a paper cup of steaming black coffee so vile Nick could smell it across the table.

Nick said, "I'm used to dealing with Detective Naughton."

The guy sniffed, chuckling at something he read, suntanned laugh lines fanning out at his eyes. "Yeah, well, he's been rotated out to Traffic. You witness a nasty accident, Mike's your man. But that's not why you're here, is it, Mr. Perry?"

"Perino."

The cop glanced up finally. His eyes were scary blue and so bloodshot they looked on fire. Another sniff. "Right. Forgive me."

"Some kind of cold you got there. Must be the air-conditioning."

"It's allergies, actually."

Nick chuckled. Allergic to sleep, maybe. "Speaking of names, you got one?"

"Thornton." He whipped back another page. "Chief calls me James, friends call me Jimmy. You can call me sir."

Nick stood up. He wasn't going to take this, not from some slacker narc half in the bag. "I came here to do you guys a favor."

Still picking through the file, Jimmy Thornton said, "Sit back down, Mr. Perry."

"Don't call me that."

"I said—sit down."

"You think you're talking to some fart-fuck, asshole?"

Finally, the cop closed the file. Removing a ballpoint pen from his hip pocket, he began thumbing the plunger manically. "I know who I'm talking to. Mike paints a pretty vivid picture." He nudged the folder across the table. "Want a peek?"

Despite himself, Nick recoiled a little. "Yeah. Maybe I'll do that."

Leaning back in his chair, still clicking the pen, Jimmy Thornton said: "You first blew into town, when was it, '74? Nick Perry, *Chiller Theater*, Saturday midnight. Weasled your way into the job, touting all this 'network experience' back east."

Nick shrugged. "Everybody lies on his résumé."

"Not everybody."

"My grandfather came over from Sicily, Perino was the family name. Ellis Island, he changed it to Perry. I just changed it back."

"Yeah, but not till you went to work for Johnny T."

Nick could feel the blood drain from his face. "What are you getting at?"

The cop's smile turned poisonous. "Know what Johnny said about you? You're the only guy in Vegas ever *added* a vowel to the end of his name. Him and his brother saw you coming at the San Gennaro Feast, they couldn't run the other way fast enough, even when you worked for them. Worst case of wannabe-wiseguy they'd ever seen."

Finally, Nick sat back down. "You heard this how? Johnny doesn't, like—"

"Know you were the snitch? Can't answer that. I mean, he probably suspects."

Nick had been a CI in a state case against the Tintoretto brothers for prostitution and drugs, all run through their massage parlor out on Flamingo. Nick remained unidentified during trial, the case made on wiretaps. It seemed a wise play at the time—get down first, tell the story his way, cut a deal before the roof caved in. He was working as the manager there, only job he could find in town after getting canned at the station—a nigger joke, pussy in the punch line, didn't know he was on the air.

"All the employees got a pass," Nick said, "not just me. Johnny couldn't know for sure unless you guys told him."

"Relax." Another punctuating sniff. "Nobody around here told him squat. We keep our promises, Mr. Perry."

Nick snorted. "Not from where I sit."

"Excuse me?" The guy leaned in. "Mike bent over backwards for you, pal. Set you up, perfect location, right downtown. Felons aren't supposed to be locksmiths."

"Most of that stuff on my sheet was out of state. And it got expunged."

A chuckle: "Now there's a word."

"Vacated, sealed, whatever."

"Because Mike took care of it. And how do you repay him?"

"I don't know what you're talking about."

"Every time business gets slow, you send that fat freak you call a nephew out to the apartments off Maryland Parkway—middle of the night, spray can of Superglue, gum up a couple hundred locks. You can bank on at least a third of the calls, given your location—think we don't know this?"

"Who you talking to, Mike Lally over at All-Night Lock'n'Key? You wanna hammer a crook, there's your guy, not me."

"Doesn't have thirty-two grand in liens from the Tax Commission on his business, though, does he?"

Nick blanched. They already knew. They knew everything. "I got screwed by my bookkeeper. Look, I came here with information. You wanna hear it or not?"

"In exchange for getting the Tax Commission off your neck."

"Before they shut me down, yeah. That asking so much?"

Jimmy Thornton opened the manila folder to the last page, clicked his pen one final time, and prepared to write. "That depends."

Sam sat in the shade at the playground two blocks from her apartment, listening to Nick go on. He'd just put in new locks at her apartment—she changed them every few weeks now, just being careful—and, stopping here to drop off the new keys, he'd sat down on the bench beside her, launching in, some character named Jimmy.

"He's a stand-up guy," Nick said. "Looker, too. You'll like him."

"You pitching him as a customer, or a date?"

Nick raised his hands, a coy smile, "All things are possible," inflecting the words with that *paisano* thing he fell into sometimes.

Natalie slept in her stroller, exhausted from an hour on the swings, the slide, the merry-go-round. Sam wondered about that, whether it was really good for kids to indulge that giddy instinct for dizziness. Where did it lead?

"Tell me again how you met this guy."

"He wanted a wall safe, I installed it for him."

She squinted in the sun, shaded her eyes. "What's he need a wall safe for?"

"That's not a question I ask. You want, I provide. That's business, as you well know."

She suffered him a thin smile. With the gradual expansion of her clientele—no one but referrals, but even so her base had almost doubled—she'd watched herself pulling back from people, even old friends, a protective, judicious remove. And that was lonely-making. Worse, she'd gotten used to it, and that seemed a kind of living death. The only grace was Natalie, but even there, the oneness she'd felt those first incredible months, that had changed as well. She still adored the girl, loved her to pieces, that wasn't the issue. Little girls grow up, their mothers get lonely, where's the mystery? She just hadn't expected it to start so soon.

"He's a contractor," Nick went on, "works down in Henderson. I saw the blueprints and, you know, stuff in his place when I was there. Look, you don't need the trade, forget about it. But I thought, I dunno, maybe you'd like the guy."

"I don't need to like him."

"I meant 'like' as in 'do business.'"

Sam checked the stroller. Natalie had her thumb in her mouth, eyes closed, her free hand balled into a fist beneath her chin.

"You know how this works," Sam said. "He causes trouble, anything at all—I mean this, Nick—anything at all comes back at me, it's on you, not just him."

They met at the Elephant Walk, and it turned out Nick was right, the guy turned heads—an easy grace, cowboy shoulders, lady-killer smile. He ordered Johnny Walker Black with a splash, and Sam remembered, from her days working cocktail, judging men by their drinks. He'd ordered wisely. And yet there were signs—a jitter in the hands, a slight head tic, the red in those killer blue eyes. Then again, if she worried that her customers looked like users, who would she sell to?

"Nick says you're a contractor."

He shook his head. "Project manager."

"There's a difference?"

"Sometimes. Not often enough." He laughed, and the laugh was self-effacing, one more winning trait. "I buy materials, hire the subs, make sure the bonds are current and we're all on time. But the contractor's the one with his license on the line."

"Sounds demanding."

"Everything's demanding. If it means anything."

She liked that answer. "And to relax, you . . . ?"

He shrugged. "I've got a bike, a Triumph, old bandit 350, gathering dust in my garage." Another self-effacing smile. "Amazing how boring you can sound when stuff like that comes out."

Not boring, she thought. Just normal. "Ever been married?"

A fierce little jolt shot through him. "Once. Yeah. High school sweetheart kind of thing. Didn't work out."

She got the hint, and steered the conversation off in a different direction. They talked about Nick, the stories they'd heard him tell about his TV days, wondering which ones to believe. Sam asked about how the two men had met, got the same story she'd heard from Nick, embellished a little, not too much. Things were, basically, checking out.

Sensing it was time, she signaled the bartender to settle up. "Well, it's been very nice meeting you, Jimmy. I have to get home. The sitter awaits with the princess."

"Nick told me. Natalie, right? Have any pictures?"

She liked it when men asked to see pictures. It said something. She took out her wallet, opened it to the snapshots.

"How old?"

"Fifteen months. Just."

"She's got her mother's eyes."

"She's got more than that, sadly."

"No. Good for her." He returned her wallet, hand not trembling now. Maybe it was the Scotch, maybe the conversation. "She's a beauty. Changed your life, I'll bet."

Yes, Sam thought, that she has. Maybe we'll talk about that sometime. Next time. "Have kids?"

Very subtly, his eyes hazed. "Me? No. Didn't get that far, which is probably for the best. Got some nephews and nieces, that's it for now."

"Uncle Jimmy."

He rattled the ice in his glass, traveled somewhere with his thoughts. "I like kids. Want kids. My turn'll come." Then, brightening suddenly: "I'd be up for a play date some time, with Natalie. I mean, if that doesn't sound too weird."

That's how it started, same playground near the apartment. And he hadn't lied, he hit it off with Natalie at first sight—stunning, really. He was a natural, carrying her on his shoulders to the park, guiding her up the stairs to the slide, taking it easy on the swing. He had Sam cradle her in her lap on the merry-go-round, spun them both around in the sun-streaked shade. Natalie shrieked, Sam laughed; it was that kind of afternoon.

They brought Natalie home, put her down for her nap, then sat on the porch with drinks—the usual for him, Chablis for her. The sun beat down on the freshly watered lawn, a hot desert wind rustling the leaves of the imported elm trees.

Surveying the grounds, he said, "Nice place. Mind if I ask your monthly nut?"

"Frankly?"

He chuckled. "Sorry. Professional curiosity. I was just doing the math in my head, tallying costs, wondering what kind of return the developer's getting."

She smiled wanly. "I don't like to think about it." That seemed as good a way as any to change the subject. "So, Nick says you wanted to ask me something."

Suddenly, he looked awkward, a hint of a blush. It suited him.

"Well, yeah. I suppose . . . You know. Sometimes . . ." He gestured vaguely.

She said, "Don't make me say it for you."

He cleared his throat. "I could maybe use an eightball. Sure."

There, she thought. Was that so hard? "Let's say a gram. I don't know you."

"How about two?"

It was still below the threshold for a special felony, which an eightball, at 3.5 grams, wasn't. "Two-forty, no credit."

"No friend-of-a-friend discount?"

"Nick told you there would be?"

"No, I just—"

"There isn't. There won't be."

He raised his hands, surrender. "Okay." He reached into his hip pocket for his wallet. "Mind if I take a shot while I'm here?"

She collected her glass, rose from her chair. "I'd prefer it, actually. Come on inside."

She gestured for him to have a seat on the couch, disappeared into her bedroom, and returned with the coke, delivering the two grams with a mirror, a razor blade, a straw. As always, a stranger in the house, one of the cats sat in the corner, blinking. The other hid. Sam watched as Jimmy chopped up the lines, an old hand. He hoovered the first, offered her the mirror. She declined. He leaned back down, finished up, tugged at his nose.

"That's nice," he said, collecting the last few grains on his finger, rubbing it into his gums. When his hand came away, it left a smile behind. "I'm guessing mannitol. I mean, you've got it around, right?"

Sam took a sip of her wine. He was referring to a baby laxative commonly used as a cutting agent. Cooly, she said, "Let a girl have her secrets."

He nodded. "Sorry. That was out of line."

"Don't worry about it." She toddled her glass. "So—will there be anything else?" She didn't mean to sound coy, but even so she inwardly cringed as she heard the words out loud. The way he looked at her, it was clear he was trying to decipher the signal. And maybe, on some level, she really did mean something.

"No," he said. "I think that's it. Mind if I take one last look before I leave?"

And so that's how they wrapped it up, standing in the doorway to Natalie's room, watching her sleep.

"Such a pretty little creature," he whispered. "Gotta confess, I'm jealous."

Back in his car, Jimmy horned the rest of the first gram, then drove to the Roundup, a little recon, putting faces to names, customers of Sam's that Nick had told him about: card dealers, waitresses, a gambler named Harry Thune, homely Brit, the usual ghastly teeth. After that, he drove to the strip mall on Charleston where the undercover unit had its off-site location, an anonymous set of offices with blinds drawn, a sign on the door reading *Halliwell Partners, Ltd.* He logged in, parked at his desk, and wrote up his report: the purchase of one gram Cocaine HCL, field tested positive with Scott reagent—blue, pink, then blue with pink separation in successive ampoules after agitation—said gram supplied by Samantha Pitney, White Female Adult. He invented an encounter far more fitting with department guidelines than the one that had taken place, wrote it out, signed it, then drove to the police tower, walked in the back entrance, and delivered the report to his sergeant, an old guy named Becker, who sent Jimmy on to log the gram into evidence. Jimmy said hey to the secretaries on his way through the building, went back to his car, moved $120 from his personal wallet to his buy wallet to cover the gram he'd pilfered, then planned his next step.

The following two buys were the same, two grams, and she seemed to grow more comfortable. Then he got bumped up to an eightball, and not long after that he rose to two. He always took a taste right there at the apartment, while they were talking, one of the perks of the job. Later, he'd either log it in as-is, claiming the shortage had been used for field-testing, or he'd pocket the light one, chop it up into grams, then drive to Henderson—or, on weekends, all the way to Laughlin—work the bars, a little business for himself, cover his costs, a few like minds, deputies he knew.

He found himself oddly divided on Sam. You could see she'd tried to cultivate an aura: the wry feminine reserve, the earth tones, all the talk about yoga and studying for her real estate license. Maybe it was motherhood, all that scrubbed civility, trying to be somebody. Then again, maybe it was coke-head pretence. Regardless, little things tripped her up, those selfless moments, more and more frequent, when she let him see behind the mask. Trouble was, from what he could tell, the mask had more to offer.

He'd nailed a witness or two in his time, never a smooth move, but nothing compared to bedding a suspect. As fluid as things had become morally since he'd started working under-cover, he'd never lost track of that particular red line. That didn't mean he didn't entertain the thought—throwing her over his shoulder, carrying her into her room, dropping her onto the bed, watching her hair unfurl from the soft thudding impact. Would she try to fight him off? No, that would just be part of the dance. Soon enough she'd draw him down, a winsome smile, hands clasped behind his neck, a few quick nibbles in her kiss, now and then a good firm bite. And was she one of those who showed you around the castle—how hard to pinch the nipples, how many fingers inside, the hand clasped across her mouth as she came—or would she want you to find all that out for yourself? Playing coy, demure, wanting you to take command, maybe even scare her. How deep would she like it, how slow, how rough? Would she come in rolling pulses, or one big back-arching slam?

Then again, of course, there was Natalie. Truth be told, she was the one who'd stolen his heart. And it was clear her poor deluded mother loved her, but love's not enough—never is, never has been. He remembered Sam asking, in their first face-to-face, about his marriage, about kids. You're not a cop till your first divorce, he thought, go through the custody horseshit. Lose. Bobby was his name. Seven years old now. Somewhere.

When he found himself thinking like that, he also found himself developing a mean thirst. And when he drank, he liked a whiff, to steady the ride, ice it. And so soon he'd be back at Ms. Pitney's door, repeating the whole sad process, telling himself the same wrong stories, wanting everything he had no right to.

* * *

Six weeks into things, he asked, "What made you get into this business anyway?"

She was sitting on the sofa, legs tucked beneath her, wearing a new perfume. From the look on her face, you would've thought he'd spat on the floor. "No offense, but that came out sounding ugly."

He razored away at three chalky lines. "Didn't mean it that way. Sorry."

She thought about it for a moment, searching the ceiling with her eyes. "The truth? I wanted to be a stay-at-home mom."

He had to check himself to keep from laughing, and yet he could see it. So her, thinking that way. "Why not marry the father?"

Again, she paused before answering, but this time she didn't scour the ceiling, she gazed into his face. Admittedly, he was a little ragged: His mouth was dry, his eyes were jigging up and down, his pupils were bloated. And his hands, yeah, a mild but noticeable case of the shakes.

"Some men are meant to be fathers," she said. "Some men aren't."

Sam let one of Claudia's Persians settle in her lap, pressing her skirt with its paws. The other cat lay in its usual spot, on the cushion by the window, lolling in the sun. Natalie sat in her stroller, gumming an apple slice, while Claudia attended to her ferns, using a tea kettle for a watering can.

"I usually charge thirty, which is already low, but I'd trim a little more, say, twenty-eight." She was talking in thousands of dollars, the price for a pound—or an elbow, in the parlance.

"That's still a little steep for me."

"You could cut your visits here by half. More."

"Is that a problem?" Secretly, Sam loved coming here. She thought of it as Visiting Mother.

Over her shoulder, Claudia said, "You know what I mean."

"Maybe I'll ratchet up another QP. I don't want any more than that in the house."

Claudia bent to reach a pot on the floor. "The point is to get it *out* of the house."

Well, duh, Sam thought, feeling judged, a headache looming like a thunderhead just behind her eyes. She was getting them more and more. "There's something else I'd like to talk over, actually. It's about Natalie."

Claudia stopped short. "Is something wrong?"

"No. Not yet. I mean, there's nothing to worry about. But if anything ever happened to me, I don't know who would take care of her."

A disagreeable expression crossed Claudia's face, part disdain, part calculation, part suspicion. "You have family."

"Not local. And not that I trust, frankly."

"What exactly are you asking?"

"I was wondering if she could stay with you. If anything ever happened, I mean."

Claudia put the tea kettle down and came over to a nearby chair, crossing her legs as she sat. "Have you noticed any cars following you lately?"

"It's not like that."

"Any new neighbors?"

"That wasn't what I meant. I meant if I got sick, or was in a car accident." She glanced over at Natalie. The apple slice was nubby and brown, and both it and her fingers were glazed with saliva.

Claudia said, "I couldn't just walk in, take your child. Good Lord." Her voice rippled, a blast of heat.

Sam said, "I'm sorry, I didn't mean—"

"A dozen agencies would be involved, imagine the questions." She rose from her chair, straightened her skirt, shot a toxic glance at Natalie that said: *Your mother can't protect you.* "Now what quantity are you here for? I have things to do."

Sergeant Becker called Jimmy in, told him to close the door. He was a big man, the kind who could lord over you even sitting down. "This Pitney thing, I've gone over the reports." He picked up a pencil, drummed it against his blotter. "Your buys are light."

He stared into Jimmy's whirling eyes. Jimmy did his best to stare right back.

"I'm a gentleman. I always offer the lady a taste."

"She needs to sample her own coke?"

"Not sampling, indulging. And there's always some lost in the field test."

"Think a jury will buy that? Think I buy that?"

"You want me to piss in a cup?"

Becker pretended to think about that, then leaned forward, lowering his voice. "No. That's what I most definitely do not want you to do. Look, I'll stand up for you, but it's time you cleaned house. You need some time, we'll work it out. There's a program, six weeks, over in Bullhead City, you can use an assumed name. It's the best deal you're gonna get. In the meantime, wrap this up. You've got your case, close it out."

Jimmy felt a surge of bile boiling in his stomach—at the thought of rehab, sure, the shame of it, the tedium, but not just that. "Like when?"

"Like now." Becker's whole face said: *Look at yourself*. "Why wait?"

Jimmy pictured Sam in her sundress, face raised to the light, hand in her hair. Moisture pooling in the hollow of her throat. Lipstick glistening in the heat. He said, "There's a kid involved."

Becker stood up behind his desk. They were done. "Get CPS involved, that's what they're there for. Make the calls, do the paperwork, get it over with."

"For chrissake, don't overthink it. Sounds like the last nice guy in Vegas."

It was Mandy talking, Sam's old best friend at the Roundup. She'd stopped by on her way to work, a gram for the shift, and now was lingering, shoes off, stocking feet on the coffee table, toes jigging in their sheer cocoon. They were watching Natalie play, noticing how her focus lasered from her ball to her bear, back to the ball, moving on to her always mysterious foot, then a housefly buzzing at the sliding glass door.

"Dating the clientele," Sam said, "is such a chump move."

"Rules have exceptions. Otherwise, they wouldn't be rules."

Natalie hefted herself onto her feet, staggered to the sliding glass door, reached for the fly—awestruck, gentle.

"He's got a bit of a problem." Sam tapped the side of her nose.

"You can clean him up. Woman's work."

"I don't need that kind of project."

"If you don't mind my asking, how long's it been since you got laid?"

Admittedly, sometimes when Jimmy was there, Sam felt

the old urge uncoiling inside her, slithering around. "To be honest, I do mind you asking."

They weren't close anymore, just one of those things. To hide her disappointment, Mandy softly clapped her hands at Natalie. "Hey, sweetheart, come on over. Sit with Auntie Man a little while." The little girl ignored her, still enchanted by the fly. It careened about the room—ceiling, lampshade, end table—then whirled back to the sliding glass door, a glossy green spec in a flaring pool of sunlight.

"She doesn't like me."

"She can be persnickety." Sam glanced at the clock. "Don't take it personally."

"You think if you let this guy know you were interested, he'd respond?"

Sam felt another headache coming on. Each one seemed worse than the last now. "It's not an issue."

"You're the one playing hard to get, not him."

Jimmy's last visit, Sam had almost thrown herself across his lap, wanting to feel his arms around her. Just that. But that was everything, could be everything. "I've given him a few openings. Nothing obvious, but since when do you need to be obvious with men?"

Mandy crossed her arms across her midriff, as though suddenly chilled. "Maybe he's queer."

Once Mandy was gone, Sam tucked Natalie in for the midday nap with her blue plush piglet, brushing the hair from the little girl's face to plant a kiss on her brow. Leaving the bedroom door slightly ajar—Natalie would never drop off otherwise—Sam fled to her own room and took a Demerol. The pain was flashing through her sinuses now, even pulsing into her spine. Noticing the time, she changed into a cinched sleeveless dress, freshened her lipstick, her eyeliner. Jimmy had said he'd stop by, and she still couldn't quite decide whether to push the ball into his end of the court or abide by her own better instincts and let it go. Running a mental inventory of his pros and cons, she admitted he was a joy to look at, had a soldier's good manners, adored Natalie. He was also a flaming cokehead, with the predictable sidekick, a blind thirst. Those things trended downward in her experience, not a ride she wanted to share. Loneliness is the price you pay for keeping things uncomplicated, she thought, pressing a tissue between her lips.

She heard a shuffle of steps on the walkway out front, but instead of ringing the bell, whoever it was pounded at the door. A voice she didn't recognize called out her name, then: "Police! Open the door." To her shame, she froze. Out of the corner of her eye she saw three men cluster on the patio—shirtsleeves, sunglasses, protective vests—and her mouth turned to dust. The front door crashed in, brutal shouts of "On the floor!" and shortly she was facedown, being hand-cuffed, feeling guilty and terrified and stupid and numb while cops thrashed everywhere, asserting claim to every room.

When they pulled her to her feet, it was Jimmy who was standing there, wearing a vest like the others, his police card hanging around his neck. The Demerol not having yet kicked in, her head crackled and throbbed with a new burst of pain, and she feared she might hurl right there on the floor.

"Tell us where everything is, and we won't take the place apart," he said, regarding her with a look of such contemptuous loathing she actually thought he might spit in her face. And I deserve it, she told herself, how stupid I've been, at the same time thinking: Now who's the creature? She could smell the Scotch on his breath, masked with spearmint. So that's what it was, she thought, all that time, the drink, the coke. Mr. Sensitive drowning his guilt. Or was even his guilt phony?

She said, "What about Natalie?" In her room, the little girl was mewling, confused, scared.

Jimmy glanced off toward the sound, eyes dull as lead. "She's a ward of the court now. They'll farm her out, foster home . . ."

Sam felt the room close in, a sickly shade of white. "Why are you doing this?"

Almost imperceptibly, he stiffened. A weak smile. "*I'm* doing this?"

"Why are you being such a prick about it?"

He leaned in. His eyes were electric. "You're a mother."

You miserable hypocrite, she thought, trying to muster some disgust of her own, but instead her knees turned liquid. He caught her before she fell, duck-walked her toward the sofa, let her drop—at which point a woman with short sandy hair came out of Natalie's bedroom, carrying the little girl. Her eyes were puffy with sleep but she was squirming, head swiveling this way and that. She began to cry. Sam shook off her daze, turned to hide the handcuffs, calling out, "Just do what the lady says, baby. I'll come get you as soon as I can," but the girl started shrieking, kicking—and then was gone.

"Get a good look?" Jimmy said. "Because that's the last you'll see of her."

He was performing for the other cops, the coward. "You can't do that."

"No? Consider it done."

Sam struggled to her feet. "You can't . . . No . . ."

He nudged her back down. She tried to kick him but he pushed her legs aside. Crouching down, he locked them against his body with one arm, his free hand gripping her chin. Voice lowered, eyes fixed on hers—and, finally, she thought she saw something hovering behind the savage bloodshot blue, something other than the arrogance and hate, something haunted, like pity, even love—he whispered, "Listen to me, Sam. I want to help you. But you've gotta help me. Understand? Give me a name. It's that simple. A name and we work this out. I'll do everything I can, that's a promise, for you, for Natalie—everything. But you've gotta hold up your end. Otherwise . . ."

He let his voice trail away into the nothingness he was offering. For Sam knew where this led, she remembered the words exactly: *I have men who take care of certain matters . . . The time will have passed for you to say or do anything to help yourself . . .*

And there it was: her daughter or her life, she couldn't save both. Maybe not today or tomorrow but someday soon, Claudia's threat would materialize, assuming a face and form but no name—the police would promise protection, but the desert was littered with their failures—and Sam would realize this is it, that pitiless point in time when she would finally know: Which was she? One of those who tried to kick and claw and scream her way out, even though it was hopeless. Or one of those who, seeing there was no escape, calmly said, *I'm ready. I've been ready for a long, long while.*

MITZVAH

BY TOD GOLDBERG

Summerlin

That Rabbi David Cohen wasn't Jewish had ceased, over time, to be a problem. He hardly even thought of it anymore except when ordering breakfast down at the Bagel Café. He'd sit there across from Bennie Savone, that fat fuck, watching him wolf down ham and scrambled eggs, or French toast with a steaming side of greasy link sausage, and his mouth would actually start to water, like he was some kind of fucking golden retriever. He didn't even think Bennie liked pork all that much—sometimes Bennie would order a cup of coffee and a side of bacon and would leave the bacon uneaten in, David assumed, not-so-benign mockery—though David knew Bennie liked letting him know who was in control of the situation.

But now, as he sat in his normal booth in the back corner facing the busy intersection of Buffalo and Westcliff, waiting for Bennie to roll up in his absurd black Mercedes that might as well have a personalized plate that said *MOBSTER* on it, he thought that he probably qualified as a Jew by now, if not in the eyes of God, then at least in his own eyes. It's not that he gave a fuck about religion—his personal motto, before all of this shit, had been "everybody dies"—but it was true he probably knew far more about the Torah and the culture in general than the people who belonged to his temple. And had he grown up with it, David was fairly certain he would have appreciated the subtle nuance of kugel.

After fifteen years, though, he still couldn't get used to the idea of baked noodles, raisins, apples, and cinnamon as a fucking entrée. Now pork loin. Pork loin was something he could get behind, especially this time of year, what with Christmas coming up. Back in the day, his wife Jennifer knew how to make it just how he liked it. Brined in salt overnight, covered with juniper berries, a bit of garlic, maybe some thyme, and then slow-roasted for three hours, until even the garage smelled like it.

Christ.

Fifteen fucking years and for what? He understood that his situation was fairly untenable these days, that those fucking Muslims had changed the way Family business was handled, particularly as it related to guys like David whose fake paperwork was fine in a company town like Las Vegas but which wouldn't even pass muster in Reno. David wasn't inclined to give too much thought to the whole Israel-Palestine issue, but he had to keep abreast of shit in case someone dared ask his opinion, though he never could confide in anyone that he shared some anger issues with the Palestinians, at least as it related to real estate, confined as he was to Las Vegas.

"Can I get you something, rabbi?"

David looked up from his reverie and saw the smiling face of Shoshana Goldblatt. Her parents, Stan and Alta, were two of the biggest donors Temple Beth Israel had, and yet here she was busting her ass on a Tuesday morning running tables. And that was an ass, David had to admit. She was only eighteen and he'd known her since she was five, but . . . damn. "A cup of coffee would be fine, Shoshana. I'm waiting on Mr. Savone, as usual, so maybe just a toasted onion bagel for now."

Shoshana took down his order but he could tell that something was vexing the girl. It took her nearly an entire minute to write the words *coffee* and *bagel* on her pad, her eyes welling up with tears the entire time. It was always like this. He'd go somewhere to just chill out, maybe smoke a cigar and catch a ballgame over at J.C. Wooloughan's Irish Pub, and next thing he knew, one of his fucking Israelites would pull up next to him with some metaphysical calamity.

"Is there something wrong, Shoshana?" he asked. When she slid into the booth across from him and deposited her head into her hands, thick phlegmy sobs spilling out of that beautiful mouth he'd just sort of imagined his dick in, he felt himself wince and hoped she didn't notice. He'd spent the better part of his life avoiding crying women of all ages, never really knowing what to say to them other than "Shut the fuck up, you stupid whore," and that hadn't seemed to help anyone, least of all himself. Whatever was wrong with Shoshana Goldblatt would invariably ruin David's whole fucking day. First there'd be the guilt he felt hearing her secrets and then there'd be the guilt associated with him finding it all rather humorous.

"Oh, rabbi," she said, "I wanted to just come in and talk to you in private, but there's always such a crowd, and my mom, you know, she's always telling me to not bother you with my problems, that you're a busy man and all, so I'm like, okay, I'll just figure it out for myself, but then, like, you're always saying that we should trust that the Torah has answers to all of our problems, right?"

"That's right, Shoshana," he said, though he wasn't sure if he'd ever said such a thing. Most of the time, he just downloaded shit off the Internet now, but it seemed plausible that at some point he'd said something like that.

"I'm just so confused," she continued, explaining to David a scenario that involved, as best as he could suss out, her having sex with three different black guys from the UNLV basketball team while a graduate assistant coach filmed the whole thing on his camera phone. It was hard for David to concentrate completely on the story since Bennie Savone had entered the restaurant about five minutes in and was stalking angrily about the bakery area, dragging his black attaché case against the pastry windows, like he was banging his cup against prison bars. So when David sensed that Shoshana had come to the basic conclusion of the issue—that she'd liked it, that she wondered what was wrong with her, but that she wanted to do it again, and with more guys—he reached across the table and took both of her hands in his.

"There's a part of the Midrash that says, essentially, we are all allowed to find enjoyment in the company of others." He'd found that if he simply dropped the Midrash into conversation, rejoined with the word "essentially," and then paraphrased Neil Young or Bruce Springsteen, people left him feeling like they'd learned something. It was true that he knew a few things from the Midrash, had even read a great deal of it, but in dealing with an eighteen-year-old girl just learning the joys of a filmed gangbang, he didn't feel the need to reach too deep. "Is a dream a lie if it doesn't come true, Shoshana? Of course not. It's something far, far worse. Do you understand?"

He let go of the girl's hands then and passed her the handkerchief from the breast pocket of his sport coat. She wiped her eyes, blew her nose, and smiled wanly at David, though now he couldn't even look her in the eye. "Thank you so much, Rabbi Cohen. I think I see that path now." She slid out of the booth, not even bothering to return his hanky.

Bennie, unfortunately, took her spot. "Fuck's wrong with her?"

"Confused about love," David said.

Bennie nodded. "Who isn't?"

It was weird. Over the course of their rather unconventional business relationship, Bennie Savone had found it necessary to use David as his father confessor too, even though he knew that Rabbi David Cohen was previously Sal Cupertine; that before he was a fake rabbi, he was a Chicago "associate" who'd accidentally killed three undercover Donnie Brasco motherfuckers on the same botched contract; and that, barring a sudden religious experience the likes of which only happened in prison movies, David's moral center was still pretty opaque. Still, David reasoned that Bennie needed to talk to someone, particularly since the one person Bennie could depend on previously had been the guy David replaced three years ago, Rabbi Ronald Kales, who also happened to be Bennie's father-in-law . . . or was until that unfortunate "boating accident" on Lake Mead claimed his life.

David knew that Bennie's decision not to fish out of the same shallow, polluted pond of local and loyal Italian women or coke-whore strippers most of his friends and coworkers had, opting instead to get connected with the real Las Vegas money—the Summerlin Jews—was still a source of some lingering organizational shame; an issue David was certainly intimate with.

"Yes, well," David said, "she's still young."

"My daughter tells me Shoshana likes black guys."

Sometimes David tried to imagine what his life would be like if he were still in Chicago, if he'd somehow had a different kind of upbringing, so that now he was selling real estate on the North Shore or running a sports bar or deli or was just a fucking Culligan man, his ends meeting, his life happy. Would he still end up on Tuesday mornings gossiping about whom eighteen-year-old girls were or were not fucking?

"I have to prepare for a talk at the Senior Center this afternoon," David said, "so I'm afraid I don't have much time to chat. Can we get down to business?"

"Of course, rabbi. I'd hate to get in the way of your busy schedule of dick and ribbon cuttings." Bennie reached into his attaché, pulled out a manila envelope, and slid it across the table. "You got a funeral on Thursday and one coming up next week too. Maybe two. Have to see how that one shakes out. Got a very sick relative. Could go anytime."

David just nodded. The holidays tended to be Bennie's busy season with murder, and now that they were flying bodies (or at least parts of them) in on private jets periodically from Chicago or driving them up from Los Angeles, David expected the news. Plus, David sort of marveled at Bennie's ingenuity; the guy seemed like a dumb crook from the outside, but on the inside he had a real aptitude for business. Stan and Alta Goldblatt might have been big donors, but Bennie Savone, with his Jewish wife and three Jewish children, was like fucking UNICEF to Temple Beth Israel. He single-handedly financed the building of Summerlin's first Jewish mortuary and cemetery behind the temple's expansive campus on Hillpointe, championed the new high school that was breaking ground in the spring, and, of course, regularly met with the esteemed rabbi over at the Bagel Café to discuss the livelihood of the Jewish faith (or whatever the fuck that shit-rag mob columnist John L. Smith in the *Review-Journal* said in one of his weekly innuendo-fests; if David ever had the desire to start killing people again, he'd start with that hack). David imagined that Bennie's long-range foresight could help a lot of Fortune 500 companies—it's not like any other mobsters had the fucking chutzpah to bury their enemies and war dead in a cemetery, or the willingness to put all the pieces in place years before they'd even see them in action. That Bennie earned most of his living from strip clubs didn't bother anyone at the temple. That's where everyone did business anyway.

"Fine," David said. "Anything else?"

"Yeah, my wife wants to know what your Hanukkah plans are this year."

"I'll be staying home," David replied, though the truth was that at least half the time would be spent at the temple making sure the young rabbi he'd entrusted with most of the social activities didn't burn the fucking place down, literally. That kid was a menace around an open flame.

"You know you got an open invitation," Bennie said. "Come over all eight nights. Spin the fucking dreidel. Eat fucking pancakes. Listen to Neil Diamond sing 'Rudolph the Red-Nosed Reindeer.' You like Neil Diamond, right, rabbi?"

What David really wanted, more than anything, was to get up from the booth, climb into his Range Rover, and drive it into a brick wall, just to feel something authentic again, even if it was pain. Because this shit with Bennie? This was an existential suffering he could do without. "The Jewish Sinatra," David said.

Shoshana brought David his bagel and coffee and discreetly set his hanky back down on the table. He looked up at her and she seemed . . . happy. Like she'd had a tremendous weight lifted from her shoulders and could now go on living her life in perfect happiness, her every orifice filled with big black cock. David felt something shift in his bowels; something he thought might be his conscience picking up enema speed.

"Listen," David said quietly after Shoshana left, "I gotta get out of here. A vacation. Something. I'm about to lose my mind. Promise me, after Christmas, you'll look at this situation. It's been fifteen years, Benjamin." He said Bennie's full first name just to piss him off a little. "You realize I haven't even left the *city limits* since 9/11?"

"Yeah, yeah," Bennie said, "sure. Talk to me again after the holidays. We'll see what we can do. Don't want you getting soft . . . Sally."

Rabbi David Cohen looked out the window again and wondered how it was he was the only fucking person who *happened* in Vegas and now had to fucking *stay* in Vegas. Put his old mug shot on a tourist brochure, then see how many people kept visiting.

When David first came to Las Vegas in 1993—back when he was still Sal Cupertine—he couldn't get over how wide open the desert was, how at night, if you weren't on the Strip or downtown, the sky seemed to stretch for miles unimpeded. At dusk, Red Rock Canyon would glow golden with strands of dying sunlight and he'd imagine what his wife Jennifer would have made of the vision. She was always taking art classes at the community college in Chicago, though never with much success, but he thought then that if she were with him in Las Vegas and had tried to paint the sunset, well, he'd pretend to love her interpretation. Used to be pretending was hard work. He was only thirty-five when he got to this place, but still felt seventeen, which meant he wasn't scared of anyone and didn't give a damn if he hurt people's feelings. It was a good skill set for his previous line of work, but David had long ago concluded it was shit on his interpersonal relationships. And the irony, of course, was that now all he ever did anymore was pretend while listening to people's problems. David was inclined to believe that his adopted religion was right about heaven and hell being a place on earth.

It was 4 o'clock on Wednesday and David was already late

for a meeting at the temple about next year's Jewish Book Fair, but he couldn't seem to shake the feeling that the previous morning's conversation with Shoshana and the one directly following it with Bennie had somehow clarified a few things that had been gnawing at his mind the last several weeks. So instead of attending the meeting, he drove his temple-purchased Range Rover the four blocks from his temple-purchased home on the fifteenth hole at TPC over to Bruce Trent Park, where he wandered among the stalls being set up for the farmer's market and tried to line up his priorities.

He stopped and smelled some apples, made idle talk about funnel cakes with the Mexican girl fixing them over what looked like a Bunson burner, watched children fling themselves over and under the monkey bars. If he closed his eyes and just focused on what he could hear and smell, it was almost like he was back in Chicago, though by now the sounds and smells tended to mostly remind him of his first days in Las Vegas when he spent all of his time foolishly searching for things that reminded him of home. It had grown increasingly difficult for David to even conjure *that* memory accurately since the landscape, both mental and physical, had changed so drastically in the intervening years. Where there used to be open vistas, the Howard Hughes Corporation had built the master planned community of Summerlin, filling in the desert with thousands of houses, absurd traffic circles instead of stop signs, acres of green grass, and the commerce such development demanded: looming casinos that eroded his favorite mountain views, Target after Target, a Starbucks every thirty paces, and shopping centers anchored on one corner by a Smith's and on the other by some bar that was just a video poker machine with a roof.

But something about today seemed to cloak everything in

radiance. Orthodox Jews tended to talk about such things as if they were moments of vast spiritual enlightenment, though David tended to think the Orthodox Jews were a little on the fruity side of things—always dropping Ezekiel's vision of the Valley of Bones like that guy wasn't a fucking whack job of the first order—so it was a good thing Temple Beth Israel was reform, which meant David just had to know some of that hocus-pocus shit, but didn't have to talk about it too much and certainly didn't have to dress in that stupid black getup. Still, his mind felt clear today, and whether it was a religious experience or just the settling of some internal debts didn't particularly vex David, because the result was the same, chiefly that he knew he needed to get the fuck out of Las Vegas before he killed himself and took twenty or thirty motherfuckers with him in the process.

That his life had become a suffocation of ironies didn't bother him. No, it was the realization that in just three weeks he'd turn fifty and yet he constantly waited for his front door to be kicked in by U.S. Marshals, that he wasn't some dumb punk anymore who could just live in blindness while other people controlled his exterior life, and, well, he missed his wife more and more with each passing moment.

The Savone family had been good to him, he couldn't deny that—they'd set him up in this life when they could have scattered him over the Midwest one tendon at a time, even had Rabbi Kales privately tutor him for two years before he started this long con, first as an assistant at the temple's Children's Center (where he actually had responsibilities for the first time in his life), and then, steadily, they pushed him up through the temple's ranks until, when it became clear that Rabbi Kales's old age and inability to shut the fuck up had become a liability, he ascended to the top spot.

He had a beautiful home. A beautiful car. If he needed a woman, Bennie took care of that too. The problem was that the world around him was changing: Locally, only Bennie knew he was a fake, all the other players having gone down in a fit of meshugass over at the Wild Horse strip club that left a tourist dead and another one without the ability to speak. Eventually, Bennie would end up getting busted on some RICO shit (or, praise be, Bennie's wife Rachel would get a fucking slit of conscience and/or retrospect and would roll on that fat fuck) and then one morning David would wake up and the U.S. Marshals would shove a big hook in his mouth and dangle him all over the press, the big fish that got away finally on the line.

And then there was the paralyzing issue of technology: When the Savone family moved him out of Chicago after the fuck-up, he had to leave everything behind, including his wife Jennifer and his infant son William. At first, it was easy to keep them out of his mind—it was either forget them or get the death penalty, which would probably be meted out by about fifteen cops in a very small cell. But as time went on and his life became a mundane series of mornings spent holding babies' bloody dicks, brunch meetings filled with whiny plasticized rich bitches who couldn't decide which charity should get the glory of their attention, afternoons spent in pink and yellow polo shirts as he golfed with men who would have fucking spit on him in Chicago, and nights spent alone in his Ethan Allen–showroom living room, flipping channels, jerking off to Cinemax, thinking about disappearing, just getting the fuck out, moving to Mexico, or Canada, or even Los Angeles, he began paving roads toward Jennifer and William.

It was so easy: He just typed their names into Google and came up with William's MySpace page. William was seven-

teen now and if his pictures were any judge, was in desperate
need of some guidance. Every single photo, his pants were
halfway down his ass, he was throwing some fucking gang sign
that actually spelled out *MOB*, and he had a Yankees cap—a
fucking Yankees cap!—turned sideways on his head, which
made him look like a retard, though not unlike half the kids
David saw Saturdays at the temple. He only saw Jennifer in
the background of a few shots and it broke his heart to see
how old she'd become, how her straight blond hair was now
silver, how her body had grown frumpy. Time and pressure
had turned her into an old woman while he was busy fucking strippers and running a goddamned Jewish empire in the
middle of the desert.

But she was there. He could see her. She existed. He
checked the archives of the *Tribune* and *Sun-Times* to see if her
name had been in any marriage announcements but came up
empty. David knew that didn't mean anything concrete, but
he also thought that if she had remarried, William wouldn't
have turned into such a fucking putz.

Over the last several months, he'd started looking at
Google satellite photos of his old house (where, according to
a simple public record search, Jennifer and William still lived).
Though all he could really see was the roof and the general
outline of the house, he could make out bits of himself too:
the pool, which he'd purchased after he got paid for his first
substantial hit (a guy he ran track with in high school—Gil
Williams—whose father was a city councilman); the towering
blue ash tree in the front yard, where he hung a tire swing for
William; the brick driveway, Jennifer's dream, which he laid
brick by brick over the course of a long weekend. Before he
understood that the photos were static and not updated regularly, David would return each day to refresh the image, hop-

ing to catch a glimpse of his wife, who he was sure he could recognize even from outer space.

Did she know he was still alive? Did she spend nights searching for him too? Did she know he'd also turned gray, but that he'd stayed in shape all of these years, working out, still hitting the heavy bag at the gym when he could, keeping himself ready, just in case, knowing, waiting, thinking that eventually, if he had to, he could kill someone with his hands again, just like back in the day. Happy with the thought. Thinking, yesterday: *You think I'm soft? I could shove that attaché case up your ass, Bennie.* And now. Now. When would things ever be tenable if they weren't now? Life, David realized, had reached a terminal point. Years ago, Rabbi Kales explained to David that when the end of days came, the Jews would be resurrected into a perfect state and the whole of the world would take on the status of Israel, and the Jews, he told him, would live in peace there. What about me? David had asked then, and Rabbi Kales just shook his head and said that he'd likely just rot in the ground, right beside him probably, in light of the experience they were embroiled in. He laughed when he said it, but David was pretty sure he meant it. Well, fuck that, David thought now. It was time to get tenable.

David purchased a small bindle of sweet-smelling incense from a hippie-looking girl with a barbell through her tongue. He'd seen this girl before—maybe fifty times, actually, since he was pretty sure she'd been there every single time he'd visited the farmer's market—but had never bothered to really notice her apart from the fact that she always stood there placidly, selling fucking incense. What kind of life was that? Selling smell. She smiled sweetly at him and David wondered how much kids today knew about the fucking world, about how things really *were*, how it wasn't all just iPods and MySpace and throwing gang signs on the Internet, that there was something permanent about the decisions being made around them. Ramifications. Spiritual and physical. If kids wanted to know what it meant to be tough, they'd take a look at the Torah, see how the Jews rolled, see how revenge and power were really exerted. David liked thinking about the Jews as Chosen People, liked thinking that maybe, after all these years, he'd been chosen too. You wander the desert for forty years—or just fifteen—you begin to change your perspective on things, begin to appreciate what you had before you got lost, begin to see signs, warnings, omens. Not everything is so obvious. Not everything has to be digitized to be real. Sometimes, man, you have to look inside of things.

"Let me ask you a question," David said to the girl with the pierced tongue. "Do you know me?"

"Am I supposed to?"

When he was young, he liked a girl with a little sass, but now it just annoyed him. "You see me here every week."

She shrugged. "If you say so."

"What do you think I do for a living?"

"Is this some sort of market research bullshit?"

Rabbi David Cohen—who for thirty-five years had been a guy named Sal Cupetine, who used to like to hurt people just for the hell of it, who killed three cops and really didn't think about that at all, never even really considered it, not even after they did an episode of *Cold Case* about it that he caught one night as he was drifting off to sleep after a long wedding at Temple Beth Israel—leaned across the small table and stared into the girl's face. "I look like a market researcher to you?"

"Everyone in Vegas is so tough," she said, and now she was laughing at him, tears filling up her eyes, and he could tell that she wasn't a girl at all, was closer to thirty, had pinched lines at the corner of her right eye, smelled like baby powder and cigarettes and dried sweat. "I'll say you sell cell phones at the Meadows Mall. Am I close?"

Thursdays were always busy for David. The children at the Barer Academy—the elementary school on the temple's campus—visited the main synagogue every Thursday for lunch and it was David's job to come by and smile at the children, say a few words to each, make them feel like God had just strolled in for a bite, and thus ensure that their parents wrote out a big fat check at the end of the month for no other reason than that their children were happy.

In truth, it was David's favorite time of the week. It wasn't that he loved children all that much—he didn't, especially, not other people's kids anyway—but that for the hour he spent going kid to kid, he didn't have to pretend. He just sat down next to them and asked them about their day, their life, how things were *going* and never how things *had been*, which was different from what he dealt with normally. With the people of parenting age, it was always about their childhood, how someone had fucked them up and only God or, if he wasn't available, David could help them deal with the past, like it was some constant growling beast that lived next door that only needed to be fed and watered and everything would be okay. The senior citizens all wanted to bitch about how things were better back then, whenever the fuck that was, and then wanted assurances that they were right, that the world had turned to shit but that they, of course, weren't to blame.

Today, though, David had a feeling he wouldn't be able to find the focus to deal with the kids, not with what he saw on the embalmer's table down at the temple mortuary. At 3 o'clock he was supposed to bury someone named Vincent

Castiglione, whose tombstone would read *Vincent Castleberg*, since Bennie liked to keep things simple. Bennie told David that morning that it was a Chicago guy so they didn't need to worry about putting on too much of a show. "I rounded up a couple old-timers to throw dirt," he told David, "so just keep it short and sweet on the last-words crap. Believe me, this guy doesn't deserve what we're giving him."

David went down to the temple's mortuary at 11:30 to check on the stiff, like he always did with the Chicago guys if they came in whole, so that way he wouldn't be surprised if it was someone he grew up with on the off chance the casket opened. Since it was a Jewish cemetery, it was always closed casket, but in the years David had been tending to the funerals, particularly those embalmed and entombed by employees of Bennie's, he noticed slightly less attention to detail when it concerned enemies of the state. Nonetheless, when he got down to the mortuary and found Vincent Castiglione belly-up on the embalming table still fully dressed in his police uniform, right down to his holster and gun, even though Vincent's head was sitting on the counter inside a plastic bag, the ligature marks on his neck bright purple, it took David a bit by surprise.

"Sorry, rabbi," the kid working the table said. "Mr. Savone said this is how he asked to be buried and so we, uh, we just, uh . . ."

David put a hand up to stop the kid from speaking. He could never remember this dumb fuck's name. He was a Mexican, some gangbanger Bennie rescued from the pound a few years back and set up in mortuary science classes out in Arizona. Two years later he was wearing a shirt and tie and was cleaning the dead for the Family. A good job, probably. Ruben Something or Other. He'd done a nice job on Rabbi Kales, David remembered that.

"Shut the fuck up," David said, and Ruben's eyes opened wide. David couldn't remember the last time he swore out loud in public, but from the look on Ruben's face, it had the desired effect. "Strip this motherfucker clean, you hear me?"

"Yes, rabbi."

"You get his clothes, personal effects, all that shit on his belt, including the gun, put it in a bag, something heavy. You got something canvas here?"

"Yes, rabbi." Ruben reached under a cupboard and came up with a large black canvas bag marked with hazardous waste symbols on either side. "We use these for our uniform cleaning."

David paused, tried to think, looked at Ruben, saw that the kid had a jade pinkie ring, two-carat diamond earrings, a thick platinum bracelet. Fucking thief was probably making six figures and he was still pinching from the dead. "You keep anything?"

"Like his organs?"

"No, you stupid wetback motherfucker," David said, feeling it now, finding the parlance again, how easy it was to hear Sal's voice in his mouth after so many years, though he felt a little sorry for calling the kid a wetback, particularly since he was probably born in Las Vegas. "You steal a clip? Maybe his badge? Something to show the boys later?"

Ruben exhaled deeply, walked back to a small desk in the corner of the embalming room, and pulled open a drawer, rifled around a bit, like he couldn't find what he was looking for, though David knew better so he kept his glare on the kid, and eventually came out with a wallet. "I think Bennie told me I could hold onto this," Ruben said, though he handed it to David like it was contagious.

"From now on," David said, because it just felt so good to be on this train again, "you don't think. Got it?"

"Yes, rabbi."

David watched as Ruben removed all the clothes from the body. Aware that Ruben was probably coming to conclusions of his own today, David tried to remain nonchalant with the process, absently thumbing through the officer's wallet. There was over three grand in folded hundreds in the wallet, along with a handful of gold credit cards. Fucking Chicago cops. When he was younger, David thought of them as the enemy even though half of them were more crooked than he was, but now he understood they were just guys with shitty jobs trying, like he had, to make the grass green. You earned it, partner.

When Ruben was finished stripping the body, he stuffed everything into the bag and then sealed it up with medical tape and set it down in front of David. "That's all of it," he said.

David hefted the bag up and bounced it a little, making sure he could feel the weight of the gun, probably a Glock. Ruben was still standing in front of him, though he didn't look too terribly respectful. He had this sneer on his face that David thought made the kid look like he'd eaten some bad clams, but which probably scared a lot of people not used to seeing how guys really looked when they were angry. The one thing about being a thug and a rabbi, David had learned, was that it was nice always feeling vaguely feared and respected at the same time. Now, though, he'd have to do a little bridge building, as Rabbi Kales used to say, if he wanted to make sure things didn't get beyond his control.

"I'm sorry I called you a wetback," David said, and handed Ruben the cash from the wallet. Ruben nodded and pocketed the money. "I got a little caught up in the moment." Ruben nodded again. Didn't anyone know how to accept an apology anymore? David took one last look around, figuring that the next time he saw a room like this, he'd be the one on the table, and then realized he'd forgotten something important. "Tell me something, Ruben," he added, back in the voice of Rabbi David Cohen, "what do you intend to do with the head?"

Ruben just shrugged. "I dunno, rabbi, what are you going to do with the uniform and gun?"

David thought about this, figured the truth would serve him here, figured that was where he was now, toward a path of more obvious truth. "I'm going to take them home, wash both, and then go from there."

As far as exit strategies went, David had to admit that his was a little hastily drawn, but when it's go time, it's go time. It was 3:15, and though he didn't need to do it, he'd gone full bore with his eulogy of the newly minted Vincent Castleberg, which didn't seem to bother the five octogenarians Bennie had assembled for the funeral. He recognized a couple of the men from other funerals, but now couldn't remember if they were for real ceremonies or fake ones. It didn't really matter, since these guys were so old and so mobbed up that even if he'd pulled out his dick and jerked off onto the casket, they'd keep quiet about it. Bennie always plied the old wise guys with lunch and a couple bucks for their time and then had his boys chauffer them back to their houses in Sun City.

But since David had decided that today was his last fucking day cutting dicks and burying pricks and listening to the world's problems while completely ignoring his own issues—the Hasidic rabbis always talked about this, David realized, saying that if you had proper remorse for your sin, you actually got closer to God, actually became a better person, whereas depression made you a sad, violent, insolent fuck, or, well, something a lot like that—he figured he ought to put things in proper perspective for the late Vincent Castiglione, née Castleberg. So he eulogized himself, instead.

He told the five men about his family life, about his father working as a union millwright, dying young from smoking and drinking (though he'd actually been thrown off a building), about how he ended up running with some guys from the neighborhood who taught him which joints broke the easiest (this got a knowing nod from the guys), how his mom ended up remarrying and moving to Florida after he graduated from high school, how he fell in love with this sweet girl named Jennifer who made him happy, how he ended up getting into the business and made some poor choices with regard to an important contract and ended up "retiring" to Las Vegas, finding God . . . and the rest was history. David changed a few important details, naturally, but found that the more he told his story, the better he felt about the choice he was about to make.

He finished with the burial Kaddish, surprised to hear the men each mutter "amen" at the proper times, and then watched as the faux mourners went about tossing clumps of dirt on the coffin. The most ambulatory of the men, dressed smartly in light-blue slacks and a white shirt, both originally purchased sometime in the '70s, walked over and shook David's hand. "A fine service," he said. "Really got the spirit of the poor fucker, if you pardon the expression. I'm not a Jew, but ten, fifteen years from now, if I die, I'd be happy to have you put me in the dirt."

David drove back to his house and packed up what he'd need for his trip—he'd been paid in cash for fifteen years and didn't spend too much of his own money, so he had enough to last him a long time if he was able to last a long time, or, at least,

Jennifer and William might have a chance for a decent life; a better life, anyway—and then took his laptop outside to poach his neighbor's wi-fi signal, purchased a one-way ticket back to Chicago using Vincent Castiglione's Visa card, first class, leaving McCarran at 7 p.m., a little over three hours away. And then David destroyed his laptop, beating it to death with the butt of Castiglione's Glock.

It felt good smashing the computer, but it felt better to have a gun in his hand again. David tried to think of the last time he'd really beaten someone good with a gun, but couldn't draw a bead. Used to be . . . well, fuck it, David thought, used-to-be's don't count anymore, just like Neil Diamond said. He worked up a nice sweat pounding on the computer, got himself warm for the task at hand.

Vincent Castiglione was a little thicker through the middle than David, but his uniform fit well enough. If he had more time, David would run it through the washer and dryer again, see if he could get the uniform to shrink, get some more of that dead stink out of it too. Still, he did stop to look at himself in the mirror before leaving the house and it was like getting a glimpse at an alternate life: Sal Cupertine looked pretty good as a cop, David decided. Sal Cupertine could have been *Sergeant* Cupertine. A real fucking mensch.

David checked his watch. It was nearly 5 o'clock. He took one last look around his home, thought about what he was giving up: the comfort of a predictable life, of money, of protection. Thought about what Bennie would look like when he saw David in a cop's uniform, thought about what Bennie would look like with a hole in the middle of his fat fucking face courtesy of Vincent Castiglione's service Glock. Thought about how, once he was on the road and the cops were swarming the airports in Las Vegas and Chicago, thinking a missing cop was on his way home, and, later, swarming the home of Bennie Savone, once Bennie's wife found him without his face, thinking the same missing cop had done the deed, particularly since David was sure they'd recognize the uniform on Bennie's video surveillance, that he'd stop somewhere and get a nice cut of pork loin for his troubles. Or maybe he'd just wait on that until he got back home.

BABS

BY SCOTT PHILLIPS

Naked City

V isitor's Center call you about a room?" I say to the woman behind the counter. It's 11 o'clock at night, and I've been in the car since 4 in the morning. I haven't yet hit the stage where the white crosses that have kept my eyes open have turned against me, but the time will be coming soon and I'll crash and sleep the sleep of the damned, and I have business to take care of before that happens.

"Oh. You're Mr. Gandy, hello. You're lucky to get something. They got the Consumer Electronics show going on right now, good thing you thought to stop at the Visitor's Center." She's shaped like a gourd, her hair long with ends split and dyed a shade of black that doesn't occur in nature. Between the elastic of her paisley slacks and the bottom of her blouse, little black hairs dance obscenely around the milky white vortex of her navel. She takes a key hanging in front of a cubby in which three envelopes sit aslant and hands it to me.

"There's mail in that slot," I point out.

"There's a fellow always gets this room when he comes through. Salesman."

So I'm subletting someone else's rented room, basically. I don't care. I'm lucky to be getting anything, as the ladies at the Visitor's Center pointed out to me when I pulled into town. It's a modest little motel, the Visitor's Center lady said, but super clean; you could eat off of those floors. I climb the open staircase to the second-floor balcony overlooking a swimming pool filled with cloudy water the color of urine. A couple are sitting next to the water smoking and glaring at one another without saying anything, and as one they swing their gazes upward toward me.

"What the fuck you staring at, faggot?" the woman says. She has on a shirt that says, *I SUFFER FROM CRS*. Her nipples are sticking straight out through the cotton, and at this moment there may not be a pair of tits on the planet I would less rather see, short of maybe Mother Teresa's; this one can't weigh much more than eighty pounds, with the emaciated face of a lifelong smoker. Even with her Jackie O shades on, her eyes look sunken.

"Seems like someone's looking to get his ass kicked," her companion says. He's so obese I can't imagine him able to get out of the lawn chair he's overflowing from, but I stare straight at him and sense that he's serious. I picture the fight and figure it could go either of two ways: He gets me down and crushes me under four hundred pounds of suet, or I dance around him and tire him out until he has a heart attack.

"Sorry!" I yell, and I head down the balcony looking for number 36. It's around the corner, facing the back ends of some houses. A dog in one of the yards starts a vicious barking jag as soon as I come into view, and keeps it up once I get into the room.

Clean enough to eat off the floors, I think after a quick walk-through, wishing I could force-feed the chipper Visitor's Center lady a nice, greasy fried egg off of the gritty shag carpet.

There's a ratty terry cloth bathrobe hanging from the clothes hook inside the bathroom door, presumably the salesman's. He must be balding, because there's hair all over the goddamned place: on the pillow, in the toilet, around the tub drain.

I'm not here for a vacation. Having spent the last few months tending bar for my stepfather's strip club in Wichita, I'm on my way back to L.A., where I am foolishly expecting to be able to pick up my old life where it left off. When I called my friend Skip to alert him of my return, he had a proposition for me: If I was coming through Vegas, he'd give me two hundred dollars to pick up a package from a stripper named Babs.

I didn't have to ask Skip to know I'd be carrying crystal methamphetamine. I'm more of a pothead myself, with a taste for the occasional hit of acid or pharmaceutical speed. Meth makes my teeth itch. But I can use the two hundred, and Skip is a good guy. (Within a couple of years, though, he'll transform into a violent monster whose ass I'll be forced to kick off my couch and out of my house in a futile effort to save my marriage. Said marriage hasn't happened yet, either, at this point.)

When I call the number Skip gave me, Babs doesn't bitch about the hour or seem surprised, just gives me directions to a bar called the Tumblin' Dice a few blocks off the Strip and says she'll meet me in half an hour. I tell her I'll be wearing a Dodgers cap.

It's past midnight and my new friends are still out by the pool. I stare as I pass by them and wink at the lady, who gives no sign of remembering me from twenty minutes ago. Her boyfriend doesn't react, having by this time fallen asleep.

The Tumblin' Dice is a monument to skank. No one here looks close to sober, particularly the lanky, disheveled bartender, whom I take at first for the victim of some exotic neurological disorder. After a long wait, he lurches over in my direction and braces himself on the bar with a big bony hand, a large bandage stretched across his right knuckles, blood starting to seep through the beige fabric.

I order a draft beer and park myself in front of a nickel video poker machine with hearts and diamonds faded to a cheerful, blurry pink. I play one nickel at a time, which proves to be a mistake.

"Fuck a duck, baby, you gotta play more'n a nickel a pop, you're fucked that way if you hit a big hand." The woman next to me is small and junkie-thin, with puffy dark circles under her eyes. I have no theoretical designs at all on the woman I'm supposed to be meeting but I can't help hoping that this isn't her.

"I'm just killing time, waiting for a friend."

"Fuck, I'll be your friend," she rasps, and then slaps my back harder than I would have thought possible, cackling. "Just kidding. I will, though. I'm Nicki." She rolls up her sleeve to reveal an amateur tattoo of a nickel the size of a silver dollar on her upper bicep. Jefferson looks pissed, like he's not happy about being tattooed onto a junkie's arm, or maybe it's the big infected whitehead erupting from his cheek. "Short for nickel's worth, get it?"

I shake my head no, even though I do.

"I done time, baby. Five big ones. Know what I did?"

"No."

"I'm not gonna tell you, either. Not till I know you better."

"Okay," I say, cursing the inborn Midwestern politeness that keeps me involved in the conversation and darting my eyes back and forth between the door and the machine. I drop another nickel and draw three nines and two queens, pat.

"Fuck, man, see that? You ain't getting shit for that, baby. You should've bet five nickels, that's the way you build up a bankroll."

"Like I say, killing time." Her short blond hair is spiky, but a stale odor emanating from her scalp makes me suspect that its body comes from a lack of washing rather than some salon product.

"What's your name?"

"Tate."

"Is your friend a lady, Tate?"

"Uh-huh."

"A lady friend, like? Like a sex partner?"

I take a good look at her, trying to figure out exactly what she's fucked up on. There's glee in her face, childish and idiotic, and I can't say whether it's malicious or not.

"Probably not."

"Cause I don't want you getting any big ideas about me, cause I'm one hundred percent dyke, baby."

"That's okay with me." I draw four clubs and a diamond, and trade the diamond for a spade.

"Aw, baby, that's a heartbreaker there. Not that it matters when you're betting nickels. You ever play one of those five-dollar machines?"

"No."

"My girlfriend, the one who died, she won a cool two grand one time. She was trying to pay me back all the money she stole."

The smart thing would be not to rise to the bait, but I'm finding her more fun than the nickel poker so I do the callous thing and bite. "How'd she die?"

Nicki leans toward me and hisses the answer in my ear, filling my nostrils in passing with a bouquet redolent of tobacco, stale beer, and gum disease. "I had her killed."

"No shit," I say, nodding, trying to strike the perfect balance between looking impressed and credulous and sympathetic.

"Bitch ran up a thirty-thousand-dollar tab on my fucking MasterCard. I said, *Bitch, you ain't getting away with that.* But I fucking loved her. It fucking broke my heart."

"Is that what you got sent up for?"

"Fuck no, that was just a little cocaine beef. This deal with Betsy was just last week. Don't you fucking tell anyone what I just told you, got it? Cause I'd hate to have to have you killed too."

"I won't tell anyone," I say, wondering how worried this should make me and cursing the white crosses popped in the course of the day's drive. Five? No, six. Seven? No, six. Three at 4 in the morning at the first motel, and three in Utah. Was it Utah?

"Cause I really would fucking hate that, cause I like you, baby. You're pretty good-looking, you know that?"

"Thank you very much," I say, the way my mother taught me to respond to a compliment.

"When I said I was a hundred percent lesbian, I meant more like eighty, if you know what I mean."

"Oh."

"You have really big lips. Just like a spade's, almost. Anybody ever told you that before?"

"Not in those exact words." I look over at the bartender, but this apparently isn't the kind of place where patrons are discouraged from bothering one another.

"I can't help thinking how they'd feel on my pooss-ay. You like the taste of pooss-ay, Tate?"

In fact, pussy is one of my favorite flavors in the entire world; at this juncture, however, my gag reflex is struggling with the back of my throat, trying to force it open to disgorge the beer I've swallowed.

A strange hand on my shoulder ought to come as a relief,

but it makes me spill my beer on the foul carpet. I turn to face a woman with long, dark hair drawn up behind her long, graceful neck in a ponytail.

"Tate?" she says, her voice high and surprisingly sweet. "I'm Skip's friend, Babs." She looks over at Nicki. "Sorry, Nicki, I need your new friend."

Babs is apparently higher than Nicki in the pecking order, because Nicki scurries back to the bar without a word. "I came in a cab," Babs says. "Can you drive?"

"Sorry about that," Babs says as we leave the parking lot. She struck me immediately as pretty, with the kind of sweet, big-eyed face I love, but the more I look at her the more character her face shows; the truth of it is she's a beauty. "If I'd've known I was going to be that long in coming, I would've told you someplace nicer." She spends a few seconds appraising my appearance, which makes me a little nervous, since I'm wearing the clothes I slept in last night. "You're a big guy. That's good."

I don't know how to interpret the remark, favorable though it seems, so I file it away for future obsessive, feverish rumination. "Kind of hard to picture you as a regular back there."

"I'm not, exactly. I own it."

"Really?" *Skip said you were some kind of stripper*, I almost add. Because I've been expecting somebody more like Nicki and less like Babs. She has on a loose-fitting shirt and jeans and not much makeup, and I can't help thinking that she sounds smarter than any woman I've talked to in months.

"Yeah, the last owner died and my boyfriend was a regular there, and I thought, what the fuck, I'll buy it and let him run it. Well, that didn't work out, did it? That was him behind the bar."

"The, uh, that guy tonight?"

"Yeah, the shitfaced guy. He didn't used to be like that. Guess I shouldn't have bought him a bar."

"I guess not." I'm stopped at a long light and a tiny old woman shuffles across. She doesn't look like she belongs in Vegas at all, let alone out on the street at 1:45 in the morning.

"Look at that poor old gal," Babs says. "We should offer to take her home, except we'd probably scare her into a heart attack. So what brings you to Vegas?"

"Going back to L.A. Bugged out after the Northridge quake and spent a few months tending bar in Wichita."

"Wichita? Are you kidding me?"

"No."

"I grew up in Wichita! For a few years anyway. My dad was stationed at McConnell. I had a little dog named Teenchie."

"Teenchie? You a *Song of the South* fan?"

"Yeah, I love it. I know it's supposed to be all politically incorrect and it probably is, but I saw it when I was little, so I can't be objective. The other one I really love is *Saludos Amigos*. Ever see that one?"

"Part of it. I wrote my master's thesis on Disney animation." As a matter of fact I didn't, my cousin did at USC, but I do know more than the average guy on the subject, and I'm truly bowled over to be asked such a nerdy question by this magnificent creature.

"Just loved all that shit when I was little. When I first started dancing, I used Teenchie as my stage name, can you believe that?"

So she is a dancer after all. I'm slightly more than half in love with her at this point in our ten-minute-long acquaintance, and I figure if the lush behind the bar at the Tumblin' Dice is my competition, I'm in like Flynn.

But it's late, so the aforementioned Midwestern politeness fails to stop me from asking the first question that pops into my head: "How can you afford to buy a bar on what a dancer makes?"

"Who said I was still a dancer?" She grins, a lopsided thing that shows a big expanse of teeth. She has, I finally notice, a slight overbite that makes her face perfect. She doesn't offer any more than that, so I don't pursue it further. "Turn left up here."

Something that should have been nagging me all along starts doing so. "Hey, you know that gal Nicki I was talking to?"

"God, do I."

"She told me she had her girlfriend murdered." When I say it, I can feel microscopic particles of Dexedrine racing up my spinal cord to my brain.

Babs snorts. "Jesus."

"Said this girl ran up a thirty-thousand-dollar tab on Nicki's MasterCard."

"Think about it, Tate. If you were the bank, would you give that crazy bitch a MasterCard with a thirty-thousand-dollar limit?"

"I guess not."

"I mean, what would she put on the application where it says *occupation*? Crack whore? Meth cook?"

This sends the Dexedrine particles back down out of my brain, and a feeling of relative calm comes over me. We're heading into a nice neighborhood now, a strangely empty subdivision. There aren't any cars on the street, not even parked, and there aren't any lights on anywhere; no late-night TV viewers or insomniac readers or dog walkers.

Finally, we get to a McMansion with all its lights blazing and two cars parked on the street in front despite a three-car garage.

"Did you ever see *The Omega Man?*" I ask. "This is sort of like his place."

"Kind of spooky, isn't it? The subdivision went bankrupt before it was all the way finished and the developer's on trial. They managed to rent out a few of 'em to people who sublet the extra rooms."

"Is this where you live?" I ask, hoping she's bringing me home, even as I recognize the pathos of the fantasy.

"Hell no. I own, in a hell of a lot better nabe than this. This is where we're getting your present for Skip. Park on the street, not too close to the streetlamp." She opens up her bag and hands me a pistol. I'm a Kansas boy and I've hunted since I was little, but I've never had a real pistol in my hands, and to her consternation I hold this one like it's a live fish.

"Hold it straight up and keep your index finger on the trigger guard."

"What's this for?" I ask.

"This guy's an asshole. I just want you to stand there and look big, and if things get tense you pull the grip out of your waistband so he can see it."

Not that I like anything I've heard in the last thirty seconds, but the thing I like least is the part where I stick a firearm down my pants. I can't stand the idea of looking weak in Babs's eyes, though, and by this time she's out of the car, so I follow her to the door.

When the door opens, an expressionless woman about seventy years old lets us in without a word. She has on a tank top and a pair of shorts that reveal a big scab on her shin. It looks like she slid all the way down her driveway with only one leg of her pants on.

There are three medium-to-hot young women in the living room watching *Cops*. The action is taking place in North Las Vegas, and they're excited because the bust onscreen is happening on a street they know.

"There's Lonnie's, look," one of them says. She has long, frizzy red hair and freckles as big as moles, and like the old lady, she has a big scab on one knee. She's picking at it with one long, red fingernail as she watches.

"I've totally seen that dude," one of her friends says.

"Which? The cop or the pimp?"

"Wannabe pimp, more like. He comes in for a drink when he's got cash."

"Gross."

"Where's Kleindienst?" Babs asks, and when they ignore her she grabs the remote and shuts the TV off, which prompts a volley of protest until she asks again, louder.

The redhead stops picking at the scab and half rises. "In the dining room, bitch. Gimme my fucking remote."

Babs throws the remote behind the television to another chorus of abuse, and I follow her through the kitchen into a dark room where a man in what I take to be a blackjack dealer's vest and starched white shirt sits with an overhead light shining down on him.

He's playing solitaire and wearing a clear green visor, which gives him the pallor of a reanimated corpse and makes him look to my eye more like a dealer from a film than a real one. Remembering my role, I lean against the doorframe and fold my arms across my chest while Babs walks up to the table. I'm expecting something out of a movie, a tense, quiet negotiation followed by a quick exit, so I'm feeling suave and invulnerable, especially with the gun down my pants. It feels pretty cool, actually, like a second dick.

Babs opens with, "You lying, ripping-off piece of shit."

This gets the man to glance up from his game for the first time. "You owe me, Kleindienst."

"I don't owe you shit." He looks over at me. I rise to my full height and move my hand toward my crotch. The adrenaline is pumping. "Who's this cunt?" he asks. "One of your johns?"

He has just insulted the woman I sort of love, and I'm still feeling the effect of too many cross-tops—I just remembered numbers seven and eight, popped at a filling station around 8 p.m. just in case—and between those and my instinctive gallantry and the drama of the thing, I commit what will in retrospect seem an error in tactics: I pull out the gun and point it at Kleindienst's face.

Babs looks at me for a millisecond, stricken. Then she pulls another pistol out of her bag and points it at the man's face as well. "Turn the light on, Tate."

"Tate?" Kleindienst says. "Your muscle's name is Tate? Oh, my goodness gracious."

I turn the light on. "Family name," I say, trying to sound like a killer.

The room is white with brass fittings and mirrors. It doesn't look as cool now as it did in the dark, and I see that Kleindienst is quite a bit younger than I'd imagined, maybe thirty or thirty-five. "Tell that bitch Darva to get in here with everything you got," Babs tells him.

He yells through the kitchen and a girl appears who looks like a teenage runaway in a TV movie, complete with cutoff hot pants and a shirt tied at the midriff. "Run fetch me the whole batch," he says. Then the three of us stand there feeling awkward, or at least the two men do. Babs looks perfectly comfortable.

A minute later, Darva reappears in the doorway holding up four good-sized packages wrapped in aluminum foil.

"Take 'em," Kleindienst says. "No hard feelings?"

"You douchebag," Babs says, and she opens one of the packages, snorts a little bit off the end of her finger. Jangly as I am, I'm relieved when she doesn't offer me a taste, and after a cursory glance at the other three packages, she seals them back up. "Don't ever fuck around like that again."

We start toward the living room and before we get there Kleindienst yells something at us. I turn to find him holding a big fucking gun pointed in our general direction. I yelp and pull the trigger, and to my horror it just makes a clicking sound. I click again and again in Kleindienst's direction as Babs fires, hitting him in the knee. He drops his gun, which sounds like a dumbell hitting the wooden floor, and falls clutching the gory knee, howling in an almost canine register. Poor Darva stands in the doorway of the dining room looking like she's waiting for someone to tell her what to do.

"You're going to need to take Billy to the hospital," she says to the paralyzed trio of *Cops* fans on the way out.

We run to the car and I peel away from the curb. I don't speak until we pull out of the subdivision. "How come mine didn't go off?" I ask, mortified by my own whining tone.

"Yeah, like I'm going to give you a loaded gun. I don't even know you," she says, and though my heart breaks a little, the events of the last five minutes have prepared me for the idea that there may be more to Babs than I previously fantasized. "Jesus, I didn't tell you to pull the fucking gun on him. That could have gotten us both killed."

"Is the mob going to hunt you down now?" I ask.

"What mob? Why?"

"For robbing a big-time dealer?"

"Billy Kleindienst? Give me a break. Billy's a fucking courier. Was until tonight, anyway, now he's just a crippled blackjack dealer. He's about as low as you on the totem pole. What we took belongs to me and my friend Sandra anyway."

"You think they're going to drive him to the hospital or call an ambulance?"

She shakes her head. "Don't give a shit, really. I did feel kind of sorry for that little Darva, though. I think she's his girlfriend, which is just as pathetic as can be." She looks over at me, shaking her head. "It all came out good, though, except for him getting it in the leg," she says with a rueful, easy smile. "Billy fuckin' Kleindienst."

I drive her to her house, in another subdivision. It's on a rise, and we can see the lights of the Strip in the distance. She's calmed down considerably, and the conversation is back in the realm of friendly flirtation. "You want to come in and taste some of this?" she asks.

"No thanks," I reply. I halfway think she's going to insist, that the taste of speed is just a pretext for taking me inside and fucking me, but she doesn't push it, just hands me Skip's share of the crank and opens her door.

"Nice meeting you," she says.

"If you ever come out to L.A., call me and we'll go see an old movie," I tell her. I wait until she gets inside before backing out of her driveway.

Heading into town, I watch those lights blinking and illuminating the early-morning sky, no longer dreading the crashed-out sleeping jag that lies ahead, and for the first time it occurs to me that there's something I really like about Las Vegas.

THIS OR ANY DESERT

BY VU TRAN

Chinatown

Six months ago, before all this, I drove into Las Vegas on a hot August twilight. My first time in the city. From the highway, I could see the Strip in the far distance, but also a lone dark cloud above it, flushed on a bed of light, glowing alien and purplish in the sky. My tired, pulpy brain at the time, I thought it was a UFO or something and nearly hit the truck ahead of me. Fifteen minutes later, at a gas station, I was told about the beam of light from atop that pyramid casino and how you can even see the beam from space, given no clouds were in the way. My disappointment surprised me.

The drive from Oakland had taken me almost a full day, so I checked into the Motel 6 near Chinatown and fell asleep with my shoes on and my gun still strapped to my ankle. I slept stupid for nine hours straight and woke up at 6 in the morning, my mouth and nostrils so dry it felt like someone had shoveled dirt over me in the night. The sun had not yet come out, but it was already 100 degrees outside. Not a cloud in the sky.

After taking a long cold shower, I walked to the front office. The clerk—Chinese probably—was slurping his breakfast behind the counter and ignored me. I thought about flashing him my badge, but instead I brandished three days' stay in advance, cash, which made him set down his chopsticks easily enough. He said nothing and hardly looked at me before handing me a receipt and walking back to his noodles or whatever the hell he was eating. When I asked him where I could get some eggs, he mumbled something in broken English, his mouth stuffed, glistening. In my younger days, I would have slapped him for his rudeness, just so I could. But I'd learned after Suzy left me to control my temper.

I did see a *phở* shop across the street and hoped they made it like she used to—the beef not too fatty, the soup not too sweet. Turned out theirs was even better, which didn't surprise me, but it reminded me of something her best friend—a Vietnamese girl named Happy of all things—once told me four years ago when she was over at the house for Sunday *phở*. Suzy had been mad at me that morning for nodding off at church, as I often did since my patrols didn't end until midnight, and though she knew I'd only converted for her and had never really taken churchgoing seriously, she chewed me out all the way home, and with more venom than usual. So when she stepped outside to smoke after lunch, I asked Happy, "What's bugging her lately?" Happy knew her better than anyone. She had been Suzy's bridesmaid, and they talked on the phone every day in a mix of English and Vietnamese I never did understand—but she just shrugged at my question. I chuckled and said, "Only me, huh? I bet she tells you every bad thing about me." But again she shrugged and said, very innocently, "She don't talk about you much, Bob." I'd long figured this much was true, but it burned to hear it acknowledged so casually. Suzy and I had been married ten years at the time. She'd leave me two years later.

At the *phở* shop, I stared out into the parking lot and watched a stout, middle-aged Asian man climb into a red BMW. It could have been him, but on his driver's license Suzy's new husband had broader cheeks and more stubborn eyes, and also sported a thin, sly mustache. DPS did list a silver Porsche and a brand-new red BMW under his name—Sonny Nguyen. The master files at Vegas Metro confirmed he was my age, that he owned a posh restaurant in town, that he once shot at a guy for insulting him—aggravated assault, no time done. It was Happy who told me he was a gambler, fully equipped apparently with a gambler's temper and a gambler's penchant for taking risks with little sense of the reward. Something in that reminded me of myself.

In my twenty-five years on the Oakland force, I'd shot at people several times, in the arm, in the fleshy part of the thigh, mostly in response to them shooting at me; I had punched a hooker for biting my hand, choked out a belligerent Bible salesman, wrestled thugs twice my size and half my age; I once had to watch a five-year-old boy bleed to death after I night-sticked his mother, who had stabbed him, coked up out of her mind; and three or six times other officers have had to pull me off a scrotbag who'd gotten on my bad side. But never, not even once, had I come close to killing anyone.

I walked down Spring Mountain Road and quickly regretted not taking my car. Vegas, outside of the Strip, is not a place for walkers, especially in this brutal heat. I'd pictured a Chinatown similar to Oakland's or San Francisco's, but the Vegas Chinatown was nothing more than a bloated strip mall—three or four blocks of it painted red and yellow, and pagodified, a theme park like the rest of the city. Nearly every establishment was a restaurant, and the one I was looking for was called Fuji West. I found it easily enough in one of those strip malls—nestled, with its dark temple-like entrance, between an Oriental art gallery and a two-story pet store. It was not set to open for another hour.

Hardly surprising that a Vietnamese would own a sushi joint—Happy's uncle owned a cowboy clothing store in Oakland. What did startle me was the seven-foot, white-aproned Mexican sweeping the patio, though you might as well have called it swinging a broom. He gazed down at me blankly when I asked for Sonny. He didn't look dumb, just bored.

"The owner," I repeated. "Is he here?"

"His name's no Sonny."

"Well, can I speak to him, whatever his name is?"

The Mexican, for whatever reason, handed me his broom and disappeared behind the two giant mahogany doors. A minute later a young Vietnamese man—late twenties probably, brightly groomed, dressed in a splendidly tailored charcoal suit and a precise pink tie—appeared in his place. He smiled at me, shook my hand. He relieved me of the broom and leaned it against one of the two wooden pillars that flanked the patio.

"How may I help you, sir?" He spoke with a slight accent, his tone as formal as if he'd ironed it. He held his hands behind his back.

"I'd like to see Sonny."

"I am sorry, but no one by that name works here. Perhaps you are mistaken? There are many sushi restaurants around here. If you like, I can direct you."

"I was told he owns this restaurant."

"Then you *are* mistaken. I am the owner." He spoke like it was an innocent mistake, but his eyes had strayed twice from mine: once to the parking lot, once to my waist.

"I'm not mistaken," I replied, and looked at him hard to see if he would flinch.

He did not. I was a head taller than him, my arms twice the size of his, but all I felt in his presence was my age. Even his hesitation seemed assured. He said, "I am not sure what I can do for you, sir."

"How about this. I'll come back in two hours for some sushi and tea. And then, for dessert, all I'd like is a word or two with Mr. Nguyen. Please tell him that."

I turned to go, but then felt a movement toward me. The young man was no longer smiling. There was no meanness in his face, but his words had become chiseled.

"Your name is Robert, isn't it?" he declared. When I didn't answer, he leaned in closer.

"You should not be here. If you do not understand why I am saying this, then please understand my seriousness. Go back to your city and try to be happy."

That last thing somehow moved me. It was like he had patted my shoulder. I suddenly realized how handsome he was—how, if he wanted to, he could've modeled magazine ads for cologne or expensive sunglasses. For a moment I might have doubted that he was dangerous at all. He nodded at me, a succinct little bow, then grabbed the broom and walked back through the heavy mahogany doors of the restaurant.

I felt tired again. *Phở* always made me sleepy. I walked back to the hotel and in my room stripped down to my boxers and cranked up the AC before falling back into bed.

People my age get certain *feelings* all the time, even if intuition had never been our strong suit in youth, and my inkling about this Sonny guy was that he was the type of restaurant owner who, if he came by at all, would only do so at night. My second inkling was that his dapper guard dog stayed on duty from open to close, and that he was just itching for the chance to eat me alive. I had a long night ahead of me. Before shutting my eyes, I decided to put my badge away, deep in the recesses of my suitcase. I would not need it.

* * *

When Suzy left me two years ago, it was easy at first. No children. Few possessions to split up. And no one we knew really cared: Her family all still lived in Vietnam, my parents were long dead, and in our thirteen years together, I'd never gotten to know her Asian friends and the only things my cop buddies knew about her was her name and her temper. She gave me the news after Sunday dinner. I was sitting at the dining table, and she approached me from the kitchen, her mouth still swollen, and said, "I'm leaving tomorrow and I'm taking my clothes. You can have everything else." Then she carried away my empty plate and I heard it shatter in the sink.

The first time I met her I knew she was fearless. My partner and I were responding to a robbery at the flower shop where she worked. She'd been in America for a year. Her English was bad. When we arrived, she stood at the door with a baseball bat in one hand and pruning shears in the other. Before I could step out of the patrol car, she erupted in an angry, torrid description of what had happened. I barely understood a word—something about a gun and ruined roses—but I did know I liked her. The petite sprightly body. Her lips, her cheekbones, full and bold. Eyes that made me think of firecrackers. We found the perp two miles away limping and bleeding from a stab wound in his thigh. The pruning shears had done it. Suzy and I married four months later.

Her real name was Hong, which meant *rose* in Vietnamese, but it sounded a bit piggish the way Americans pronounced it, so I suggested the name of my first girlfriend in high school, and *this* she did give me, even though her friends still called her Hong.

Our first few years were happy. She took over the flower shop and I'd stop by every afternoon during my patrol to check in on her. We had a third of the week together and we spent it trying out every restaurant in Chinatown, going to the movies (she loved horror flicks), and walking the waterfront since the smell and the waves reminded her of Vietnam. At first I didn't mind losing myself in her world: the Vietnamese church, the crosses in every room, the food, the sappy ballads on the stereo, all her friends who (with the exception of Happy) barely spoke a lick of English, even the morbid altar in the corner of the living room with the gruesome crucifix and the candles and pictures of dead grandparents and uncles and aunts. That was all fine, because being with her was like discovering a new, unexpected person in myself. But after two years of this, I finally noticed that she had no interest in discovering me: my job, my friends, my love for baseball, my craving for a burger or spaghetti now and then, the fact that until her I had not thought of Vietnam since 1973, when my unit just barely missed deployment. Vietnam was suddenly everything again . . . until she made it mean nothing. The least she could do was share her stories from the homeland, like how poor she'd grown up, or what cruel assholes the Communists were, or how her uncle or father or neighbor had gone to a concentration camp and was tortured or starved or *something*; but she'd only say her life back there was *difficult* and *lonely*, and she'd only speak of it with this kind of vague mysteriousness, like she was teaching me her language, like I'd never get it anyway. So I got nothing.

When we made love, she'd whimper, a childlike thing a lot of Asian women do, only her whimper sounded more like a wounded animal's, so that eventually it was just another way of making me feel like a stranger in her presence. An intruder.

I suppose our marriage became a typical one: petty arguments, silent treatments, no sex for months, both of us spending our free time more with friends than with each other. And still we kept at it, God knows why, until I came to believe, in an accepting kind of way, that she was both naïve and practical about love, that she'd only ever loved me because I was a cop, because that was supposed to mean that I'd never hurt her.

The night I hit her was a rainy night. I'd just come home from a shooting in West Oakland, where a guy had tried robbing someone's seventy-year-old grandmother and, when she fought back, shot her in the head. I was too spent to care about tracking mud on Suzy's spotless kitchen floor, or to listen to her when she saw the mess and began yelling at me. Couldn't she understand that brains on a sidewalk is a world worse than mud on a tile floor? Shouldn't she, coming from where she came, appreciate something like that? I told her to fuck off—which I rarely throw at anyone. She glared at me, and then she started with something she'd been doing for the last few years every time we argued: She began speaking in Vietnamese. Not loudly or irrationally like she was venting her anger at me, but calmly and deliberately, as if I actually understood her, as if she was daring me to understand her, flaunting all the nasty things she could be saying to me and knowing full well that it could have been fucking gibberish for all I knew and that I could do nothing of the sort to her. I usually just ignored her or walked away. But this time, after a minute of staring her down as she delivered whatever the hell she was saying, I backhanded her across the face as hard as I could. It shut her up, sent her bumping into a dining chair.

I had never before raised my hand at her. I'd arrested men who'd done worse to their girlfriends and wives, and I always remembered how pathetic and weak those guys looked when I confronted them. But when I felt the sting in my fingernails, saw the blood curling down Suzy's busted lip and her just standing there in a kind of angry stubborn silence, I hit her again. She yelped this time, holding that side of her face and still staring at me, though now with a look of recognition that told me she'd never been as tough as I thought, which somehow annoyed me more. Would I have stopped if she had hit me back, as I'd expected? Her nose began bleeding. Her eyes teared up. But her hand fell from her face and she stood her ground. So I hit her a third time. She stumbled back a few steps, covering her mouth with one hand and steadying herself on the dining table with the other, until she finally went down on one knee, her head bowed, like she was about to vomit. She spat blood two or three times. As I walked upstairs, I heard the TV from the living room and the rain pummeling the gutters outside and then the kitchen faucet running, and everything had the sound of finality to it.

In the divorce, she was true to her word and I was left with a house full of eggshell paintings and crucifixes and rattan furniture. Months later, someone told me she had moved to Vegas. I sold the house and everything in it and tried my best to forget I had ever married anyone. I also went on a strict diet of hamburgers and spaghetti.

But then a month ago I bumped into Happy at the grocery store. To my shock, instead of ignoring me or telling me off, she treated me like an old friend. She had always lived up to her name in that way, and actually she looked a lot like Suzy, a taller and more carefree version of her—and, in truth, a version I'd always been attracted to. I asked her out to dinner that night. Afterwards, we went home together. We drank wine and went to bed and it wasn't until we finished that I realized my other reason for doing all this. With her blissfully drunk and more talkative than ever, I finally asked about Suzy.

She told me everything: how Suzy had become a card dealer in Vegas and met up with this rich, cocky Vietnamese poker player who owned a fancy restaurant and a big house and apparently had some shady dealings in town, and how they got married and she quit her job, and how everything had been good for more than a year.

"Until he begin losing," Happy declared soberly, sitting back on the headboard. She said nothing more and I had to tell her several times to get on with it. She glanced at me impatiently, like I should already know. "He hit her," she said. "She hit him back, but he very strong and he drink a lot. Last month, he throw her down the stairs and broke her arm. I saw her two week ago with a sling, her cheek purple. But he too rich for her to leave. And he always say he need her, he need her."

I stood from the bed, a bit tipsy. I knocked the lamp off the nightstand.

Happy flinched. After a moment, she said, "Why you still love her?" There was no envy or bitterness in her voice. She was simply curious.

"Who said I did?"

She checked me with her eyes as though I didn't understand my own emotions.

I tried to soften my voice, but it still came out in a growl: "Is it just the money? What—is he handsome?"

"Not really. But you not either." She patted my arm and laughed.

"You know what? I'm gonna go to Vegas and I'm gonna find this fucker. And then I'm gonna hit him a little bit before I break his arm."

This time she laughed hard, covering her mouth and looking at me with drunken pity.

"You such a silly, stupid man," she said.

* * *

I returned to Fuji West at 7:30 that evening, just as the sun was setting. I drove this time. The parking lot was half full, mostly fancy cars, and I immediately spotted the silver Porsche in the back row. Sure enough, those were the tags. I rechecked the five-shot in my ankle holster. My hands felt bruised from the hot, dry air.

Inside, the restaurant was cool and dark and very Zen. Piano music drifted along the ceiling beams overhead. Booth tables with high wooden seats, lighted by small suspended lanterns, lined the walls like confessionals. Candlelit tables filled in the space between the booths and the circular sushi bar, which stood in the center of the restaurant like an island, manned by three sushi chefs in white who with their hats resembled sailors. Flanking the bar were two enormous aquariums, filled with exotic-looking fish that were staring out calmly at the twenty or so patrons in the restaurant, most of whom easily out-dressed me.

I asked for a table near the bar and ordered a Japanese beer and told the hostess I was waiting for a friend. I'd barely wet my lips before Sonny's young doberman appeared and sat himself across from me, just as casually as if I'd invited him.

He was now dressed in a black pinstripe suit, set off by another beautiful pink tie, looking very ready to be anyone's best man. He waved at a waitress, who swiftly brought him a bottle of Perrier and a glass with a straw. Pouring the Perrier into the glass, he said to me, "So you did not like my advice." His voice was gentle but humorless.

"I appreciate the wisdom—but my business with Sonny is important."

"I know it is," he said, nodding agreeably. "Except my father has no business with *you*." He sipped his Perrier with the straw like a child. In the aquarium directly behind him, a long brown eel swam slowly through his head.

"Your father, huh? Well, I guess that makes some sense." I downed half my beer, wiped my mouth with two fingers. "So how do you know who I am?"

"Your friend Happy is also a friend of mine. She visits here often. She came to me last week and told me what you have been planning to do. She told me for your sake. She likes you, Mr. Robert, and she knows you can be a foolish man. She did not tell Suzy, of course, or my father. So only I know that you are here. And that, Mr. Robert, is a good thing."

"Because your father is a dangerous man?"

He eyed me sternly, drawing together his dark handsome eyebrows. "Because my father does not have my patience."

A waiter came by and whispered something into his ear, and Sonny Jr. looked to the front doors where two large parties of customers had just appeared. He stood from the table and gestured at the hostess, who walked quickly over to our table, and he gave her and the waiter rapid orders in Vietnamese. He glanced at me, a bit distractedly, then turned again to them and went on with his instructions. He watched them walk away and continued watching as they saw to the parties. His father might have been a poker-playing gangster or maybe a gangster-playing poker player, but I was getting the feeling that Junior was nothing more than what he appeared: the young manager of a restaurant.

He appeared to sigh and finally turned back to me, adjusting his tie, his face once again as calm as the fish. "You are a police officer, so I should not show you this. But I know you are here with other, less official concerns, however silly they might be. Please come with me then."

"And where are we going?"

"As I said, you are the police officer here. It should be me who is nervous."

I offered him a smile, which he did not return. I stood and followed him to the kitchen.

We passed two private tatami rooms, each being prepared by the staff for the new parties. Foolishly or not, the presence of so many people eased my mind a bit.

The kitchen was staffed by Mexicans and Asians, all in white uniforms. No one paid us any attention as we walked to the back, toward a door marked *Office*. Junior unlocked it, and once we stepped inside he relocked it and approached a huge, life-size oil painting of a geisha walking up a dark flight of stairs. There was a clock on the wall beside it, which he set to midnight, then he turned the minute hand three revolutions clockwise and two revolutions counter-clockwise. The painting slowly swung open from the wall like a door, revealing a passageway and a dark descending staircase. He walked down and without looking back at me said, "It will close again in five seconds."

We reached a long dim hallway and passed six closed doors, each with a keypad over the knob. At the end we stopped at a door that was set much further away from the others. He punched a series of numbers on the keypad and something clicked. He pushed the door open completely before moving inside.

I heard soft Oriental music. The room glowed bluish and shimmered. It was no more than a thousand square feet, but felt cavernous, with walls of glass surrounding us—behind them water and fish. I had entered a gigantic aquarium. Each wall showed the flushed faces of four separate tanks, framed in quadrants like enormous television monitors, their blue waters filled with stingrays and sharks and what appeared to be piranha and other odd-looking fish, all swimming around beds of corral and white gravel. Against the brick wall behind me were three aisles of smaller aquariums, with smaller fish, stacked on two rows of iron shelves. On a large Oriental rug in the center of the room stood a black leather couch, two dolphin chairs, and a glass coffee table.

Sonny Jr. went to the table and took a cigarette from the pack lying there, lit it, and approached the tank of stingrays. I felt a movement behind me and turned to see, at last, the seven-foot Mexican standing in the hall just outside the doorway, his forehead out of view. God knows where he'd come from. His white apron looked like an oversized bib, and he still wore that heavy, dull-eyed Frankenstein expression. Junior spoke Vietnamese to him and he stepped inside the room, bowing to do so, and closed the door. So that was at least three languages the Mexican understood.

"Is Dad making an appearance too?" I asked.

"He is not here, Mr. Robert," Junior replied calmly, and ashed into an ashtray he held in his other hand—yet another annoyingly formal mannerism. He gestured at the entire room and said, "But I have brought you to meet his fish. These are all illegal, you see. And all very expensive. This one here," and he pointed at a foot-long fish with a huge chin and an elongated, undulating body, "is a silver Asian arowana, also called a dragonfish, as you can see why. Our clients will pay over ten thousand dollars for one."

"I can sell you my car for half that."

He turned his back to me, ignoring the comment, and continued, "We installed a couch and a stereo because my father likes to come here and relax. The fish, the lights, and the music give him peace. For all his flaws, he is a man who values peace."

I took a step toward him and heard the Mexican shuffle his feet behind me. I spoke to Junior's back: "I've met your fish. Why else have you brought me here?"

He turned around and expelled smoke through his nostrils, dragon-like. "I have brought you here to tell you a story." He licked his lips and brushed ash from his breast. "You see, my father appreciates these fish because they are beautiful and bring him a lot of money. But he also appreciates them because they remind him of home—they *bring* home to him. It is the irony, you see, that is valuable: a tiny tropical ocean here in the middle of the desert; all these fish swimming beneath sand. The casinos in this city sell you a similar kind of irony, but what we have here is genuine and real, because it also keeps us who we are."

"*Who you are?* No irony, you think, in you and your father owning a Japanese restaurant?"

"Shut up, Mr. Robert, and listen." He put out his cigarette and walked over to take a seat in one of the dolphin chairs. He unbuttoned his jacket and crossed his legs elegantly. He offered me the face of a boy, but sounded like an old man. "More than twenty years ago, my parents and I escaped Vietnam by boat. Two hundred people in a little fishing boat made for no more than twenty, headed for Malaysia. On our second night at sea we hit a terrible storm and my mother fell overboard. It was too dark and stormy for anyone to see her or hear her cry out, and the waters were too rough to save her anyway. She drowned. I was seven at the time. I will not bore you with a tragedy. I will only say that her death hardened my father, made him more fearless than he already was.

"In any case, after sixteen days, our boat finally made it to the refugee camp in Malaysia, on the island of Pulau Bidong. The first day my father and I were there, the ruffians in the camp made themselves known and threatened us. My father was once in a gang back in Vietnam, so he was not afraid. He ignored them. A week later, one of them stole my rice ration. The thief slapped me across the face, pushed me to the ground, ripped the sack out of my hand. To scare me even more, he grabbed my wrist and ran a knife across it, barely cutting the skin. I ran to my father, bawling, and he shut me up with a slap of his own."

Junior stared at his hands for a moment, like he was studying his nails. Then he went on.

"He took me by the arm and dragged me to the part of the camp where the ruffians hung out. He made me stand under a palm tree and ordered me to watch him. There were many people there, minding their business. A few shacks away, the man who had attacked me was kneeling and playing dice with two friends. On a tree stump nearby, someone butchering an animal had left his bloody cleaver and my father grabbed it and marched up behind the man and kicked him hard in the back of the head. The man fell forward and his two friends pounced at my father, but he was already brandishing the cleaver at them. They backed off. My father then grabbed the man by the back of his shirt and dragged him to the tree stump. In one swift motion, never once hesitating, he placed the man's hand on the stump and threw down the cleaver and hacked off his hand at the wrist.

"Blood spurted and the man screamed. I do not remember how horrified the people around me looked, but I remember hearing a few women shriek. My father dropped the cleaver, bent down, and muttered something in the man's ear as he writhed on the ground, moaning and clasping his bloody forearm to his chest. His severed hand still lay on the tree stump. My father wiped his own hand on his pants and held mine as we walked back to our shack. We stayed in that camp for two more months before we came to the States, and those ruffians never once bothered us again."

Sonny Jr. stood from the chair and walked over again to the stingrays. He took out a handkerchief and wiped the glass where his finger had pointed at the arowana. He turned to me thoughtfully.

"I still occasionally have dreams about that afternoon. But I have not told you this story so that you will pity me, or anyone for that matter. I have told you so that you will understand what kind of man my father is—and in a way respect it. Think of this conversation—this situation—as an exchange of trust. Remember that I have brought you, a police officer, here to see my father's illegal business. I am trusting that you will forget your plans in this city, go home, and not say a word of what you have seen. In exchange, since I have made this rather foolish gesture for you, you will trust that I am trying to help you, and you will do all those things. A man of your sentiments should appreciate the sincerity of this offer."

I watched him neatly fold his handkerchief and place it back in the breast pocket of his suit. His logic was giving me a headache. I walked over to the couch and sat down, facing him. I hadn't smoked since Suzy left me—another part of my detox plan, since smoking together was one of the few things we never stopped doing. But now I took a cigarette from the pack and lit up. It was my turn to talk.

"Why do you want so badly to help me?" I said. "Why do you care what happens to me? Is it really *me* you're protecting? Or is it your father? Because somehow I feel he's no longer—maybe never was—the hard man you say he is. And I'm guessing maybe you made up that dramatic little story just to scare me. But even if it's true, I've dealt with scarier people.

Now why you've chosen to show me all this fish stuff is still a mystery to me—though I'd wager you just like getting off on your own smarts and impressing people. You've either read too many books or listened to people who've read too many books. Either way, it's not my fault that I can't understand half the things you say. But what I do understand is this . . ." I leaned forward on the couch and looked at him squarely. "Your father is a thug. Not only that, he's an asshole, and a coward too. He threw a woman down the stairs and broke her arm. Who knows what else he did, could have done, or might do in the future, but men like him only have the guts to do that to a woman. And the fact that you haven't blinked yet tells me all of this is true. You're a smart boy, and you seem to be a good enough son to want to protect him. That's fine. It's even admirable. But my business with him has nothing to do with you. So fuck off."

I stood up and walked around the table and stopped a few yards from him. I took a long drag off my cigarette and then flicked it at his feet. "I have police buddies who know exactly where I am and who your father is, and if I don't say hi to them next week, they'll know where to come find me. And they all hate sushi."

He was glaring at me. Behind him, the stingrays swam languidly around his thin, stiff figure like a flock of vultures.

His eyes looked past me and he nodded his head, and before I could turn around I felt the Mexican's enormous arms wrap around my chest, hugging me so tightly I could hardly breathe. I soon felt a fumbling at my ankle holster, and then saw Sonny Jr. with my five-shot, which he deposited in his jacket pocket. He said something in Vietnamese, and the Mexican pushed me down to the floor, forcing me flat onto my stomach. With his knee digging into my lower back, he twisted one of my arms behind my back and held my other arm to the floor before my flattened face. I could do nothing but grunt beneath him, a doll in his hands, the tile floor numbing my cheek.

I looked up and Sonny Jr. had taken off his jacket. From his pant pocket, he now pulled out a switchblade, which he opened. The Mexican wrenched my extended forearm so that my wrist was exposed. Sonny Jr. kneeled and planted his shoe on my palm. Then he steadied the blade across my wrist.

"Wait!" I gasped. I struggled but could hardly budge under the Mexican, his boulder of a knee still lodged in my lower back.

Sonny Jr. slowly, gently dragged the blade. I could feel its icy sharpness slice the surface of my skin. The pain was no more than an itch, but waiting for it had made me clench my jaw so tightly that it now ached. Sonny Jr. lifted his shoe. A thread of blood appeared across my wrist.

"You and I," Junior murmured casually, "now share something." He wiped the blade with two fingers, closed it, and returned it to his pocket. He stood and I could no longer see his face, but his voice came out bitter and hard, like he was shaking his head at me: "I know exactly who you are, Mr. Robert. The minute you arrived at our door, I knew. You are a man who has nothing to lose. But that does not make you brave, it only makes you naïve. Happy told me you were a silly, stupid man. What were you going to do—kill my father? Break his arm? Yell at him? Everything I have told you is true, and I meant every sentiment. And yet you are too sentimental to listen. You want to come here and be a hero and save your former wife from a bad man. You want to know how he has hurt her, and why. But in the end, the only thing you *really* want is to know why she would leave you for slapping her, and then stay with a man who threw her down a flight of stairs and broke her arm."

His shoes reappeared before my eyes, a foot from my nose. He was now speaking directly over my head like he was ready to spit on it. "You see, we keep most of these fish separated not because they will eat each other—though that is true—but because they like it this way. Just like *we* like it this way. Why do you think, when you walk into any casino in this city, that nearly every dealer is Asian, and nearly every Asian dealer is Vietnamese? Because we enjoy cards and colorful chips? *No.* Because we flock to each other. We flock to where there are many of us—so that we will belong. It is a very simple reality, Mr. Robert. A primal reality."

He bent down, speaking closer now to my ear.

"What made you think she ever belonged to you, or more importantly that *you* ever belonged with her? America, Mr. Robert, is not the melting pot you Americans like to say or think it is. Things get stirred, yes, but like oil and vinegar they eventually separate and settle and the like things always go back to each other. They have made new friends, perhaps even fucked them, but in their heart they will always wander back to where they belong. Love has absolutely nothing to do with it."

He sighed dramatically and stood back up.

"That is enough. I am tired of speeches." With this, he lifted his shoe and stomped on my hand with the heel.

I screamed out and he let me. The Mexican dismounted me then. After a long writhing moment I forced myself to sit up. I was holding my injured hand like a dead bird. I couldn't tell if anything was broken, but my knuckles and fingers felt hot with numbing pain, right alongside the ache in my shoulder where the Mexican had twisted and held my arm.

Junior now stood before the tank of piranhas, in his jacket again and with his hands in his pockets. As though he was ordering a child, he said to me, "If I ever see you again, I will do much worse. You will now go with Menendez here, and he will take you back outside. Remember, you have seen nothing here. If necessary, I will hurt my new mother at your expense. I like her, but not that much."

He handed Menendez my gun and Menendez led me out of the room by the arm, almost gently.

Junior's voice followed me out: "Go home, Mr. Robert, and try to be happy."

I let the Mexican drag me to another door, which revealed another staircase, which ascended into another office, which opened out into what looked like the pet store next door to the restaurant. Everything was dark, save for the shifting shadows of birds in their cages, dogs and rodents in their pens. We passed aquariums with goldfish and droning water pumps. Something squawked irritably in the putrid darkness.

I was released outside into a rainy, windy night. It was like stepping into another part of the country, far from the desert, near the ocean perhaps. I must have looked at Menendez with shock, because he said to me, in a gruff but pleasant voice: "Monsoon season." He handed me my five-shot, closed the door, and I saw his giant shadow fade back into the darkness of the store.

I drove down Highway 15, toward California. My right hand was wrapped tightly in a handkerchief. I could move my fingers, but didn't want to. It was 10 o'clock, an hour after I had left Fuji West, and the rain had not yet stopped. On my way out of town, I saw three car accidents, one of which appeared fatal—a Toyota on its side, a truck with no front door, no windshield, a body beneath wet tarp. I had worked so many of these scenes in my time, and yet that evening they spooked me—chilled me. Rain must fall like an ice storm upon this town.

I kept thinking of the night I hit Suzy. But soon I was remembering another hot rainy night, many years ago, when I came home from work all drenched and tired and she made me strip down to my underwear and sat me at the dining table with a bowl of hot chicken porridge. As I ate the porridge, she stood close behind my chair and hummed one of her sad Vietnamese ballads and dried my hair with a towel. I remember, between spoonfuls, trying to hum along with her.

Sonny Jr.'s parting words flashed through my mind. What did he know about other people's happiness?

I took the very next exit and turned around and began driving in the direction of their house. I had wanted all along to avoid this—I knew she might be there. It took me half an hour to find it. By the time I turned into the neighborhood, the street curbs were overflowing with ankle-deep water and I could feel my tires slicing through the currents.

Their house, like many of the others, was a two-story stucco job with a manicured rock garden and several giant palm trees out front. It looked big and warm. All the windows were dark. A red BMW sat in the circular driveway behind the brown Toyota Camry I'd bought Suzy eight years ago. Who knows why she was still driving it with what he could buy her now.

I parked by the neighbor's curb and approached the side of the house, beneath the palm trees that swayed and thrashed in the wind. The rain was coming down even harder now, blinding sheets of it, and I was drenched within seconds. On their patio, I saw the same kind of potted cacti that stood on our porch years ago, except the pots were much nicer. And also, there in front of me, like I was staring at the front door of our old house, was a silver cross hanging beneath the peephole.

The rain soothed my injured hand. I unwrapped the wet handkerchief and tossed it on the driveway. I tried to make a fist and realized I could, though the ache was still there, and also some of the numbness. I rang the doorbell and stood there waiting, shivering. I didn't know who I wanted to answer the door, but when the porch light turned on and he finally opened it, I understood what I wanted to do.

He looked exactly as he did on his driver's license, but was shorter than I expected, shorter than both Suzy and his son. He was wearing a white T-shirt and blue pajama bottoms, his arms tan and muscular, his face a mixture of sleepiness, curiosity, and annoyance. "Yes?" he muttered.

I noticed the tattoo of a cross on his neck. I raised my gun at his face. He snapped his head back, but then froze. He was looking at me, not the gun. There was a stubborn quality in his expression, like he'd had a gun in his face before, like he didn't want to be afraid but couldn't help it either.

"Open the door and then put up your hands," I ordered calmly.

He did as I said, slowly, withdrawing into the foyer of the house, then into the edge of the living room as I followed him inside, leaving some distance between us. I kept the front door half open, then turned on a small lamp by the couch and caught the familiar scent of shrimp paste in the air.

Their house was furnished with all the fancy stuff required of a wealthy, middle-aged couple, but what caught my eye was the large aquarium against the wall, the tall wooden crucifix above the fireplace, and the vases everywhere filled with fresh flowers. Daffodils, pink tulips, Oriental lilies, chrysanthemums—I had become used to all of them over the years.

The rain was pummeling the roof above us—a steady, violent drone. I watched him watch me and imagined what I must have looked like to him: a pale bald stranger with a gun, still pointed squarely at his face, standing there in his dark living room in drenched clothes, dripping water onto his wife's pristine carpet. She used to yell at me for merely walking on the carpet in my shoes.

"You take what you want," he said in a loud whisper. "I not gonna stop you. My wallet right there." He nodded at the table beside me where his wallet lay by the telephone and some car keys. Behind the phone stood a photo of him and Suzy on a beach. "Take my car too," he added. "Just go."

I picked up the phone, listened for the dial tone, and then placed it face-up on the table.

"Anyone else here in the house?"

"No," he said immediately.

"No? Your wife—where's she?"

I could see him about to shake his head, like he was ready to deny having a wife, but then he realized he had all but pointed out the photo.

"She not here. She sleep at her mother house tonight. Just me here."

"Then why are there two cars in the driveway?"

"What do that matter? I tell you, it just me here tonight." He sounded irritated now, but his eyes were still wide and wary.

"So if I make you take me into the bedroom, I won't find anyone in there?"

He didn't say anything at first. He glanced toward the dark hallway to my left and then returned his scowl back on me. "I told you," he growled, but then lowered his voice. He didn't want to wake her. "Take my car. My wallet. Take anything you want and go."

"I tell you what," I said. "I'm gonna let *you* go. Walk out the door. Call for help if you want. You're free to leave."

"What?" He lowered his hands a bit.

"Go."

"What wrong with you?"

"I'm giving you a chance to leave without me shooting your face in. If no one's here, then you have nothing to worry about."

He just glowered at me. Then his hands fell. "Who are you?" he said in a thick voice. "What you want?"

I took a step closer to him, and he slowly put up his hands again without adjusting his glare on me.

"Last chance," I said.

"I not going anywhere."

I could still see fear in his eyes, but there was an angry calm in his demeanor now, in the flimsy way he held up his hands like I was an annoying child with a toy gun. I decided to believe everything his son had told me, and it filled me with both disappointment and relief, and then suddenly a heavy decisive sadness, like I no longer recognized that shrimp paste smell in the air or any of the outlandish flowers in this strange house—like a stone door had just closed on the last fifteen years of my life.

I edged closer but he did not budge. When my gun was finally within a foot of his face, I said, "Okay then," and struck him across the cheek with it. He staggered back and threw up a hand to shield himself.

I backed away. With his hand on his cheek, he watched me move toward the front door. I glanced at the hallway, at the doors in the darkness, wondering which room was their bedroom, which room might she be sleeping in, which door might she be standing behind right now, cupping her ear to the wood, holding her breath. I took a last look back at Sonny. His cheek was bleeding, his eyes dark and wide. How many more times would he save her like tonight?

I turned and ran out into the rain, stumbling across the gushing lawn, through the surging water in the street, toward my car. My engine roared to life. As I drove frantically past the house, I glimpsed Sonny standing on their front porch with his arms at his side, watching me speed away. I could have sworn I saw a darker, slimmer figure looming behind him.

I drove like a maniac for a few miles, cars honking at me as I passed them one by one. Then I slowed down. I turned on the radio. I reentered the highway. My body felt cool and the rain was soothing on the roof of the car. I turned off the radio and let the droning rain fill my ears. The night was like a tunnel. I drove a steady clip down the highway, promising myself that I would never again return to this or any desert.

PART II

Neon Grit

BENNIE ROJAS AND THE ROUGH RIDERS

BY PABLO MEDINA

West Las Vegas

for Chris Hudgins

T he morning Bennie Rojas boarded the plane for Las Vegas, he was convinced he'd just gotten a new lease on life. Cuba, that small island rocked by politics and hurricanes, was already beginning to fade into the past and all his troubles were but flickering specks in a distant black sky. In the seat to Bennie's right was one of the cooks from the Tropicana, the grandest nightclub in the world. To the left was a taciturn man with a scar that ran from his ear to his chin. He'd gotten on board in Miami, where the plane stopped on its way west, and had said nothing for four and a half hours. Naturally, Bennie assumed he did not speak any Spanish. Tough guys, Bennie thought. There's nothing you can do about them. And so he spent the whole trip talking to the cook, a fellow from Matanzas with a pencil-thin mustache and a head the shape of an eggplant. His name was Orlando Leyva.

They promised me a job, Orlando said nervously. Rivulets of sweat ran down his face and moistened his collar. He was a man given to perspiring and every time the plane hit an air pocket more sweat poured out of him.

They promised me a job too, Bennie said. I'm not worried. I'm told Lansky is a man of his word.

Unless he isn't.

Unless he isn't, Bennie had to admit. If it weren't for politics, Havana would be paradise. Maybe Las Vegas is paradise.

Las Vegas is in the desert.

Where do you think the Garden of Eden was located, *chico*, in the Caribbean?

Waiting for his bags in the claim area, it occurred to Bennie that Vegas was definitely not paradise but it sure was better than being unemployed in Havana living with a wife he couldn't stand. Besides, the revolutionaries considered all casino employees to be part of a vast conspiracy of corruption: worms feeding on the dung heap of capitalism. It was only a matter of time before they came after Bennie and put him in one of their decrepit jails.

But Bennie was an honest man. Not once during his ten-year career as a twenty-one dealer did he skim, not once did he pass chips or take a hit or sell a customer short. And he didn't get involved in politics or union business. All those complaints about unfair business practices and worker exploitation were not for him. He knew his bosses were not the most honest people in the world, but that wasn't his concern. He did his job, put his time in, had a Cuba libre (a *mentirita*, people were calling them lately) with the other dealers after his shift, and went home to his hysterical wife, whom he referred to as Juana la Loca. No one had anything on him, except that, in this particular case, he was on the wrong side of the fence.

For a while after Fidel took over the casinos remained open and Bennie went to work as usual. There were still American tourists coming to Cuba, suckers willing to have their money taken while they drank themselves silly on *daiquirís*. Bennie's job was to be a card dealer, not a priest. He'd see the *Americanos* at the table with a couple of gorgeous Cuban redheads wrapped around them and say to himself, Man, if I only had the money, I'd be right there next to them. Then one day two men came around asking if anyone wanted to go work in Las Vegas.

Las Vegas? Where the hell is that? Bennie asked. In the middle of nowhere, one of the guys said. But soon it's going to be the next Havana. You schmucks want to stay here and rot? Schmuck was an English word Bennie had never heard. The guy doing the talking kept straightening his tie as he spoke. He looked like a movie gangster except that he was very young, maybe twenty years old, and he spoke in a reedy falsetto.

I have a wife, Bennie started to say, then he remembered he hated his wife. This was a perfect opportunity to escape the clutches of his lousy marriage, to escape all he sensed was coming to the island.

Six other dealers volunteered that day as well as eight cooks, twenty showgirls, and an unknown number of musicians. Two weeks later Bennie was at the Las Vegas airport, waiting for his bags and making small talk with Orlando and three of his culinary colleagues. The taciturn man with the scar led the five of them to a Ford station wagon and drove them to a motel off Rancho Drive. It was mid-July and the heat rose from the asphalt, turning the station wagon into a pressure cooker. The heat of Havana was nothing compared to this. Bennie mentioned his discomfort to the cooks but they, used to the infernal atmosphere of commercial kitchens, thought nothing of it. Paradise indeed.

Another man met them at the motel and gave each of them a room key. Bennie's was number 207.

Good number to play, he said to Orlando. Number two is butterfly. Number seven is seashell.

Mine is 112. One is horse. Twelve is whore, Orlando responded. Not too good. That Chinese system is foolishness. There are better ways to make money.

Then the man announced that someone would be by for them the next morning at 7:30 and left.

For seven years Bennie lived in that motel, caught between a present substantially narrowed by a dead-end job and a suffocating nostalgia for the glories and joys of a past that was neither glorious nor joyous. His one friend, Orlando, was a man of limited intellectual capacity and no imagination to speak of. His conversations never strayed from the perfect demi-glace he'd concocted that morning or the bread he'd baked for lunch or the celebrity who'd entered the kitchen and offered his compliments on the salmon mousse. When Bennie tried to engage him in more expansive topics, such as baseball or women, a blank look came over Orlando's face and at the first opportunity he'd switch the conversation back to kitchen matters. Bennie worked the graveyard shift because nights were hardest for him to spend alone. He'd sleep mornings as much as he could, until about noon or so. Then he'd shower, pick up the local paper, and go to a cafeteria on Sahara where he'd have two eggs fried over easy, bacon, toast, and bad American coffee. The rest of the time was his to do as he wanted. He napped, read the paper again, and, in the cool months, took long walks on streets that led nowhere but back into themselves. His shift began at 11 p.m. but more often than not he did a double, starting at 3 o'clock and going straight through until 7 the next morning.

Making money wasn't the object; he simply had too much time on his hands and no way of whiling it away. The summer was too hot for anything but sitting in air-conditioning; the winter was high season and Joey, his pit boss, threw as much work at him as he could handle. His wife, who had since moved to Miami, sent him divorce papers, which he signed and sent right back. There was no ocean to look at like there was in Havana; only desert and fancy casinos where the tourists dropped their money. Mostly there was a lot of dust which got in his eyes and made him teary, as if he wasn't teary enough already. There were plenty of women, beautiful ones, but none was accessible to him, a simple dealer from the tropics with a thick Cuban accent—like Desi Arnaz chewing on a raw steak, Joey once said—and the looks of a Galician grocer. The way to attract women, an uncle of his told him long ago, is to impress them with your power and your wealth. Good looks will only go so far. The woman needs to see you as a god, and those attributes are the closest we humans have to divinity. And just when Bennie had resigned himself to a life of celibacy, he met a woman, a round Mexican who cooked him fiery dishes and made love like a Zapotec beast. She always brought food—enchiladas, tacos, moles—enough for him and for Orlando who lived downstairs. Her name was Mercedes. She took care of both of them, in more ways than one, but she had her eye on Bennie. *Barriga llena, corazón contento*, she would say with a sparkle in her eye, expecting any moment he would say back to her the magic words.

As he sat outside his room on his day off, Bennie heard a commotion on the first level of the motel, followed by a woman's voice that sounded very much like Mercedes screaming, *Puto, cabrón, hijo de la chingada*. He rushed down the steps to the first level and saw Orlando the cook on the floor, leaning against the brick outer wall of his room with a butcher knife stuck halfway into his chest. His eyes were glazed and a string of bloody saliva hung from his lips. Orlando babbled something about someone taking twenty thousand and said nothing else. He looked up at Bennie before letting out a long sigh like a balloon deflating; then his eyes lost their bearing and his head drooped softly to the side.

Bennie's first instinct was to go back upstairs and forget what he had seen, let someone else deal with the situation. Instead, out of deference to his friend, he looked around to make sure no one else had witnessed the killing, maneuvered Orlando away from the wall with great difficulty—he was a bulky guy, as cooks tend to be—and dragged him back into the room. Bennie shut the door and turned the air-conditioning as high as it would go, figuring it would help preserve Orlando. He sat on the unmade bed and tried to light a cigarette. His hands were shaking so badly it took four tries before he could bring the match to the tip and take the first drag. Sure, he'd seen plenty of people die, like his mother and her sisters, and a cousin with leukemia, but never like this, with a knife sticking out of them and their last words about money. This would never happen in Cuba, he thought, then thought again. Of course it would. Still, at this moment he wanted to be back there in his old apartment on Lagunas Street where his parents had lived and their parents before them, now occupied by his revolution-crazed cousin Aleida, who had beautiful eyes but farted like a foghorn.

Bennie surveyed the room and spied a half-full bottle of Don Q rum on the dresser, which he could reach without having to stand up. Two healthy swigs settled him somewhat and he considered the situation. Calling the police was out of the question. They'd snoop and his bosses weren't fond of snooping. So he called Joey, his pit boss at the casino—he'd know what to do—and waited for him to show up.

It took Joey three hours to get to the motel. When he saw

the cook lying on the carpet, his first words were Holy fucking shit. Orlando's face had acquired a blue pallor and *rigor mortis* was beginning to set in, no matter that it was damn cold in the room. Those were Joey's second words: It's damn cold in here, followed by, What was your fight about?

Fight? Bennie kept to himself the fact that he heard Mercedes screaming just before he found the cook. Joey, he said, I didn't kill Orlando. He was my friend.

Friends kill each other all the time. Why didn't you take the knife out of him? The longer he's dead, the harder it's going to be. And next time, put a shower curtain under him. That way the blood won't get on the rug.

You do it, Joey. You take the knife out. I couldn't even watch my mother kill a chicken.

Didn't they teach you anything in that damn country of yours? Fucking Latin lover can't get his hands dirty.

Joey looked long and hard at Bennie, then he kneeled next to Orlando and jiggled the knife handle. Blood's pretty much set. We won't be needing the curtains. And before he'd finished saying the word curtains, he had the knife out and was holding it next to his head. It was a huge nasty thing. For an instant Bennie had the image of the blade entering Orlando and causing massive damage to his inner organs. The thought made him shiver.

This is a job for the rough riders, Joey said, and made a phone call. In ten minutes two men showed up, a tall slim guy in a gray suit and a short heavyset one in a blue shirt and beige linen trousers. Bennie noticed that the short man had a tomato sauce stain on his right pant leg. The men looked at dead Orlando on the floor and proceeded to ransack drawers, pulling them out of the dresser and upending their contents on the body. When they were done with the drawers they took the bed apart, then started on the closet and rifled through Orlando's clothes, discarding them this way and that and making a huge mess. Finally, one of them turned to Bennie, who was now standing in a corner of the room, and said, Where's the money?

Money? Bennie asked, trying to be as sheepish as possible. Now the three men were looking at him, waiting for an answer. I don't know about no money. Bennie's legs were shaking and his throat was beginning to tighten as it did every time he was nervous, making him cluck like a chicken.

We better cut him up, one of the men said. It'll be easier that way.

Bennie made a move for the door.

Where you going? said the man in the blue shirt.

I live upstairs, said Bennie. I just thought I'd lie down for a while. I work tonight.

You staying right here, Jack. He turned to the man in the suit. Bring the tools.

Bennie needed to sit down but the mattress was up against the window leaning over the two armchairs. The only other chair was on the opposite side and he'd have to step over Orlando. He looked at Joey, who shrugged.

Joey, please, he implored him, I don't want to watch this.

I don't either. They'll do it in the bathroom.

But I can hear.

Cover your ears.

After the two men carted Orlando's pieces wrapped in wax paper and tied neatly with butcher string out of the room, they came back in and stood on either side of Bennie and asked again where the money was.

Bennie's lips were shaking so badly they couldn't meet to form words, to say simply, I don't know, I didn't take it.

Despite the very real danger he was facing, however, there was a spot of coolness inside him that kept him from falling apart. It surprised him. He'd always thought of himself as a coward. That coolness led him to conclude with absolute certainty that Mercedes had taken the twenty thousand but he wasn't about to tell these guys that. Right now every little bit of knowledge he kept from them was to his benefit.

Then Joey saved him. Guys, he said, Bennie don't know anything. He's a stupid Cuban. All he knows is dealing cards. Leave him alone.

The two men looked at each other, then back at Joey. The small one said, We don't take orders from you.

Listen fuck-head, Bennie here doesn't have the money. And if Archie gives you any grief, tell him I answer directly to Meyer and he can go suck a moose.

The men grumbled some curse words at Joey and left to drop pieces of Orlando all over the desert. Bennie asked Joey what was going on. Either Joey didn't know or he didn't let on. Later that night, as the two of them shared a six-pack of beer, Bennie asked Joey how he knew these thugs.

I got some juice in this town, Bennie. Me and Meyer grew up on the same block in the Lower East Side. You can't fuck around with Lansky. He owns everyone in Vegas, including me. He owns you, except you don't know it. Orlando tried to pull a fast one and he paid for it.

What did he do? Bennie asked.

I'd like to know that myself. The whole thing's unsavory, I know, but there's nothing to be done about it. Joey used the word unsavory with great delicacy, saying every sound as if it were a precious jewel. You sure you don't know anything about that money those guys were talking about?

Bennie shook his head.

I have a feeling you do, Joey said. He finished his beer and left.

Bennie didn't see Mercedes for two weeks, and every day of those two weeks one of Archie's men came by asking about the money. Joey's so-called juice was the only thing between Bennie and the butcher's block. It was the loneliest period of his life. He worked, he ate, he came home, and he sat by the door to his room until it was time for bed. Day in and day out without a holiday, not even Christmas, on which he worked a double shift and made five hundred dollars. The money didn't matter that much to him. He had nothing to spend it on. He didn't like whores and had no need for a car. He paid a full twenty dollars a week for his room. His work clothes were provided for by the casino and he had no family to care for, not in Vegas or Miami or Cuba. As he pondered his sorry state, cursing the day he ever decided to leave the island, he heard a knock at his door and Mercedes's plaintive voice asking to be let in.

Where have you been? he asked.

I was in Mexico but I'm back now.

I can see that, he said. What happened between you and Orlando?

He tried a nasty thing on me, *ese cabrón*.

You didn't have to kill him.

He wouldn't stop. There was a knife there. I just try to scare him but he kept coming and so I hit him with it. I just try to scare him.

By now Mercedes had grown very agitated. Her eyes were wide open and her lips were spread into a grimace, like those Mixtec goddesses you see biting into the hearts of men. *Hijo de la chingada*, she grumbled.

Bennie wanted to shut the door on her and forget she ever existed. What about the money? he asked.

Mercedes was silent for a moment and grew meek, hunching her shoulders downward and looking up at him with beseeching eyes.

I didn't steal it. I just found it.

Oh, to be back in Cuba right now, he thought. Communism had to be better than this.

Mujer, are you crazy? You know half of Vegas is looking for you? What did you do with it?

Mercedes was silent.

If you don't return that money to its owners, they're going to grind us up into *picadillo*. You understand?

Mercedes straightened up and narrowed her eyes into fierce slits. Let me tell you three things, she said. First, the money is hidden; second, I ain't giving it to nobody; third, you are a big *pendejo*.

Why do you come here? You are incriminating me, he said to her, which was stupid, considering he was incriminated the moment he landed at the Vegas airport.

I miss you, *güerito*. I want you to go away with me and we can be rich together.

That's when he took her by the arm, shoved her out of the room, and slammed the door. When he turned around he saw a letter-size white envelope lying on the dresser. Bennie sat on the bed and stared at it, not knowing whether to pick it up and count it or flush it down the toilet or simply ignore it as if it were never there. He did the latter for a few hours until his fantasies got the better of him and he started thinking of everything he could do with the money. He could buy himself a fancy car. That would draw the women. He could buy a house. That was a smart thing to do. Or he could escape Las Vegas once and for all. Go to Miami, open up a barber shop, run a small book on the side, marry a nice *criolla* who would give him lots of children.

What about Mercedes? After all, she was the one who had killed Orlando and took the money. She worked incessantly, the poor woman, doing laundry, cleaning houses, and selling herself when the opportunity availed itself to lonely men like him who lived in cheap motels without a hope in the world. Most of what she made from her menial labors she sent to her family in Mexico like a dutiful daughter. At least she said she did. Eventually Bennie's sense of fair play won out. Mercedes was foul-mouthed and overweight but not a bad sort. If he squinted really hard, he could see traces of María Félix in her features. If she killed Orlando she did it in self-defense. How many women would not have done the same under similar circumstances? The more he stared at the envelope the more he thought, Mercedes, Mercedes with that singsong Oaxacan accent of hers and hair like black milk and ever-so-dim resemblance to the most beautiful actress of all time.

He called in sick to work and sat on the bed consumed by an idyll he had never before experienced. He imagined himself in Mexico, owner of a hacienda surrounded by acres and acres of *maguey* and a distillery bearing his name, Benjamín Rojas, Producer of Fine Tequilas. He imagined a stable of black *paso fino* horses and a herd of gleaming prize zebu cattle that were the envy of every *ranchero* in the *comarca*. He built a whole architecture of fantasy with him at the center: cars, women, presidents, prime ministers, cardinals, all currying his favor. What Mexico needed was a Cuban with balls, *coño*, who would create an empire of liquor that would rival the great distilleries of the world—Bacardi, Jack Daniel's, Hiram Walker—and with those twenty thousand dollars Mercedes had given him, by God, he could do it.

That's when someone knocked at the door.

Bennie picked up the envelope and stuffed it into the

back of his pants. He looked through the peephole and saw that it was Joey.

Jesus, Joey said as he walked into Bennie's room. It's freezing in here. You'd figure Cuba was in Siberia the way you guys like the cold.

It's on its way there, Bennie said.

Joey sat on the bed and lit up a Cuban Churchill, every puff of smoke round and sweet and perfect.

You have the money, Joey said. As a matter of fact, I'm willing to bet my left testicle you have it on your person even as we speak.

Bennie felt his throat tightening. He sat on the armchair, took out a handkerchief, and blew his nose. The cigar smoke was getting to him. How about Mercedes? he said. You know, the Mexican.

Yeah, the one you wiped your sword with. A man needs that every once in a while. Joey blew a puff of blue smoke up toward the ceiling. You fucking Cubans can sure make cigars, he said. It's about the only thing you're good at. Mercedes is taken care of. Twenty G's is pocket change for Meyer, but he just hates to be swindled. Why don't you give me the money, spare yourself?

Bennie hesitated. All those dreams of women and *paso finos* and thousands of acres of *maguey* plantings going up with Joey's smoke. He reached behind him and handed Joey the envelope.

I'll make you a deal, Bennie. I keep fifteen and I'll give you five. Call it a reward for a job well done. Just between you and me. Nobody else has to know.

Joey counted out the five G's and passed them back to Bennie, who took the money without hesitation and put it in his pocket. As he did so he felt his blood thicken and his heart slow a few beats.

After Joey left, Bennie pulled the shades shut and lay on the bed. He tried to summon up his fantasies but all he could think of was the money in his pocket. What was fat Mercedes to him anyway, and Orlando with that eggplant face of his? Five thousand wasn't twenty but it was enough for a down-payment on a small house. The wife and the book operation would come eventually. So would the juice. Without his realizing, the coolness inside had turned to ice.

BITS AND PIECES

BY CHRISTINE MCKELLAR

Green Valley

The grinding rumble of heavy construction equipment awakened Madison Feldon an hour before her alarm was set to go off. She swung her short, muscular legs out of bed and stumbled into the master bathroom of her two-bedroom condo.

"Those rude bastards," she grumbled as she sat down on the padded toilet seat. "It's not even 7 o'clock and already they're at it."

Madison sat for a few minutes moodily contemplating the day ahead of her. She was a fitness trainer at a prestigious private club in Green Valley, a burgeoning upscale suburb of Las Vegas. She had a small but steady clientele. Madison was disciplined and very knowledgeable about nutrition and physical therapy. "It's the social shit I can't get a handle on," she muttered. She sighed as she stood up, then went to the sink to wash her hands.

The face reflecting back at her from the mirror, the only mirror in the condo, wasn't necessarily attractive even on a good day, much less after a night of restless tossing and turning. Madison's brown eyes had puffy bags beneath them and were slightly bloodshot. At twenty-nine years of age, her skin had a mottled look from too many summers in the dry, windy desert. Madison was stocky and compact. She was the only child of Louie and Rachel Feldon. The Feldons had carved a niche in the Las Vegas Valley in the real estate market. Along with their good friends, Al and Lois Clavell, they also owned a small local casino that was a virtual cash cow.

It was spring in the high desert, and Madison had left her sliding bedroom door open to take advantage of the cool night air. Now, mingled with the noise of the machinery, she could hear the occasional shouts and curses of workers on the construction site. With much more force than necessary, she went and slammed the glass door shut. Madison stood, hands on her hips, glaring at the men in hard hats. Clouds of dirt rose and swirled in the air like masses of swarming angry bees. A chorus of muted honking began as commuters vented their frustration over the congestion caused by the project.

Madison could feel the tic begin in her eyelid. She could never see it when she looked in the bathroom mirror. But it was there, she knew it. She could feel it. Just like she'd felt every nuance of her father's subtle and not so subtle criticisms. It was his short, micro jabs that had caused the most damage. Not the clean, hard thrusts or stabs that Madison could—and did—parry or fend off.

"It's not my fault I'm not the son he wanted," Madison mused out loud to the oblivious construction workers. "He would forgive me even that, I suppose, if I looked like Mother. At least he'd have a showcase daughter he could marry off to some money."

Madison looked like her father. Short, stocky. Brown nondescript hair and eyes, an overly large nose, and a slightly receding chin. Her mother was tall and had a willowy figure that looked elegant even under the worst of circumstances. Madison couldn't recall one single time when her mother looked anything less than composed and perfectly coiffed.

Her father, on the other hand, was loud and obnoxious.

Louie seemed to revel in exemplifying the typical Jewish tycoon. Everything was a crisis to him. And he was merciless when it came to picking on his only child.

"You want that I should spend fifty grand on a bat mitzvah for you when you look like a schlump?" he'd screamed at the chubby, prepubescent teenage girl. As always, her mother seemed to fade gracefully into the background during one of Louie's tirades. Louie laid down the law. There would be no rite of passage for Madison, not until she lost twenty pounds. Madison lost the weight. That was when the tics started.

Later on, one of her therapists expressed her horror at what went on for years at the Feldon home. While Louie and Rachael were wined and dined most evenings, the housekeeper strictly monitored Madison's diet. Every morsel she ate had to be accounted for. Every carb and every calorie. Madison attended a private school and her humiliation was without measure when her father showed up at the dean's office. Madison was called from class and had to sit in an agony of embarrassment as Louie made it loud and clear she was to eat only the meager lunches provided by her parents. The cafeteria was off limits.

Her stomach growled and Madison noticed one of the hard hats across the street seemed to be looking into her second-floor window. "Eat this," she sneered, and flipped him the bird. She brushed her teeth and went downstairs to the kitchen. Madison ground fresh coffee beans and began brewing a pot of coffee. Then she opened the refrigerator door and stood looking thoughtfully at its contents.

Madison was unaware that the tic had moved from her eye to her upper lip. The refrigerator was stocked, like the tiny pantry, almost to the point of bulging. Unopened packages of deli meats, cheeses, and bagels and cream cheese in all flavors were crammed inside. There were pints of yogurt, bottles of chocolate milk, and doggie bags full of uneaten meals. Madison poked through the contents of the refrigerator before pulling out the only item that wasn't covered in mold, curdled, or decayed: a carton of egg whites.

As she scrambled the egg whites in a Teflon-coated pan, Madison thought about the new client she was to begin training later that morning. He was a walk-in referral. Garvey Kendall sounded nice enough over the phone. He'd actually seemed a bit nervous. Madison smiled as she measured one and a half ounces of egg onto a paper plate. She had a mental picture of Garvey: tall, geeky. Probably wore glasses and was eager to put some muscle on his skinny frame.

Her cell phone rang, its shrill intrusion into her breakfast moment causing her to drop a plastic forkful of egg onto the dirty parquet floor. "Damnit!" She glanced at the caller ID. Her stomach relaxed when she saw it wasn't her mother calling. It was her shrink's office. Dr. Golob's secretary briskly informed her that tomorrow's appointment would have to be rescheduled. The doctor had a family emergency.

Partly due to her mother's insistence, but also partly due to simply needing someone to talk to, Madison had been in therapy for years. In school she hadn't been that popular to begin with, then word had gotten around about her father's dietary directive. She became the constant source of entertainment for her creatively cruel classmates.

The strict diet she was forced into seemed to interfere with her pubescence too. While other girls her age were whispering and giggling about bra sizes and tampons versus pads, Madison remained flat chested and untouched by the monthly curse. It wasn't until she was fourteen that she got her first period. Even so, she remained ridiculously unendowed with breasts.

It was Dr. Golob who'd suggested Madison study nutrition and fitness training. He'd pointed out she could modify her body type with a regimen of a proper diet and exercise, so why not make a living out of it? "People will *have* to talk to you, Madison. Actually, your clients will be counting on you. Trusting you to help them improve their bodies. You really need the socialization. Consider it part of your therapy."

Her last session with Dr. Golob hadn't been a fruitful one, to say the least. She'd been complaining about the construction surrounding her. Vegas was booming. Old familiar buildings and hotels were being imploded and demolished. High-rise condos and towering casinos were vying for space in the once clear blue sky of the valley. Lake Mead was like a gargantuan bathtub with a faulty plug and a bad case of ring-around-the-ninety-foot rim.

Madison had moved to the suburbs six years ago to escape the congestion. Now the Green Valley area was pretty much a metropolis of its own. "Did you know, Dr. Golob, that years ago on Tomiyasu Lane there was a vegetable farm owned by a Japanese man named Mr. Tomiyasu?"

Her stomach growled again when she remembered plump red strawberries and sweet ears of corn that the housekeeper would bring home. Madison was so hungry all of the time back then that her sense of smell had sharpened considerably. She would imagine that by drawing in deep breathes through her nose she was actually tasting the fresh produce. This was something she never shared with the therapist.

Nor did she share with Dr. Golob how deeply affected she was by the constant cycle of destruction, then resurrection, surrounding her. Even at night, machines were digging and scraping away at the soil, leaving deep scars in the million-years-old earth. Machines that in the yellow lights used by the construction workers looked like something from a Martian collective.

Cold and relentless, they jabbed and dug and poked; just like her father had jabbed and dug and poked at her, Madison would think. Then the builders would come and layer by layer cover up the blemishes and pockmarks. They would be followed by the landscapers who planted trees, bushes, and flowers that really had no business in the arid soil of the Nevada desert. So, too, had Madison built walls of concrete around her, and layered her façade with cosmetics and apparel foreign to her nature.

"Oh no! Gotta go!" Madison, lost in her mental ramblings, was running late. She quickly showered, then dressed in her usual training ensemble: blue shorts, white shirt, socks, and Nikes. Her short curly hair needed only a dab of mousse to keep it in place. She applied mascara to her sparse lashes, a hint of blush to her cheeks, and some lip gloss on her narrow mouth.

Madison strode purposely to her old BMW, then inched her way out into the traffic on Silver Springs Road. She wasn't too concerned about upsetting her client with her tardiness. She knew she could blame it on the construction work surrounding the area.

Lately, Madison was blaming everything on the construction, from her lack of sleep when she woke up drenched in sweat as the machines chewed and gnawed their way through the night (she never did remember the nightmares about her father) to her increasing desire to eat the food she would only allow to rot in the refrigerator. (Her stomach seemed to rumble more and more each day in a synchronized cacophony with the backhoes and loaders.)

Madison pulled into the club parking lot and got her gym

bag out of the trunk. Three women dressed in short colorful tennis skirts walked by, bright sunlight flashing off the diamonds on their fingers. They were laughing, oblong bags slung across their backs. Thin, blond, and full-breasted, they passed by Madison without so much as a glance.

Garvey was waiting by the water cooler in the gym. To her surprise, he wasn't tall and skinny. He was short and stocky like her. His hair was black and longer than the current buzz-cut fashion. He had shy brown eyes and perfectly unblemished olive skin. She soon found out his mother was Latina. His father was Caucasian and owned a concrete-mixing company.

Madison eased Garvey through the usual trainer's monologue. What were his goals? How committed was he to meeting those goals? What were his eating habits? Where did he want to see the most improvement? She weighed him in and calculated his body-fat index, then took him through thirty minutes of a light workout on the weight machines.

Two clients later, Madison was ready to call it a day. On her way home she decided to stop at Starbucks for her one indulgence in life, a caramel macchiato. Hot beverage in hand, she picked up a copy of a local alternative weekly and wandered out onto the patio.

"Miss Feldon?"

Madison squinted into the bright light. Garvey Kendall was smiling shyly down at her. He had a cardboard cup in one hand and a small brown bag in the other. He shifted nervously from one foot to the other.

"Mind if I join you?"

For a moment, she *did* mind. She minded, all right, because she could smell the cinnamon coffee cake with its thick sweet icing that was nestled in the bag he set down on the round metal table. She minded because she didn't appreciate him intruding on her solitude. She minded because he was a client, just an eighty-dollar hour, of which her cut was only forty percent. She minded because he was a man, and Madison knew from past experience that men didn't like her.

Five years ago, Madison's only friend, her cousin Sarah, had come to Las Vegas to celebrate spring break, and that was when Madison had lost her virginity. The cousins were the same age, born just weeks apart. Sarah had a clear complexion, long brunette hair, and sparkling blue eyes that matched her upbeat personality. Sarah was the darling daughter among three sons. Sarah's family lived in Chicago.

A new hotel-casino had opened not far from Madison's condo. It was the vivacious Sarah who suggested they should go to dinner at the hotel. After dinner, the two women went out onto the casino floor to play poker. Madison found she was actually enjoying herself. The pile of chips in front of her was gradually increasing.

One of the seats at the table opened up and was quickly occupied. Madison glanced at the newcomer, then almost knocked over the cocktail at her elbow. She'd seen him at the sports club many times. While she couldn't remember his name, she certainly remembered how he looked while he was working out. (Muscles taut and straining under his glistening, tanned skin.) Madison felt a flush of warmth as she recalled how she enjoyed surreptitiously tracing with her eyes the vinelike pattern of pumped-up veins along his hard body.

The handsome man was sitting beside Sarah, and the two were obviously flirting with one another. The chips in front of Madison began to dwindle. She was paying more attention to the action between her cousin and the bodybuilder than to the poker game. Madison had just asked the bored-looking

Asian dealer to cash her out when Sarah stood up and motioned to her.

"Let's go to the nightclub downstairs. Bradley's going to join us." Bradley was looking at the two women, but his eyes passed right over Madison. He nodded at Sarah as if to signal he'd be joining her shortly.

The club was packed. Madison and Sarah had to wait in line for ten minutes. Bradley caught up with them, but the only place the trio could find to sit was on one of the large divans on the sprawling outdoor veranda. Bradley seemed to know everyone. Martini after martini began to appear. Madison quickly got drunk enough to attempt small talk with Bradley. Her cousin seemed to have lost interest in the body-builder once he'd introduced her to a mangy-looking rock-star wannabe.

People were thronging around the patio. Soon total strangers were sitting or reclining on the divan—laughing, drinking, kissing, and fondling their partners. Madison was pressed against Bradley. The close contact with him again sent a heated sensation throughout her body.

When Madison stood up to go use the powder room, she was unsteady on her feet. She was vaguely aware of Sarah shaking her arm and pointing to Bradley. The next thing she knew she was home—and Bradley was with her. Sarah had cajoled him into driving Madison to the condo.

Madison wasn't simply home with Bradley. She was in bed with him. His breath reeked of vodka and vermouth. His kisses were sloppy, and he was groping at her thighs. Madison didn't remember taking off her clothes, but she was naked. Bradley was wearing only his shirt. She could feel his bare muscled thighs against hers.

"Wait a minute, wait a minute." The ceiling seemed to

spin. "Brad, I think I'm going to be sick." Madison struggled to move out from underneath him.

"No you're not." His words were slurred.

He was lying completely on top of her, his weight pressing her down, down, down.

Brad managed a drunken laugh. "Shit, girl, you really are flatter'n a pancake."

Madison felt bile rising in her throat, but she managed to suppress the gag reflex. Bradley was now fully between her spread legs, and he began to position himself to move inside of her. Madison had read enough romance novels in her years of isolation to expect that her first time with a man would be somewhat painful. (Later, she would reflect that romance novels, like everything else in her life, were filled with nothing but lies and bullshit.)

When Bradley forced himself into Madison, she cried out. She was a fairly strong woman, and she pushed at his shoulders and thrust with her legs. She almost succeeded in bucking him off. Bradley stopped the invasion of her body for a moment. "Oh shit. You a virgin?"

Madison began sobbing. It wasn't that she didn't want to have sex with him. But this was supposed to be *her* moment. Her first time with a man was supposed to be seductive, romantic. The man who deflowered her was supposed to be gentle, compassionate, and bring her slowly from orgasm to orgasm. Not treat her like some blow-up doll.

Madison managed to say yes to the man looming over her. A man whose face she could barely see in the darkness of her bedroom. A man who said to her with obvious annoyance in his voice, "Oh well. Let's just get this over with then." And he did. And that was it.

At the gym, Bradley didn't avoid Madison; he simply ignored her. It was as though they'd never met. Madison didn't tell Sarah what happened that night. She never even told her shrink, Dr. Golob. Sex was one topic Madison Feldon avoided at all costs. She never picked up another romance novel at the grocery store, either. Now here she was being invited to sit intimately and alone with a man.

"Hey, are you all right?"

Madison detected a note of genuine concern in Garvey's voice. "Yeah, I'm fine." She motioned with her hand. "Go ahead, have a seat."

"I don't mean to bother you. I just wanted to tell you that I know I'm in good hands." His smile was simple and genuine.

"Thanks. I appreciate clients who appreciate me." She smiled back.

A cement truck lumbered by on the congested street, bits of rock bouncing out of the revolving drum and skittering along the sidewalk near the coffeehouse. Madison winced and let out a harsh, irritated breath. She could feel the minute twitch begin in her left eye. Her uninvited guest didn't seem to notice her distress. He kept rambling on about the importance of fitness and nutrition.

Garvey opened the brown bag and offered to share the coffee cake with Madison. Now her eye *and* her lip were twitching. She looked at everything but the tempting pastry and the man sitting across from her.

"I hardly think *that's* nutritious. It's all empty calories and major carbs, you know." Madison's mouth flooded. She clenched her hands under the table.

Garvey laughed. He had a good laugh. It was light and easy, almost infectious. She found herself responding to the sound. Madison Feldon giggled.

* * *

Two weeks later, Madison was at the gym with Garvey. He was a dependable client. He hadn't missed a single one of his tri-weekly sessions. He was eager to please and quick to pick up on the nuances of working with weights. They were both sweating when the hour ended, and Madison hurried to the showers in the women's locker room.

No one at the club had ever seen her naked except for Bradley, but then he didn't really see her That Night, and he certainly never saw her again. Wrapped in a big towel, Madison kept her eyes averted from the potpourri of nude bodies around her. Fat, lean, wrinkled, smooth, young, old; from the corner of her eye she glanced at them, these naked females who moved unself-consciously through the rituals of blow drying their hair, moisturizing their bodies, and chatting on cell phones.

Garvey was waiting for her outside the club entrance. He asked if she'd like to meet him at Starbucks. Madison shrugged. "Only if you promise not to buy any junk food." Again, that easy laugh of his.

Over coffee, Madison shared her thoughts about the growth and construction in Green Valley.

"These developers are eco-rapists. They don't care about the environment. They don't design or plan with any thought to water conservation or traffic flow." Madison scowled. "When I first moved to Green Valley, you could hear coyotes yipping and howling at night. Now all I hear is the beep-beep of backhoes and loaders." She looked at Garvey. "Where do you think the coyotes have gone?"

"I don't know, Maddy."

Madison flinched at his use of the nickname. Only the Feldon's housekeeper had ever called her that. Despite having been designated as the enforcer of Madison's diet, Mrs. Anson was kindhearted. On occasion she would treat the ever-hungry young girl to something special: a frozen Popsicle or a sorbet. They had to be careful since Louie Feldon demanded that his daughter weigh herself in his presence every morning. Her whole body twitched at the memory of the invective Louie would rain down on her naked body if the digital scale reflected so much as a gain of one ounce.

Garvey was shredding a paper napkin into a little pile in front of him. "I think you'd be surprised at what goes into the building process. Everything follows a plan. Water, sewer, gas pipes have to be laid down. Houses have to be wired for phone and electricity."

He pushed the torn bits of paper onto his palm, then dumped them in the unused ashtray. "I don't know if I mentioned it but I'm taking classes at night in architecture at UNLV."

Madison murmured a polite response.

"My dad's cement company has the contract for a new housing tract up in Roma Hills. Want to go there with me this weekend? Maybe if I explained the construction process to you, you'd better appreciate it."

Madison stood up abruptly. "We'll see. I've been busy with a project at home. You have my cell number. Why don't you give me a call Saturday or Sunday?"

She was gone before he could respond. Back at the condo, Madison looked around the combination living room/dining room with sudden distaste. Unopened copies of the *Las Vegas Review-Journal* were scattered about. An assortment of gym shoes and dirty socks lay abandoned near the couch and around the base of the dining room table.

She went to her messy bedroom to change into sweatpants and a T-shirt. Madison had long ago given up the habit of making her bed in the morning. The project she'd told Garvey about lay in bits and pieces on her dresser. Madison swept everything onto a tray and carried it to the living room. Her stomach told her it was dinnertime, but she knew that if she drank lots of water and got busy with her hands, she could put off the inevitable for another hour or so.

Madison had taken up beading as a hobby. She would sit, focused for hours, stringing different shapes and shades of glass and crystal beads along thin wires. She made necklaces, bracelets, and earrings. Bit by bit, piece by piece, she created objects of beauty. Strands of sparkling cosmetic jewelry were strewn all over the condo; they hung from the windows; they lined the counters and tabletops. They were in the bathroom, in the shower, on all the doorknobs.

They reflected light just like her first and only formal gown at her lavish bat mitzvah. Louie Feldon had been louder than usual that night. The party wasn't so much about presenting his young daughter as it was about showing off his wealth. The rite of passage and elegant celebration had been a blur to Madison. She was severely anemic at the time, but no one was aware of it.

When she could no longer ignore the hunger pangs, Madison set the beading aside. She didn't even bother to open the refrigerator. She went straight to the pantry and pulled out a can of powdered whey protein. *Breakfast is the only important meal of the day. Carbs at night are unnecessary. Carbs and calories make you fat.* Louie's voice was loud in her head. Of course, it wasn't really her father's voice. Louie Feldon wasn't talking to anyone these days. Louie Feldon had died of a massive heart attack a few months after Madison fled the family home and moved out to the suburbs.

"He ate and drank himself to death," Madison told the

unconcerned reporter on the television. Her mother, Rachael, had seemed unfazed by the passing of her husband. But then, she'd had a lover keeping her company during her thirty-five-year marriage: Prince Valium and his court of Soma, vodka, and prescribed diet pills.

With Louie gone, Madison's mother no longer had to keep her diary updated.

It had been Rachael's assigned duty to keep a daily record of every morsel Madison put in her mouth. It was also her job to report nightly to her husband every act of misbehavior on their daughter's part. Whether it was that Madison hadn't used her napkin properly, or that she'd sat with her legs slightly apart and not crossed at the ankles, Rachael had logged every malefaction.

Garvey phoned Saturday while Madison was at the gym with a client. Madison left the messages, unheard, in her voice mailbox. The construction behind her condo seemed to have increased in urgency. The crew was working night and day in a frenzy to complete yet another high-rise condominium complex.

Madison had called the county office to complain. She was told the developer had a permit to work at night. She quit grinding coffee beans in the morning. The grating sound of the blades reducing the hard little beans into fine grounds seemed to be a mocking echo of the outdoor machinery shredding her nerves.

Madison noticed Sunday afternoon, when she began to work on a necklace for Garvey, that she'd developed a tremor in her hands. She'd never designed a necklace for a man, and she'd been looking forward to the challenge. However, instead of gliding onto the long wire strand, the black and silver beads rolled from her useless fingers and onto the mottled carpet.

Madison's cell phone beeped incessantly in the background. Her mother could go for weeks without contacting her daughter, then she'd get manic and speed dial Madison. In a salute to the departed Louie, Rachael would demand to know Madison's weight and if she were sticking to her diet.

The doorbell rang and Madison froze. Aside from the occasional annoying salesperson or Jehovah's Witness, no one came to 5555 Silver Springs Road. Madison looked through the peephole. She was fisheye to fisheye with Garvey Kendall. Should she pretend she wasn't home? Should she step outside and send him away? Should she, could she, would she just let him in?

Madison opened the door a crack.

"Hey, Maddy, I hope I'm not bothering you, but you haven't answered your phone and I was wondering if you're all right." *That shy smile and those cocker spaniel eyes.*

"I'm fine, Garvey. How'd you know where I live?"

"I saw you turn in here after we left Starbucks the other day. Your name's on the mailbox ledger."

Thoughts and images raced through Madison's mind. Louie, Rachael, Mrs. Anson, and Bradley all vied for her attention. She jerked her head as though to fling them out of her consciousness. Finally, she opened the door for Garvey to come in. He didn't seem to notice the dirt and the clutter. Rather, he noticed immediately the strings of scintillating beads that adorned the small condo. The sunlight seemed to capture and magnify the many facets, sending little rainbows dancing around the drab interior.

"Nice. Did you make all of these?" His voice was admiring.

Madison nodded. She offered him a bottle of water. They

talked for some time about the role of progress versus environment. Garvey shared with Madison some of the conflicting thoughts she had inspired in him regarding his father's livelihood and its impact on the Las Vegas Valley. Garvey took one last swallow of water and stood up.

"Do you still want to go out to the site with me?"

He may as well have been asking a much younger Madison if she wanted to sit on her abusive father's lap. Her lip, her eye, even her shoulders began to twitch.

"What's wrong?" Garvey looked at her in alarm. "Madison, what's with you?"

"Nothing, nothing. I'm just a little anxious. Look." She bent over and picked up a length of twisted wire and a few black and silver beads. "I was making you a necklace, Garvey, but the noise out back began bothering me."

Garvey stepped closer. He took Madison's face in his hands. "You're such a different kind of girl."

Was it her imagination or did his eyes flicker on her flat chest?

"Madison, your face is like one big teardrop just waiting to fall."

She pulled back abruptly. *Teardrops, fear drops.* So, it showed. Her life was written all over her homely face. Out in the open for everyone to see. Something inside of her burst like a festered boil. She could actually feel all twenty-six feet of her intestines relax. Madison smiled at Garvey with a look of gratitude.

"I'm going to finish this necklace for you. Turn around so I can measure your neck."

That night Madison made dinner. She set the dining room table with linens, her mother's fine bone china, and candles. It didn't matter that the baked potatoes had wormy little sprouts poking out of their fat, warm skins. It didn't matter that the salad leaves were black and slimy.

Madison began to carve the slightly warm meat. The sharp knife slid cleanly through tissue, then gristle, then bone. She was a vegetarian, but that didn't matter. Madison wasn't about to partake of this feast. This was the feast of atonement. This was the blood sacrifice for sin. Just as her Hebrew ancestors centuries ago had offered up the blood and flesh of goats, so too was Madison going to petition God for His mercy. This was Madison's Yom Kippur.

The knife grated on something hard. Madison sighed in exasperation, then plucked a silver bead from the gory mass in front of her. Everything was in order. It was time for her to go. Carefully, she began to roll bits and pieces of Garvey into remnants of the filthy carpet she'd also sectioned up. There were six construction sites in her neighborhood alone.

Madison had to make four trips to her BMW. Two legs, two arms, one torso, the surprisingly heavy head. The midnight sky reflected the beam of the giant Luxor pyramid thrusting its shaft of light heedlessly through the dark womb of stars and galaxies above. Madison drove out of the parking lot without thought, without feeling.

Early morning found Madison not far from her condo. She didn't remember where she'd been, but she knew she had one last stop to make. Madison stood among broken soil, a heavy blood-sodden lump of carpet cradled in her arms. The eastern sky was beginning to brighten into a jaded pink. The lights of the Las Vegas Strip seemed to wink at her.

Madison was poised before a slab of semi-hardened concrete. Silent pieces of heavy equipment surrounded her: hulking dark masses that loomed against the backdrop of the dawn sky. Reverently, she knelt on the cold foundation and laid her burden down. Madison wondered briefly if the cement contractor would appreciate the sacrifice his son had made.

From the valley below, the slow hum of machinery warming up began to fill the air. Bit by bit, the thriving city came to life. Madison rose to her feet and picked her way carefully back to her car.

Safe and secure in her condo, she began to methodically gather every strand of jewelry she'd ever made. Piece by piece, Madison fed the necklaces, earrings, and bracelets into her garbage disposal. Perhaps now the tics would stop. Perhaps now Madison Feldon could move beyond the shadow of her bullying father.

Madison was training one of the tennis women she so admired from afar when a detective came to see her the following week. Detective Nick Latkus's face looked like an orange that had been left too long in a fruit bowl. His freckled skin hung in folds of crepe around his deeply lined mouth. His hair, mustache, and eyebrows were a faded red. Tall, thin, and stoop-shouldered, the only remarkable thing about the man was his eyes. Beneath droopy lids, they were as green and knowing as a feral cat.

He waited patiently for Madison to finish with her client, then asked where he could speak to her in private. Detective Latkus followed Madison upstairs to the club café. After exchanging a few pleasantries, the detective abruptly asked her if she was aware she was missing a client. The local media had been in a frenzy for the past week over the discovery of body parts at construction sites throughout Green Valley. The victim had been ID'd as Garvey Kendall; Madison's client.

Even a seasoned veteran like Latkus would never forget,

when he arrived at the first crime scene, the agonized mask that was Mr. Kendall's face. The cement contractor was actually cradling the severed head in his arms. He'd refused to relinquish what was left of his son, his only child, until the screams of the newly arrived Mrs. Kendall pierced the air.

"Ms. Feldon, we traced several calls from Garvey to your cell phone last Sunday. He was first reported missing the following morning when he didn't come home. Did you see him that day? Mind telling me what you talked about?"

Madison looked steadily into the detective's eyes. Nothing twitched. Not her eye, not her lip. Even her heart felt as though it was on standby. She was as placid as the waters of Lake Mead in the early-morning stillness of high summer. Madison sighed.

"Garvey was a true loner, detective. He had a serious self-image disorder. And that's why he came to me." Madison shook her head in much the same manner as her mother would after one of Louis's tirades. "Garvey was obsessed with his diet. He wasn't comfortable in his own body. He wanted me to help him reinvent himself. He was also consumed with a need to impress his father." Madison smiled sadly. "I did see him Sunday, detective. He came over to tell me that he'd had an epiphany."

"An epiphany?" Nick Latkus's splintered alley-cat eyes bored into the dull brown of Madison's.

"Yes." She dropped her eyes to the stubby fingers that were folded primly in her lap. Madison noted her ankles were neatly crossed; her mother and father would have approved. For the first time ever, she felt composed, assured, and completely in control of her environment. "He told me he knew he could never measure up to family expectations." Madison leaned forward and looked earnestly into the detective's face.

"Garvey realized he had to stop his father's madness. He simply needed someone to show him the way. There had to be atonement, you see. Garvey was special. He was worthy of sacrifice. I set him free."

Latkus snorted. "So you decided to cut this young man up into bits and pieces as a *favor* to him?"

Madison nodded. Her eyes seemed to glaze over. She had no doubt she would soon be behind bars. Only she was aware she would be in a reverse form of prison. Madison was already dreaming of the indulgences behind thick concrete walls, away from prying eyes and nagging voices. Three hot meals to be eaten every day. No digital scales to haunt her. No construction noises to interrupt her sleep. Madison arose, and like a small child, obediently allowed the detective to escort her to his unmarked white car.

After all, she thought, gazing out the window as the tree-lined streets of Green Valley flashed by, *once I get some time by myself to pull myself together, there's always the possibility of parole.* A cloud of dust from a back loader drifted across the road. Madison Feldon smiled.

CRIP

BY Preston L. Allen

Nellis

They called him Crip, and you could find him at night seated on his throne outside the Gold Man's Gentlemen's Club.

He wore a mustard-colored suit and a ruffled party shirt. His round-eyed shades were mustard-tinted, and his narrow-brimmed hat was mustard too. He carried a gold-tipped cane. But he was a nobody, just a big, ugly coal-black man with a twisted face and a brain that divided the world into absolutes. Black and white. Right and wrong. Loyal and disloyal. What he like and what he don't like.

He was not exactly a bouncer, but he was. He was not exactly a valet/bodyguard, but he was. He was not exactly associated with the Gold Man's Gentlemen's Club, but he was. What he was, was a man with a face so ugly that the Gold Man himself found him useful and kept him around for special assignments.

Usually he just sat outside the entrance with his hat and his cane in his lap, keeping watch over things. Making sure the college boys didn't start any trouble when you turned them away for being underage. Making sure the flyboys from Nellis Air Force Base weren't too drunk already before they went in. Making sure nobody tried too hard to put the moves on Candy Apple, the pretty little thing who checked IDs and collected cover at the door. Yeah, there was a security guard out there, little Josh Ho the Hawaiian, all decked out in his black-on-black uniform—but everybody knew the real power was the Mustard Man. Crip never said much. He never had to. He just had to stand up and walk over to you. He loomed well over six-foot-five—and he had to be pushing three hundred pounds. The twisted, scarred face. The unsettling mustard tints. If he told you, "Get to steppin'," then you did, no matter how drunk you were pretending to be.

He had a work ethic that was admirable. He never called in sick. He never caught a cold. He never took a night off. The only time you didn't see him on his throne was when he went to take a leak or refill his drink. Bourbon on the rocks, with not too many rocks. When he wasn't in that chair it signaled trouble for somebody, big trouble, because the Gold Man had summoned his Mustard Man upstairs.

So that night he left his throne and went upstairs, where Snake told him, "Gold Man wants you to babysit."

Crip nodded and went into the nursery. Crip was surprised to find an actual child sitting there, because it was not really a nursery. It was where they held you and sometimes worked you over to make an example of you. He took his seat next to the child. She didn't look like trouble, so he relaxed and rested his cane and hat in his lap, and waited for the Gold Man's door to open.

Through the walls, he heard the Gold Man say, "Her? Don't worry about her. She's okay. For now. It's *you* that you should worry about."

And the nursery door swung open. A beet-red face, the child's father, peeped in. Got a good look at his precious little one sitting next to the big mustard suit. That black skin. That twisted face. Then the door closed. Through the walls, Crip could hear Snake's cruel laughter. Then he heard the Gold

Man laying down the terms. The other voice, the sobbing voice, that was the girl's father.

The little girl said, "How'd you get so black? I've never seen anybody so black."

"Huh?"

He looked down at her. Usually he tried not to look at them, unless they seemed like trouble. He looked down at her, and she was staring up at him as though she expected an answer. Well, little blond-haired, blue-eyed, pink-cheeked child, one day I took a paint brush and dipped it in a big can of black and slapped some more on my face because I didn't think I had enough problems already. Instead of answering, he scowled at her, trying to scare her, but she kept staring at him until he turned away.

Through the walls came, "Scumbag. Degenerate. You piece of shit. I want my money. I want my money or I will do bad things to you. Very bad things."

The little girl said, "I like the color of your suit, though. It's pretty. Where'd you get it from?"

Hand tailored. A gift from the Gold Man. Got three more just like it at home. One of them's double breasted. One of them's got tails. One of them's got a matching vest. Got an image to uphold. I am Crip, the Mustard Man. He felt something on his knee. The little girl's hand. He glanced at her. Her smile was gone. Tears were rolling out of her eyes, down her cheeks into the lacy collar of her nightgown. The kid was probably in bed dreaming about sugar plum fairies when Snake and Radney and Goggles went to collect her and her old man. The kid was leaking tears, but she was quiet about it—just a sniffle here and there. A brave little girl she was for eight or seven.

The Gold Man's voice: "If I don't get my money, I'm gonna lose my temper. I haven't lost my temper yet but I will."

"The payment plan," the father sobbed. "I'll stay on the payment plan this time, I swear it."

"You'll stay on the payment plan, you'd better. Five hundred every five days."

"Ohmygod. God. God."

"Five hundred every five days, and you don't owe me seven grand anymore. Now you owe me ten."

"Ohmygod. God. My daughter."

"I'm done talking to you now. Snake, Radney, show this bum the door."

"My little girl—"

"Show it to him hard."

The little girl had her hand in his lap and tears in her eyes and he took her hands in both of his and said to her, "I painted it on."

She sniffled, "Painted what?"

"I painted on an extra coat of black."

She smiled. "You can't paint yourself. You're lying. People are born with skin."

"And I grew the suit from pumpkin seeds."

She was smiling, sniffing back sobs. "No way. That's silly. You can't grow suits from pumpkin seeds. You buy suits in a department store."

He winked at her with his twisted face. He made his bug eye jump in the socket to spook her. The little girl wasn't afraid of it at all. She was holding his hand when Goggles came through the door and called him over, whispered to him: "Gold Man says to pack her up."

"What do I know about kids? I never done a kid before."

"Pack her up is what he said."

"What do they eat? What do they drink? Kid'll end up dead living with me. Do they drink bourbon? All I got is bourbon."

"With a father like what she's got, this one'll probably end up dead anyway. He's into us for a lot of dough. He's in over his head."

Crip looked over at the little girl in the cotton nightgown and she looked back at him, rubbing the redness out of her nose with her little hands. He said to Goggles, "Well, I'll figure it out. It can't be that hard. We was all kids once, right?"

All night he thought about the kid. At 5 in the morning, things had slowed down enough for him to get off the throne and head on home. He went upstairs to collect her. She had fallen asleep in the chair. Her hands and feet were bound, and she had duct tape over her mouth. There was no need for that, but the Gold Man was trying to send a message. This is not kid's play. People could get hurt. The stripper who had been assigned to watch her was snoring in the other chair. He shook her awake. "Did she eat? Does she have any other clothes? What do you feed a kid like this?"

He pulled out his blade and cut the bonds on her little arms and legs. He checked her neck and face for bruises, and he was glad when he saw that there were none. She awoke as he was removing the tape from her mouth. She looked about to cry, but they made eye contact, and he told her with his eyes, *Don't cry.* She held it back. She was a brave kid. She didn't cry.

He gave the stripper a hundred to follow him home. Crip lived, if you could call it that, on the second floor of a distressed property in the 1400 block of Vegas Valley Drive, in the shadow of the South Maryland Parkway, and not too far from the hospital where he sent a lot of the people who owed the Gold Man money. Degenerates who borrowed more than they could ever pay back. Like this Air Force boy from Nellis with the pretty little daughter. The scoop he got from Goggles was that the boy was typical. A country boy from Tennessee. Second year in the service. Stationed in Las Vegas. First time in Las Vegas. He gambled more than he could afford. He moved up to borrowing from the high interest check cashers, one of which was owned by the Gold Man. When he couldn't pay them back, he started writing bad checks. When his CO found out about it, it was too late. The Air Force has its standards. The best the CO could do was to arrange an honorable discharge. So now the kid is cut loose. He gambles, he wins. He gambles, he loses. He's got a baby he left back home from some girl he knocked up in high school. The girl gets killed in a car wreck. The sickly grandma ships the poor little orphan off to Las Vegas to be with her military man daddy—only he's not in the Air Force anymore, but is too ashamed to tell anyone. The Gold Man gets tired of waiting for his money and calls the boy in for a little chit chat. So the Mustard Man gets to babysit the collateral until the Gold Man gets his dough. Typical. Typical stuff.

Crip opened the door to his apartment, and both the stripper and the little girl gasped. There was a mattress with a pillow on it. That was it. Other than that mattress, there was no other furniture. No TV. No bookshelves. No tables and chairs in the kitchen area. Nothing on the stove. If you opened the cabinets, nothing in the cabinets, no plates, no glasses, no forks and spoons, nothing. If you opened the refrigerator, you'd find a bottle of water and two bottles of bourbon. There were two bedrooms in the apartment, and both the doors were locked from the outside. At the moment, he was not babysitting anyone except the girl, but it was his practice always to keep those doors locked. There was stuff in there that maybe you didn't want to see. There was one closet, the hallway closet; if you opened that door, you'd find his clothes in it—his other suits and underwear and shoes and whatnot. But that door was locked too. There was stuff in there that maybe you didn't want to see.

The stripper set the bag of groceries and other supplies down on the kitchen counter. Now she understood why they had gone to the twenty-four-hour Wal-Mart and bought a fry pan and paper plates. A bottle of Crisco. Crip led the little girl to the mattress and made her lie down. There was a clean sheet on the mattress, and he covered her with it.

The stripper, who was called Sapphire, threw up her hands. "Shit. I'm gonna need more than this. I'm gonna need lettuce and apple juice. Some cups. Some milk. Some of everything. Shit, you got nothing in here, Crip."

He gave her three more hundreds. "Get whatever you need. Get it quick and get back here. And don't curse in front of the kid no more, you hear? Don't make me hafta smack you around a little bit."

While the stripper was gone, he sat down on the floor next to the little girl on the mattress. He listened to her sweet, innocent breathing.

He said to her, "Sleep, little girl. Sleep." Poor thing, to have a father like that. Poor little thing. Bad parents was one of those things Crip put on his *Don't like it* list. Owing money was one of those things he put on there too. Hurting kids? Well, that was at the top of the *Don't like it* list. But that was one of those things he had control over because this time, it was he who was the babysitter.

Once upon a time, a long, long time ago, he had a mother and a little sister and a babysitter who was not in her right mind. He would watch her do things to his sister that he should have told his mother about, but didn't. He loved his baby sister Ta'Shana and he did not believe the woman when she said that she was Ta'Shana's "other" mother, but he didn't do anything about it. All day long the babysitter would keep changing Ta'Shana's clothes, dressing her in outfits that she had snuck into the house in her bag and asking him, How does she look now? Doesn't my baby look nice now? And he would say, She looks fine, and go back to watching cartoons with a heavy heart. When the babysitter opened her shirt and pulled out her creamy peanut butter brown breasts, he would feel a coiling of his privates in his pants. She would sit there with her shirt open tugging her thick brown nipples and asking him how they looked. Were they big enough yet? Did they look big enough to suck on yet? He would say, They look fine, and not do much else because he really did not know what to do about it at six or seven. Then she would pick up Ta'Shana and push one of the thick, wrinkly nipples into her mouth, and say, There, there now, my baby, as Ta'Shana sucked. This troubled him so much that he would go into his room and stand in the corner like somebody had put him on punishment.

He always blamed himself for what happened the day the babysitter's boyfriend came over, because he should have told his mother about all the other stuff, he should have told her, he should have told her, but he didn't.

The babysitter's boyfriend, who was not supposed to be there when his mother was not home, had snuck over many times before to be with the babysitter, so he was no stranger. This time, like all the others before, the boyfriend and the babysitter took their clothes off and got on top of each other on the couch and started pumping and huffing and growling and panting and screaming and laughing and shouting profanity.

Crip, who was called Leon back in those days, had seen it

all before so he went into the room he shared with Ta'Shana and closed the door. A few minutes later, the boyfriend and the babysitter burst into the room and started punching him and slapping him around, accusing him of being disloyal and spying on them, and they said they knew all about his plans to tell his mother on them, but they knew a way to punish his black ass, Oh, they knew a way—they would take *their* baby and leave him behind. He cried and screamed and pulled at them and begged them not to take his sister, as they grabbed Ta'Shana from her crib and dressed her in a sailor suit and red shoes the babysitter had in her bag. They laughed at him and slapped him some more. He ran into the kitchen and came back with a butcher knife. He was going to stab them and save his sister, but the boyfriend snatched the knife from him, then picked him up and threw him against the wall three times. It could have been more than three, but after three is when he blacked out.

When he woke up, he was in a hospital. There were police there. There was his mother crying hysterically. His sister was gone. His body was broken. His face. His legs. A few years later, his mother was gone too. Out a window.

Two nights in a row, Crip got to his throne four hours later than he normally did. On the third night, he did not show at all. On the fourth night, when he got there four hours late again, Snake was waiting for him.

"What the fuck?"

Crip said, "What do you mean, *what the fuck?*"

"I mean what the fuck when I say what the fuck. Where you been? What's been happening to you?"

"The hell with you. What are you, my mother?" Crip pushed past him and sat down on his throne, and set his hat and cane in his lap. He scowled at Snake, which usually would have been enough to scare him off. But tonight, something was missing in his scowl. Snake stood his ground. Crip grumbled, "What do you think has been happening, man? What do you think? I gotta take care of the kid. I gotta feed her. I gotta make sure one of the girls is there with her while I'm here. Last night, the kid was sick. Had a temperature of a hundred and one. Sapphire was supposed to come sit with her. That bitch Sapphire never showed up. I'm gonna wring her neck when I get ahold of her. I got this kid, what am I supposed to do? Leave her there watching TV all night?"

"You got a TV now?"

"Yeah, I bought a TV. And a VCR with tapes. Cartoons and stuff. Yeah, that's right. Is that a problem? What am I supposed to do? She's a kid."

Snake said, "You should just tie the brat up like you do the rest of 'em. She'll still be there when you get back."

"She's a kid. You think I'm gonna tie up a kid?"

"I would."

Crip's voice was cold as ice. "I would fucking tie you up, Snake. I would tie you up real tight. So tight you couldn't breathe."

This time the scowl was working. Snake backed away with his hands raised in surrender—he backed all the way into the club. It was only when Snake was gone and Crip sat back down that he realized he had stood up out of his seat as though ready to go after Snake. Little Josh Ho the security guard and Candy Apple were staring at him. They had never seen him talk so much. He gave them the scowl too, and they went back to doing their jobs.

On the fifth night, he had to get there early, he just had to, but he got there late once more (Sapphire didn't show again—he had to wait for Diamond to show up, but she showed up high, so he had to wait for Ebony Rainbow, who was drunk, but what the fuck, he had to get to work), and just as he got there, lucky break, he saw the father go into the club. Crip put on his hat and he gripped his cane, and he waited. When the father came back out, with a blackened eye and a kerchief against a bleeding nose, Crip gripped him by the arm and took him around back where the cars were parked. He drove off with him in his Lincoln, took him to an alley that was nice and dark. He said to him: "You know you have a sweet kid. Do you know what you have?"

The father whimpered, "Ohmygod. What have you done to her? What have you done?"

"I've done nothing to her," Crip said. "What have *you* done to her? She's got no mother. She's got no grandmother. And you, you, look at you. She's got no father. Do you realize the Gold Man will kill you? He will do it. I've seen him do it. I've helped him do it. He will kill you, and then what's gonna happen to your kid? Look at me. I grew up with no mother, no father, no beauty to me at all, and this goddamn limp. The world is an ugly place. Your beautiful girl will become a whore, I can tell you that. She will suck dick and take it up the ass from the ugliest forms of life you have ever seen, and I know because I have seen these ugly forms of life. I live with 'em. I'm one of 'em. We're like this goddamn city. We're all dressed up, and we twinkle with all these bright lights, but behind it all we stink rotten like a sewer. You're her father. You're supposed to protect her. You're supposed to give her a chance at the good life. This kid, you know what she tells me she wants to be when she grows up? She wants to be a nurse. I tell her, Nurse? Why not be a doctor? She says, Okay, I'll be a doctor. I can be anything I want to be, she says. And she can be, but not if her father is throwing away every penny he has in these god-damned casinos. Casinos are for suckers and men who want their daughters to sell ass. I don't wanna see that happen to that kid, do you hear me?" At that point, he had the father by the collar and was shaking him. The bloody kerchief fell from his nose. "Do you hear me? Do you hear me?"

The father whimpered, "I hear you."

And Crip released him and patted down his shirt, which he had rumpled up in his rage. The father's eyes were the little girl's eyes. He was a man with beautiful eyes, despite the shiner. They were teary eyes. Crip said to him, "I got something for you. I got some money for you."

"What?"

Crip reached into his mustard jacket and pulled out the envelope with the ten grand in it and pressed it into the father's hand. "It's all there. It's everything you need. Give this to the Gold Man the next time you come. Then be a father to your daughter."

"Ohmygod," the father said, looking at the thickness of green bills in the envelope. "Ohmygod. Thank you. Thank you."

"Don't mention it. I gotta get back to my life. Babysitting kids is way too hard."

On the sixth night, Crip got there on time. Slap her around a little and Sapphire not only stays off the weed real good, but she shows up where she's supposed to show up and on time. Crip was happy. In a few nights, it would all be over. The father would pay the Gold Man and the kid would be free to go on and grow up to be a doctor. Plus, it was a nice crowd tonight, no troublemakers, no college guys, mostly tourists, men in their fifties and sixties wanting to see the titties dance, wanting to maybe get a little bit of the old special treatment in one of the back rooms.

When Goggles came out, Crip was on his throne, sipping his bourbon like the way it used to be, with his hat and his cane in his lap. He smiled at Goggles trying to put the moves on Candy Apple, riding his hand on her ample buttocks during a slow spot in the line. Candy Apple was a good kid, working her way through college. A man like Goggles was not her type. Thank God.

Goggles caught Crip smiling at his failed attempt with Candy Apple and sauntered over to the throne and slapped him five. "What are you smiling at, old black man?"

Crip grinned his lopsided grin. "Smiling at you, no-game white man."

"So you didn't go with 'em, huh?"

"Go with who?"

"Snake and Radney."

"Go with 'em for what?"

Goggles lowered his voice. "Shit. They didn't tell you about that asshole? The father?"

Crip's heart sped up. "Whose father? The kid's?"

"Asshole went into the casinos last night and blew a big wad. Huge. Then he packed up his shit and caught a plane outta the country. One-way ticket to Germany or some shit like that. Don't look like he's planning to come back—"

Crip jumped out of his chair and hobbled as fast as he could to the parking lot to his car. He knew the deal. He didn't have to stick around to hear Goggles say the rest: "—so the Gold Man sent Snake and Radney to deal with the collateral."

If all they were going to do was deal with her, then, well, her old man did owe the money, and a debt is a debt. You gotta pay back your debts. But she was such a pretty little girl, and

Snake was not called Snake for nothing. Crip punched the accelerator and the Lincoln roared through the glittering nighttime streets. He was praying the only prayer he knew—*"The Lord is my shepherd, I shall not want"*—and sustaining himself with a vision of the girl all grown up and wearing all white with a stethoscope around her neck and a name badge on her chest that said *Doctor*.

When he was a boy, he had wanted to be a doctor, but he had grown up in the streets and become a killer. Maybe it had something to do with the seven foster homes he had run away from. Maybe it had something to do with how ugly he was. Maybe it had something to do with the babysitter who had stolen his sister and caused his mother to give up on life and jump out of that window. He had hate in his heart, a hate uglier than his face. A doctor is not much good if he has hate in his heart. And the only thing this pretty little girl had in her heart was hope and courage and good wishes for everybody, all the things that make a good doctor. And the only chance she had was him.

When he got to the house, the light was on inside and Radney was standing guard outside, which meant Snake was alone in there with her. Radney watched him as he lumbered up the stairs. Radney had his gun hand under his coat and fear in his eyes.

Crip just wanted to get close enough to him before he took that gun out. He was halfway up the stairs when he waved at Radney and said, half-joking, "What? You guys start without me? What, you break into my house when I got the key right here? You're gonna pay to fix my door, I swear to God."

Radney, showing his teeth, withdrew the gun hand from the coat. "Don't blow a fuse. It's Snake. He said we hadda do it now. He outranks me."

Crip was at the top of the stairs with Radney smiling at him. Crip smiled back and shoved the blade between Radney's ribs, stepped over him when he fell, and pushed through the front door. In a flash, he took it all in. The TV was on. He could hear Sapphire locked inside one of the bedrooms, pounding on the door and screaming to be let out, probably because of what she saw in there. You didn't want to be locked in one of those rooms, alive or dead. Snake was on the bed—there was a bed now. And the girl was on Snake's lap and his hand was under her shirt and his other hand was pointing the gun straight at Crip, who lurched forward because there was nothing else he could do. He was her only hope.

The first shot ripped through him, though he didn't feel it much, but his blade was gone, so maybe the shot through his ribs had caused him to drop it. But he wasn't worried too much about that because his hands were around Snake's neck now. Trying to muster his strength. Rolling on top of Snake on the bed. Trying to snap his neck. He was slippery as a snake. The second shot, that one he felt. That one went through the guts, zapped his strength. The girl screaming. Sapphire pounding to be let out. The TV on too loud. Snake was slippery as a snake. Trying to stop Snake from raising the gun. Snake was trying to shoot him in the head. He lowered his head. Face to face like he was kissing Snake. His stinking gold-teethed mouth. The pervert. The child molester. He found his strength. He felt it and heard it loud when Snake's neck snapped. It felt like his own fingers had snapped too. He lay on top of Snake like a lover and caught his breath.

Crip called the girl over, told her to stop screaming, stop crying. She was a brave kid. She stopped crying. He told her, Take this key, go to the closet, close your eyes, don't look inside, there's stuff in there I don't want you to see, get on your knees, feel around for shoes, there's something in the shoes feels like a wad of paper, bring it back to me. She did as she was told and she came back with all the money he had left in the world. He took the money, four grand in hundreds, and rolled over on his back next to Snake. He told her, Now take the key, go get Sapphire out of the room, then close back the door, don't look inside, tell Sapphire to come here.

A moment later, the pounding and pleading to be let out stopped. When he opened his eyes, Sapphire was looking down at him. He handed Sapphire the money. "You gotta get her back to Tennessee. You gotta get her there now. She's got a grandmother. You can't find her grandmother, find somebody. An aunt. An uncle. Somebody. She has to have somebody. What money's left over, you keep."

Sapphire said, "Gold Man is gonna kill me. What about Gold Man? What about him, huh?"

"Come here," he said to Sapphire. "Lean down." When she leaned down, he grabbed her by the throat and slapped her around a little bit. "Get the kid outta here. Get her back to Tennessee. You hear me? She's just a kid."

"Okay, okay, I'll do it. Okay," said Sapphire, hollering and crying.

Then he called the girl over again and shoved a couple hundred in the pocket of the pants he had bought her. "Run," he told her. "Run. Soon as you get a chance, run. Grow up and be a doctor. Save lives."

Then he scowled at her and made his bug eye jump in its socket to make her laugh one more time. She hugged him around his face as he died.

A nobody.

Just an ugly, coal-black man who didn't take kindly to people hurting kids.

* * *

That was back in the early '90s, about fifteen, twenty years ago. You look around Las Vegas today and you'll see the casinos are more lavish, more prosperous, and the gamblers are even more desperate. They still don't have a state lottery in Nevada, only casinos. And they still got that Air Force base at Nellis. Still got problems with the boys stationed there and their gambling. The Gold Man's Gentlemen's Club is still doing good business with those who like to see the titties dance, though the Gold Man himself is partially retired because of his stroke. He has a son who runs the place now. The son has a degree in business from UNLV, but he's just as cruel as his old man and just as slimy as his brother they used to call Snake.

Of course, the Mustard Man is gone, and if you want to see the only sign that he ever existed you've got to know what you're looking for and you've got to look real close to see it. It's right outside the Gold Man's Gentlemen's Club. Barely perceptible. Four smooth grooves in the polished marble tile where a throne used to rest.

Well, there is one other sign that a coal-black man with a twisted face and a tender heart once did exist, but you'd have to fly to Tennessee to find it.

She's a young, very pretty pediatric physician who's married to another doctor, a general practitioner by the name of Dr. Eli Yates McKitrick.

They named their firstborn son Eli Mustard McKitrick.

Not too many people know why they did that.

THREE TIMES A NIGHT, EVERY OTHER NIGHT

BY LORI KOZLOWSKI

North Las Vegas

His guitar was out of tune and he was fiddling with the strings when he heard her voice.

"It's my wedding and I'll curse if I want to!" the bride growled, flipping her veil behind her, whipping her new father-in-law in the face.

Wally recognized the voice. His head began to hurt, and he rubbed his temples, touching his calloused hands to his unruly sideburns.

A wedding party paraded into a dark-walled Irish pub inside a locals' casino on Tropicana Avenue, which was crowded at that hour—bustling with quick-handed dealers and green gamblers who couldn't count.

Brenda, the bride, was carrying her train in one hand and a bottled beer in the other. She took two more steps and then murmured, "Isn't that right, baby?" nuzzling her face into her new husband's neck. The groom just smiled, gazing at her, pushing up his wire-rimmed glasses, saying nothing.

The wedding party took seats in the middle of the room, so they could see the round stage. She placed herself front row, center.

Wally Whittaker, the Irish singing wonder who played three times a night, every other night at the pub, eased out from behind a heavy burgundy curtain. He cleared his throat.

The lights dimmed, though she remained glowing. She was a big stark white reminder in the middle of the room.

"Tonight's a Wednesday, folks, and all the good people of Las Vegas have come to see me. We're gonna have some fun, my fellow drinkers. Why don't I tell you a wee story about a girl I used to know," he began, strumming his guitar, sitting on a wooden stool. "There once was a girl named Sherry. But Sherry had no cherry. I said that's okay, hun. We can still have fun. Cause the hole still works where the cherry came from!"

Some people giggled. Some blushed. Wally guffawed at his own limerick, then immediately burst into song. His laugh was phony, and his voice was off, but he was getting through the verses.

He looked at her.

The bride was clapping with her mouth open. She was a shade too tan for that time of year and a little too pudgy for her dress. Bright orange swells of skin for arms squeezed out of short white satin sleeves. She yelled "*Baum, baum, baum*" into cupped hands as a vocal representation of the horn section in Neil Diamond's "Sweet Caroline." And as Wally serenaded her, singing, "The good times never seemed so good," the bride cannoned back, "SO GOOD! SO GOOD! SO GOOD!"

They caught each other's eyes. She raised a drawn-on eyebrow. He looked away.

He had slept with Brenda just once. She was nothing like his Linda. But that's what drew him in. She was just a fun party girl he thought he could enjoy for a moment and soon forget.

She tipped well, wore low-cut tops and piles of shiny gold jewelry. She drank until sun up, chain smoked, and a never-ending heavy metal concert played in her head.

Several years back, she began attending all of his performances, every other night, wherever he played in town. Sometimes she wore green plastic leprechaun hats. It was almost as if she wanted to be Irish. He thought she was strange and annoying at first. She often lingered around the pub too long, trying to get his attention. After he played, she always wanted a hug. She was his biggest fan.

Usually he just smiled at her, acknowledging her support of his music. He was always friendly to his crowds. From the kids to the kooks, he thought he knew how to read people. Give them what they want. Sometimes she was so into his whole act, he'd sing directly to her. It was just good showmanship.

But as he saw her more, her allure grew. On Tuesday nights, she showered him with compliments that made him feel taller, smarter, and like the musician he wanted to be. Sometimes she brought him gifts. Heart-shaped ashtray. Engraved silver hip flask. Tortoise shell guitar pick with his initials embossed on one side.

She wanted to be possessed. He was willing to surrender. One too many Jack-and-Cokes, and he willfully fell into bed with her. He hadn't seen Brenda since their coital encounter two years prior.

Sabrina "Brenda" Marie Rosetti. She was a busty blond Italian who said her father was so-and-so in the Mafia. Wally never paid much attention to her mob talk at the bar. Who in this town didn't think they knew something about the mob? He had heard it all. It was always a cousin of a friend who had some small encounter in some obscure place. Everyone was fascinated with bodies buried in the desert and mysteries of the city's history. Everyone thought they really knew particulars about the Bugsys, Tonys, and Moes.

Whenever she spoke, he hardly listened. Wally was never interested in her for her mind, and could care less about who she thought she knew. He just shook his head, pretended that she was significant, and continually drank the whiskey she bought for him.

Brenda was tattooed all over her back in navy and emerald inks. There was a snake over her left shoulder and a dragon covering her right. He knew her tattoos well. He had counted them once, tracing that inked back with cold fingers.

When he had taken her to his apartment nearby, he thought of Linda the whole time. Closing his eyes.

Brenda was wild, as he knew she would be. She kept laughing at odd moments. Halfway through, as she was being her most obnoxious, Wally heard a dull clank as car keys fell onto taupe carpet. He had peered up from the bed and saw Linda standing right there. He swiftly pushed Brenda away, stood up, and reached out in one big panic. "She means nothing." He scrambled, pulling pants over himself, and knocking Brenda to the floor. Linda just stood there, stiff. Her eyes welled up, but tears did not fall.

As he practically crawled after her out the door, Brenda lay on the rug, bruised and watching him. She clenched her jaw.

When Wally moved on to his next number, Brenda kicked both feet up onto a chair and sucked on a cigarette, blowing the smoke out of her nose. Right then, she appeared much like the dragon on her shoulder, who also puffed fire and flames. The two reptiles peeked out from behind her headdress. Snake, dragon, snake, as the veil swept back and forth on her back.

There was something about it. Her veil, the tats, the thrashed blond hair. Her raspy laugh. He was attracted all over again.

Brenda was showing off—shimming and shaking up and

down the front row. Tanned bust, shoulders, and back. Wally was trying his hardest not to find her sexy. But he was watching her every move. She put her bare feet in the groom's lap. Her toes are fat, Wally thought. Fat-toed Brenda. That's what he would think of her. Who would want to be in bed with those fat toes anyway?

Surrounding the couple, the wedding party made a collective toast. The maid of honor was covered in tattoos of lime tree frogs, the best man was stamped with a giant house fly.

The groom just sat there, so plain and placid. Run-of-the-mill tux, standard dull black shoes. He could be a computer programmer or an insurance salesman, Wally thought, as he strummed his guitar a bit harder. He could be an associate named Tim at Coldwell Banker. He could be a tax accountant. Counting Brenda's fat toes.

He looked as straight-laced as they came. But when he embraced the bride, it was obvious: She captivated him. Coldwell Banker Tim couldn't help himself either.

The crowd continued to grow, and Wally scanned the blooming room. This was just one of several Irish pubs he played around town. Locals' casinos had become hot spots for the egalitarian atmosphere they provided. Warm enough for grandmas playing penny slots, dark enough for serious drinkers, and raucous enough for everyone in between. The rumor was that the casino pubs were actually authentic, broken down in the U.K., imported in large boxes, and then reconstructed. The walls were made out of old ships. The floorboards and the scaffolding from Celtic drinking halls. The décor had become familiar to him, but that night, Wally could feel the spell of the ancient—ghosts in the ship wood, eyes in the floor. A thousand dead soldiers swaying to his song.

Wally pulled at the collar of his buttoned-down plaid

shirt. He couldn't get comfortable. His neck was tense, his old knee injury was flaring up again. He tried to adjust himself on the stage, and still feign the merriment. His cheeks were sore from smiling. He scratched at his itchy sideburns. Taking off his velour jacket, he kept clearing his throat and looking around, noticing half-drunk highballs and the eager audience waiting for him to play on.

Three hollow-eyed dealmakers sat at a corner table. They appeared to be there simply for business—leaning in, making plans. They wore gray suits. They did not tap their toes. Wally thought for a moment that the one in the middle was glaring at him. His paranoia grew.

As a lounge singer, Wally saw hundreds of faces. All sorts of late-nighters. Those drowning their sorrows usually sat in the back. The real partiers always took to the middle of the room or the front row so that they could hear him better. On really rowdy nights, Wally could hardly hear himself because the crowd was singing along so loudly. He liked that, when it happened. His voice was lost among voices and it was as if they were the ones singing to him. Sometimes there was a stand-out, a personal singing telegram just for him.

That night, Brenda was the overpowering Siren. Her voice was distinct—half like a baby doll and half like Mae West. It wasn't even 10 p.m. and she was already drunk. She spilled brown ale on her lavish wedding dress. The gown was all iridescent sequins and baubles and loops of lace, and there were ashes on the edge of the train where she was flicking her Marlboro.

Wally trembled. The one woman he thought he'd always have was gone, and in her place was the one reminder of his loss. Brenda was back and this time he was scared. As he sang each tune, he threw out jokes and put on the same faux smile that he smiled every night, but his shivering continued. He thought he saw Linda's face in the round wall clock. She was mine, Wally thought. What he loved most about her was the way she walked. Slow and deliberate like she had a secret between her legs.

But Linda wasn't in the pub.

Brenda was in her place, and she was doing an Irish jig all over his scar tissue, ripping him open with every heel-toe. He knew that she had come to the pub just for him. To rub it in. To show him that someone wanted her enough to marry her. She kept eyeing him. Winking or twirling a finger around a perfect yellow ringlet, when she caught him looking.

His palms were sweaty. And for the first time in a long while he felt nervous as he played.

"All right, lassies and gents, why don't we take a wee break, so I can wet me whistle," he finished.

He strolled past the wedding party, giving Brenda a cordial nod, trying to be polite without getting too close. Her eyes were surveillance, recording him. She was smacking purple gum.

Sitting at the bar, the singer coughed and ran a hand through his chestnut hair before sipping his pint. Wally thought more about Linda and how if she were there he would be having a drink with her right now. He would be smelling her clean hair, instead of standing alone at the corner of the bar in the middle of a crowded room. It amazed him how alone he felt in crowds of people. Though he was an entertainer—and not half bad, he thought, compared to the other hundreds of flimsy acts in town—when it came time to be part of the group, the circles of people around him made him dizzy. The feeling was always difficult for him, yet with her there he could usually get by, taking in her stories about work, how her day went, who she saw, what she bought. But now the lounge singer was alone in his own arena.

The middle man in the gray suit was examining him closely. Wally started to perspire through his clothes.

He wanted to leave. No one'll notice if there's no second half, he thought. But who was he kidding? It was packed for a Wednesday night. And even though he could afford the night off, he couldn't lose this gig. The manager would never have him back if he left midway through a show.

Swallowing down his black and tan, he could feel the thickness of the room: the ad-hoc drinking songs and the clinking of shot glasses and the ringing of bells when someone hit the jackpot on the dollar slots.

He tried to concentrate on his beer, focusing on the top of it, thinking how by now Linda's bright pink lipstick would be pressed onto the rim of the glass. He secretly liked the taste of her lipstick, and when she wasn't looking he would drink specifically from that part of the glass. She could make an ordinary beer into a first-rate cocktail, he thought.

But now there was no kiss on the side of his glass, and this beer was just like every other beer. Just a beer. Nothing more.

He gulped down the rest anyway, flicking two dollar bills onto the bar.

He turned around to see the bride standing behind him.

"Hey, lass. Congratulations on your day," he offered, leaning away from her.

"Yeah, thanks, man. You're the bomb."

"You too, hun," he said, not quite knowing what the bomb was, wishing she'd go away.

Her French-manicured acrylic nails became claws closing in on her glass. She smiled, looking up at him. Right then, she actually seemed sweet in her fancy gown, her eyelashes curled and black. He remembered how much she used to adore him. He missed being adored.

"You know, I'm not really Irish," he said, softening.

"That's okay, I'm not really blond."

They both laughed. Her giggle was fake. His chuckle was nervous.

"Why are you doing this to me?" he asked.

"Because I can. Because I wanted you to see me in my pretty white dress. Don't you think I'm pretty?" she said, leaning over her drink, tipping her cleavage out even further.

He hated her right then, but he was attracted too.

"You're a cruel woman."

"It's part of my charm," she smiled.

"I like your lipstick." He couldn't help himself.

She bit her bottom lip just slightly.

"The color is called *Tempt*. Are you tempted?" She smiled wider, then walked away, looking over her shoulder. She wiggled.

He told himself that he had to quit this jester-like job and find better pay doing something more normal. He was tired of cover songs and dark walls. He was tired of running into shades of his past. He wanted to emerge on the other side of this a better man.

He stared at Brenda's train as it slithered away on the dirty floor. Not marrying Linda was the biggest mistake he'd ever made, and he knew it right then. Graceful Linda with long limbs and blue eyes. She left him and Vegas. He had heard she was with a wealthier musician now. Probably touring around Europe. Eating French cheese from the hands of that rich man. Bathing with him in an Alps-sheltered chateau.

Wally was stuck in the same pub, and he had one more

set to play before he could pick up his paycheck on the fourth floor, drink a Guinness for breakfast, and then walk out of the well-lit casino into the 6 a.m. sun.

He exhaled, moving back to his half-moon stage, feeling more himself as he stepped away from the pack of people.

The middle man in the gray suit came to the stage with a twenty-dollar bill for the tin tip jar. Wally swallowed.

Middle man had long fingers and big teeth. His hair was white and slick.

"What would you like to hear, my friend?" Wally asked.

"Why don't you play 'Danny Boy.' I like that one," the old drinker said, straight-faced.

"Oh, yeah, sure. It's my favorite," Wally lied.

He quickly belted out the old hymn, not concerned if it was perfect or even if it sounded good. He was sick of singing and sick of being there and sick of seeing Brenda jiggling her parts all over the pub. That middle man was making him nervous, and he knew he had to get out.

Ending just after 11 p.m., he no longer cared if he left early. He grabbed his guitar case and stumbled off the stage, hurriedly heading up to the fourth floor to grab his check. Rushing through the tawny casino, a million little lights all around him. Cigar smoke rising. The face of a huge masked joker bolted to the wall. Bold baccarat signs and spinning roulette wheels. G-stringed cocktail waitresses sauntering through the aisles. Pit bosses sternly standing by, arms folded. One-armed bandits stealing money left and right. Cherry, seven, six.

He stabbed at the elevator button, wanting to hurry up and run out of the whole place. Out of the casino, out of the parking lot, and maybe out of town.

As soon as he got into the brassy elevator, he was locked inside a private funhouse. The mirrored interior gave Wally eight different images of himself. He hated every one. He stared at the floor. Grotesque casino carpet was better to look at.

His head was bowed. His heart was near his knees. It was a long ride. As the elevator ascended, for a moment he wondered if you go to hell, do you feel like you are going up instead of down? The devil's parting trick.

Finally floor four came, and he dashed out down the hall to human resources. He had reached the end of the hallway when he heard a steel door click shut, then a swishing behind him. He turned around and at the other end of the hall, near the stairwell, he saw her.

There she was in all her tan and white glory. Psycho, fattoed Brenda. The deranged harpy was up on the fourth floor, she'd followed him up there. Holding out the sides of her wide dress as wings.

"What are you doing?" he uttered, scurrying toward an emergency exit.

"Shut up." She grabbed him and then kissed him hard and dramatically, jolting her head and her veil from side to side. She tasted like cheap rum.

She pulled up her white dress and unzipped his trousers in what seemed like one swift movement. His back was against the long beige wall. Sure, he had already had her. But this. The veil. The virginal white. He was overtaken. She tilted her head back, and as she did, Wally noticed the elevator doors opening. Out walked the three men dressed in gray suits.

"Sabrina! What in the hell are you doing?" the middle man yelled.

"Daddy?"

"I never took my daughter for a tramp!" he said, yanking her from Wally.

The singer slid from the wall to the floor, trying to inch

away. He thought of every bad thing he'd ever done. Every one night stand, every unreturned phone call, every cheat, every lie. False hope handed out, cigarettes stolen, rent money gambled away. He wanted to confess. He wanted to plead.

Brenda looked at him cowering on the ground and grinned. She flipped her veil, hitting her father in the face.

Johnny growled.

"And you! You sick son of a . . ." Johnny Rosetti didn't finish his sentence and he didn't care. He was a man who did not like his principles marred in any way. He leaned down, grabbed Wally by the collar, and pistol-whipped him in the side of the head.

Dazed, Wally edged down the hall, still trying to escape.

Slowly, Johnny walked over to the singer's body. His wingtips squeaked, and Wally cringed as he heard each footstep, closer and closer. The mad father looked down upon him.

With one open eye, Wally could see Johnny's angry face. Those big teeth grinding together. Possible punishments ran through Wally's mind. His detached head rolling down the hallway like a bloody bowling ball. Eyes plucked out with the antenna of a rusty car. Meat cutter through his middle. Thrown from the hotel roof. Legs sawed off. Something worse?

For all the fantasy, all Johnny did was reach for his gun. The quickest way was a lead projectile. Johnny harrumphed at the cowardice he saw below, then he shot the singer point blank.

Wally bled into the carpet, making the red parts redder, staining the gold squares. The amber hallway lights grew softer, and as he lay there, he watched Johnny address the other two suited men: "Get this cleaned up."

Then the man turned to his daughter, disgusted.

Johnny grabbed Brenda's arm, squeezing her thick tricep and the white satin wrapped around it.

DISAPPEAR

BY JAQ GREENSPON
Sunset Park

The best place to watch the sun set in Las Vegas was at the east end of the airport, just underneath the landing jets. Staring west, as the sun slipped behind the Red Rock Mountains, the obsidian, angled shape of the Luxor fell into sharp relief against the stretched-out orange glow. Sundown in the desert beat out any other geography, hands down. On the water the sunset would linger, bouncing on the waves, but in the desert there was nothing for the light to hold on to, nothing to trap it, bribe it to stay any longer than absolutely necessary. It ran, fled after the day like a scared rabbit. It was my favorite time of day. I loved it out here, for however long it lasted. I thrived in the liminal time, the gray area between light and dark. Playing with shadows was how I made my living.

And it was a good living. Most nights, after watching the sun go down, I'd be getting ready to earn that living. I'd be filling my pockets with cards, setting coins, writing predictions which I knew would come true later in the evening. A few years ago I'd be doing all this in a tuxedo, but not anymore. Now the uniform of choice, what the casinos wanted, was the street look. Dressed in jeans, T-shirt, and loose-fitting coat, sporting a few days growth I wasn't exactly comfortable with, I fit in well with the tourists at the Manhattan Resort and Casino. They didn't suspect a thing until I walked up and asked them if they'd like to see something amazing. Then I'd amaze them for a few seconds with a magic trick I learned when I was still in high school—nothing any of them couldn't do with the right book and three minutes of practice—then send them back to the casino floor. But not tonight. I was off tonight, asked for it special.

I lit a cigarette. I watched the glowing cherry at the tip of my Turkish Camel. If I timed it right, the light from the sun would vanish, leaving just the glowing ember to illuminate my face. I waited for it, slowing my inhalation. The dark overtook me, the red glow giving my face a Stanley Kubrick look. I sucked in, drawing down to the filter. Smiling, I flicked the butt out toward the landing lights of the next plane coming in. I turned left and started to walk toward the park. I had an appointment to keep and I didn't want to be late.

In reality, I couldn't be late. She wasn't going anywhere until I got there. She was waiting for me. I knew it, even if she didn't know I knew.

Her name was Raven, though she didn't acquire the name at birth. She hadn't been ushered into the waiting arms of loving parents who took one look at her and decided then and there what to call her. No, she was pushed out and virtually abandoned into the apathetic arms of grandparents who had no desire to raise another screaming, ungrateful child. But they did the right thing and took in Baby Girl Miller, which is what they called her for the first six months of her life. They had figured if they didn't give her a name, they couldn't get too attached, and then, if it all became too much, who would really miss a Baby Girl? But like it always happens, the prospect of another life to ruin became too much of a temptation to resist. Of course, that's not how they see it, but then, who really ever sees the damage they cause? By six months they knew they would keep her, at least until she turned fourteen and left on her own accord, with their blessing, and, it must be noted, to their great relief. With this realization, though, came the following thought, that Baby Girl might be fine for now, but wouldn't see her through her teenage years. Instead, they'd need a name that would sum up the unusually quiet little girl who had been born with a massive shock of dark hair and a preternatural fascination with shiny objects. A day trip to the Grand Canyon via helicopter to celebrate their twentieth wedding anniversary introduced them to Indian mythology, and by the time they'd gotten home and retrieved Baby Girl from the neighbor, they had decided to call her Raven.

I knew her as well as anyone, I guess. She'd jumped boxes for me back when I did that kind of thing. I'm sure if I ever went back to the big illusions, she'd be there for me. That's probably how she knew where to find me. I had a warehouse nearby, a place for storage and rehearsal. I shared it with a couple of other guys, workers who had scored nice variety act spots when the big production shows started closing down. It was a good deal for all involved and it was walking distance from where I was now, albeit in the opposite direction.

This was my area of town. This was where I lived and created, where I prowled and hunted. She had come here looking for me. I determined I wasn't going to be hard to find. As I sauntered into the park I saw her. Even in twilight that figure was hard to miss. She was looking in the other direction. I could easily have ducked behind a tree or jogged to the playground. Hell, I could have just sat down at a picnic table and she would have kept staring right through me. But no, I wanted to get this over with. I stopped short and just stood still, inhaling the ozone-filled desert air. It would rain soon, the clouds were making their way east even now. Tomorrow

I wouldn't be able to see the sun as it went down behind the gray, threatening sky. But then, depending on how this meeting went, it might not matter what the sky was like. There was a very good chance the sunset I had just enjoyed might be my last.

Eventually, she saw me and headed in my direction. She smiled like she caught me unaware. This was the difference between an amateur and a professional. In magic, it was marked by the outs. I never screwed up a trick, even if it didn't come out they way I had originally intended. No matter the situation, I had an out. But then, I'm a professional. An amateur, they have no outs. They only have one way to do something and if things don't go as planned, well, that's when the fur starts to fly. And I didn't want that to happen. Not yet at any rate. So I fought my instinct and closed my eyes and inhaled deeply. It wasn't often Vegas had that wet smell permeating the air. I concentrated on breathing and stood my ground, letting her do this her way. I didn't want her thinking she had no other options. Without options this wouldn't turn out well for anyone.

She walked up to me and stopped a foot away. Her head tilted up to look me in the eye. Her face was illuminated by the distant glow of the basketball court lights. Where we stood, by the picnic tables, was meant only for daytime use.

"Hi, Remy," she said.

I nodded. I wasn't going to make it easy for her. I had some ideas as to what she was doing here, I knew she was looking for me, but there was no sense diving in when I didn't know how deep the water was.

"I've been looking for you."

I nodded again. Magic is all about what the mark thinks they see, not what really happens. So one secret to a great trick, then, is knowing when to talk and when to let the audience make the connections for themselves. This was the latter. Whatever was really happening was secondary to whatever Raven thought was happening, and since I wasn't sure of either, I kept my mouth shut.

"Things have gone a bit pear shaped," she laughed nervously. Her eyes reflected the far-off light, giving them a depth they didn't actually possess. It made her look thoughtful and contrite. I didn't buy it. Not for a second.

"Do tell," I countered.

"I fucked up."

"That much I know. I was there for that part."

"No. After that."

"There was an 'after'?" Now we were getting somewhere.

"I thought everything was clear."

"Everything *was* clear. All you had to do was walk out of the building without touching anything. If you could have done that, walked past the pretty rocks and kept your hands to yourself, everything was clear. But you couldn't do that, could you?"

The tears streaming down her face glistened in the halflight. "How was I supposed to know they were counted? They were just there, sitting out, like fruit in a bowl or a candy dish at the dentist's office. How could they miss a couple?"

"I told you they'd miss them, that's how you were supposed to know." I shook my head in disgust. I had trusted her with my secrets but she couldn't control herself, and now . . . I stopped. I still didn't know why she was here. If they wanted me, she would have taken me out already. Or at least she would have tried. I wouldn't have let her get close if I didn't think I could protect myself, but they would have known that. That was why I let myself get caught. I figured she was just a messenger doing what it is messengers do. I would listen, nod wisely, and then dispose of the body.

I wasn't prepared for this. It seemed like she was asking me for something but wouldn't come right out and say it. And I couldn't parse it.

A plane went by overhead. I didn't dare look up, not with her standing so close. But she couldn't resist—she glanced at the underbelly. I knew she would and now I had a decision to make with not much time to make it. I opted for the safer of my two choices and stepped in toward her. I closed the distance between us and reached out with my left hand to grab her right arm. Pulling quickly, I spun her around and into me. My right arm wrapped around her chest while my left continued to hold her arm tight behind her back. To anyone walking through the park now, we looked like two lovers enjoying the nighttime amenities of the dark and the grass. I held her and placed my face close to hers, peaking over her shoulder like an evil Jiminy Cricket. We'd held this position many times before under much more pleasant circumstances. I breathed in deeply, letting her scent carry me back in time, just for a moment. My mind wandered old, worn pathways of almost forgotten emotion . . . but my hands held firm. I resisted the temptation to kiss her. Almost.

"Remy," she pleaded.

"What did you do?"

"They found out."

"They were diamonds, for god's sake. *Their* diamonds."

"But that's all."

"Those little rocks are money and blood and power and energy. They are never 'that's all.'"

She turned her head just enough. Our lips were barely separated. Our cover was a breath away from becoming reality. "Remy."

My arms instinctively tightened around her, a Pavlovian response to her whispering my name, at least that's what I told myself.

"You're hurting me."

"What did you do, Raven?" She smelled good. I could taste her scent on the back of my tongue. Jasmine and honey and the wetness of the air all mingled as I looked into her eyes. I didn't want to let her go. I didn't want her to stop hurting. I didn't want her. "Why are you here?" I held her tighter. She clenched. Her body's weight seemed to rest on my arm. Her eyes flinched but they never left mine.

"I need you. I need your help."

"Why me?"

"Because you're the only one who can make me disappear."

I faltered and relaxed my grip. She started to fall forward. I caught her and lowered her to the ground. She wasn't going anywhere and I knew she wasn't an immediate threat, so I lit another cigarette. She needed time to breathe. My coffin nail would give it to her. The smoke and nicotine I sucked deep into my lungs took her scent with it. She peered up at me and I knew I had to look away. In the distance, a late-night pickup game of basketball was just getting started. I watched the "skins" beat the "shirts" until I had smoked down to the filter.

In the silence, she had decided to tell me everything. I could feel her move around, turning so her back rested against my legs. Neither of us looked at the other anymore, yet I didn't know if we'd ever been closer. The first time I kissed her had been here, at the park. And the second. It held memories of us in the blades of grass and the pocket knife–carved picnic tables. It felt like the park was reclaiming us for its own.

"They caught me."

"And sent you to get me."

"No!"

I turned at the urgency of her denial.

"No," she continued, softer, still staring off into the distance. "They don't know about you. They asked but I didn't tell them."

"I'm sure they did more than ask."

"I got away."

I didn't want to know what she did to get away or what it cost her. It wasn't any of my business. What was my business was what she was doing here and why she needed me to make her vanish. Her motives were crystallizing in my mind. She hadn't told them about me. No matter that by giving them my name, she would have been in the clear. She could have simply looked them in the eye, told them "Regal Remy" had done it, had orchestrated the whole thing, given back the diamonds she stole, and her path would have become miraculously unblocked. Of course, as penance, they could have sent her to get me, which is exactly what I figured had happened.

Evidently, I was wrong.

She stood up and took my hand, leading me toward the trout-stocked lake in the middle of the park. It was a favorite for late-night lovers, consummating passions under the watchful eye of the Easter Island statue ensconced on a spit of land in the center. Our illusion was complete.

"They figured it out a few days ago. I was at work, like you said. I was casual and relaxed, making tips and laying low. Pierre came in. I didn't think nothing of it. He's been in before, you know?"

I did know. Pierre Charon was the "personal assistant" to Scott Wyld, hotelier extraordinaire. He was a former enforcer on the local minor league hockey team who found work much more in line with his calling in life after a career-ending fight took him off the ice. He was also well known at the higher end of the local strip club spectrum. I know because we used to go together. We were together at one of those clubs the night I first met Raven.

I'd been hired to work the smaller room in one of Wyld's casinos. It wasn't a bad gig and I was mostly filling 250 seats a night, six nights a week. I'd been working with a girl called Catherine, blond and pretty, and she knew how to jiggle when I needed her to distract the audience. But there was nothing there. She was passable as an assistant, but she was a lousy actress. No one bought it when she looked at me lovingly. I was surprised when the audience thought she even liked me. I was a job and nothing more. When she asked for a week off, I gladly let her go. Charon suggested we get Raven to fill in for her. He had a thing for the exotic-looking stripper, and since he worked for my boss, I took his suggestion with a little more seriousness than maybe I should have. He went with me when I asked her to be my assistant.

"Really? I've never done that before. I don't know if I'd be any good."

"Sure you would, sweetie, it's easy. Anyone can do it," explained Pierre.

That wasn't exactly true, but the reality wasn't far off. It took looks, the ability to move and smile and point in the right direction at the right time—this was the heart of helping out a magician. Sure, there were others, partners, who did more, who knew more, but what I was asking this girl to do was climb in a box and wiggle her toes at the right time. It wasn't brain surgery. She looked at me for confirmation. I nodded and smiled my approval.

"Yeah, I think you'd be perfect," I said. She never looked at Pierre again.

We met up the next day to rehearse. After an hour I knew she'd be able to handle the gig. After two I left a message on Catherine's machine telling her not to come back. Raven and I played it big. Her looks and my magic had us turning 'em away at the door.

Eventually, though, things went the way they've always gone with me. I found myself spending a little too much of my paycheck on the tables before I could get out the door. Then it was more than my paycheck and I found myself doing odd jobs for Wyld himself, paying him back by using sleight-of-hand skills honed in years of practice to fuck with big casino winners or illusions to make people believe things which couldn't possibly be true. And through it all Pierre was there, protecting his boss's interest. Evidently, those interests included going to see Raven at the club the night before last.

Raven was still talking, still putting the whole story together for me. I guess she thought she owed me that much. "So he comes in and I see him and smile, right? Like always. I was hustling a little bit, over by the bar. I figured I'd wait a few songs and then go say hi. When I looked back, though, he'd been taken to a table in the back, away from the stage."

I shook my head. "He always likes to be close to the action."

"That's what I thought. But Cinnamon took him to the back table and then she came over and whispered in my ear that he really wants to see me. The way she said it, I knew he meant now. So I went over."

"Those are dark tables. Anything can happen back there."

Raven smiled. She'd been part and party to a few of those anythings.

My first thought, however, was anything but sexy. Those back tables were the strip club equivalent of a dark alley. You never knew what was waiting for you. Usually you had the bouncers to watch your back, but when those guys worked for the guy who wanted to see you, you had no outs.

And yet she was here, walking and talking.

"I went up to him. I could barely see him, sitting all the way back in the booth. He asked me what I was doing there, now that I was rich."

I would have expected that. It wasn't in his nature to waste time. She continued her story. I stopped listening to generalities. I just wanted to know the details. Charon knew about the diamonds. He took her out the back door of the club, cutting her shift short. She ended up in the rear of a van, sucking on a .45 while good ol' Pierre told her they knew she was in on it. They knew she wasn't alone, that she couldn't have done it alone. She was hurt at the insinuation but couldn't refute it. He never explained how they had pinched her and she never told them it was me.

According to her, my name was on a laundry list of possible masterminds, all minor operators and petty thieves, and she didn't give up anyone. There was only one other name on that list, besides mine, that was of any concern. I figured that name was the reason I was still alive. Paul Robbins was a thief, and a damn good one. He worked all sorts of odd jobs. I only met him once and he stuck me for the bill. I didn't think he knew Raven, but then, I wasn't sure who she knew. All his name told me was they didn't know for sure I was in on it and there was no profitability in taking out one of your best on a hunch.

"How did you get away?"

"He threw me out the back of the van."

"Just like that?"

She paused. "He fucked me first, gun still in my mouth."

That also sounded like him.

"While he did it, he said he was going to do the same thing to whoever helped me."

I thought about it. I had to ask the question. "And you decided to come to me? They already think I'm guilty, why put me in the thick?"

"They don't think you're guilty. They think it was Paul. They just threw your name in to scare me. Pierre never liked you."

"He liked me fine."

"Not after we started working together."

"That why he fucked you?"

"That's why he didn't like you."

I let it sink in. According to her, I was in the clear. I could keep working like nothing ever happened. "So what do you need from me?"

"I told you, I need you to make me disappear. Just because they let me go doesn't make me free."

She had a point.

"You make me vanish and I'm gone for good. No one's the wiser."

I turned around.

"Remy?"

I could hear the shake in her voice, the need.

"Remy, please."

"Not here." I started walking away. I could feel her scamper up behind me. "The warehouse."

The warehouse was in an industrial area about a quarter-mile from Sunset Park. We shared a block with a custom furni-

ture place, a photographer, and an Internet porn company. I
opened the plain front door and let Raven in first. She turned
on the lights. I locked the door behind us.

After David Copperfield built Butchy's Lingerie, the false
storefront to mask his warehouse, all the magicians in town
wanted to do the same. Unfortunately, we didn't have Copperfield's money. I shared the warehouse with two other magicians, both of whom used it primarily as a storage facility. It
helped pay the rent. The front office at our place looked like
a fabric shop, but that was because it was where we did all
the sewing. No hidden doors or electrified toilet seats here.
We had the front office, complete with conference/cutting
table, a ratty green couch along the wall, and a mini-fridge
that was almost never stocked with anything Raven wanted.
She looked anyway.

"Still drinking that crap, I see."

"Help yourself." She took out a bottle and tossed it to me.
It was an old ritual, one we fell back into easily.

I opened the door to the rest of the building. The back
area held a decent-sized space filled with props, illusions, some
tools, and, tucked away in a far corner, a stage for rehearsals.
It was crowded but not packed. The walls were covered with
show posters, autographed pictures, and pin-ups. It made the
place look smaller than it really was. I turned on the stage
lights rather than the work floods. No need to really light the
place.

Raven walked around as if reacquainting herself with an
old friend. "It's been awhile."

She looked good, slipping in and out of shadows amongst
the illusions. It had indeed been awhile. Too long. She walked
up to the "Artist's Dream" and stopped. I sipped my beer and
watched her. It was a simple illusion, a way to produce an

assistant. On the front panel was a picture of the girl. It was briefly covered and then, just like that, the girl was standing there and only a silhouette remained on the panel. Very Galatea . . . or My *Fair Lady*. Either way, the artist was bringing to life the girl of his dreams. I smiled as she pulled down the front panel. It was still set with her photograph. I hadn't done the trick since she left. I think that pleased her.

Raven and I had stopped working together, professionally, about a year and a half earlier. The jobs dried up for the big shows in town and I really didn't want to work the ships. They weren't my kind of crowds. They were looking for safe and I equated that with boring. At least doing what I was doing, hustling tourists to give them the "street magic experience," gave me the opportunity to keep my close-up chops. Doing nothing but boxes on a cruise was death to me. Besides, the ships didn't really approve of you laying a week's salary on red. So I didn't go and Raven quit being my assistant. We stopped seeing each other personally not long after. Seems I wasn't fulfilling potential, was only hurting myself, and she was tired of supporting me and my bad habits.

That's the thing about habits, though, everyone has them. And I was Raven's. Just because we'd stopped dating didn't mean she wasn't available for a quick fuck whenever I was in the mood. We had something together neither of us had alone, and for her it was a driving force.

"Do you have an idea?" she asked without looking at me. She had made her way to the stage. It was the first time I'd seen her completely lit in months. She still took my breath away. Did I have an idea? There was a mattress propped against the wall behind the stage. It wasn't clean but it was more comfortable than the floor.

"I might."

Maybe she could hear my thoughts in my voice. Maybe she knew me as well as I thought I knew her. Maybe it was all part of the game we were both playing, but she turned and stared across the room at me. She smiled. A sad smile. "I like fresh sheets these days, remember? It's not like it was."

We'd been on that mattress more times than I could count. It was what we did during rehearsals, after shows, before breakfast. But she was right. It wasn't like it was. She was in trouble and I was here to help. She wanted me to be her white knight, but I was rusty. I drained my beer. The right lubrication can ease any passage.

"Did you give back the diamonds?"

She looked at me like I was a black man at a Klan meeting.

Of course. Charon pegged her for the body, not the brains. I wanted to laugh. The layman realizes how little the illusionist actually does, though. The magician dances out his choreography while the assistant does all the work, squeezing and running and hiding while the props move around them. One false move and it's the girl in the box who's getting impaled while the magician wields the blade. "Charon didn't know you took them." It was the only explanation. "And he didn't know anything else was gone."

She reached into her pocket and pulled out a handmade velvet bag. I'd seen it before. She got it when she bought a necklace from a beach vendor in Santa Monica. She used it to keep her valuables.

"And now he knows either me or Paul has 'em and I'm sending you away?"

"You can have half."

"I'm covered, thanks. I got what I was after."

She turned toward the back door. "This was a mistake."

I could have let her go. I could have let her walk out the

door and face whatever was beyond it. That would have been the smart thing to do. "Wait." I was never that smart.

She turned back, grateful. I didn't move. She crossed the floor and into my arms, hugging me hard. I didn't want to but I hugged back. It was a reflex. "Oh, Remy," she whispered in my ear. "Thank you. I was so scared . . ." The words trailed off as I turned my head. Her fears melted into passion. Just another emotional outlet.

I lifted her up, her lips still locked with mine, and set her on the "Impaled" table. The floor would have been more comfortable. The bottom half of "Impaled" was the receptacle. Perched above it, Murphy-bed style, was a rack of sharp metal spikes. Real ones. It was part of the gag. The magician would prove the spikes were real while the assistant was being chained to the table. A light would be positioned behind her and a thin curtain in front, so the audience could see her struggling. There was a time limit, artificially imposed, something to add more drama to the situation. When the clock ran out, the spikes would fall, and if the girl was still there, well . . .

At just the right time, though, the light went out, the spikes fell, and the girl reappeared someplace else, safe and sound. It was foolproof. There was a safety catch so the spikes couldn't fall if the girl was still chained up, and she had a foot switch to release the spikes when she was in position. It looked dangerous and evil. It was the kind of illusion I could never perform on a cruise.

It was a new prop in the warehouse and I'd never before used it for this purpose. It supported our combined weight nicely, creaking and groaning along as if it were an active participant in our lovemaking.

Afterwards, we lay there in each other's arms, slowly becoming aware of the cold metal table beneath us. She laughed as I shivered.

"Can you really get me out of here?"

I held her face in my hands and looked directly into her eyes. "I'm gonna get us a blanket first."

She laughed again when I rolled off the table. I bumped my hip as I got to my feet. I looked over at her. She was beautiful. For just this moment, it was like it was. I went into the front office to grab a blanket. Raven had rolled over, away from me, when I returned. She was still naked.

I stopped and looked at her, wishing she didn't have to go away. But I knew there was no other choice. If she was still here it was dangerous for everyone involved.

As I approached the illusion I hit the foot release.

I made myself watch as the spikes came down.

She turned her head at the sound, but there was no chance to get out of the way. She didn't even have time to scream. With an illusion, there's no point in a slow death. Of the forty spikes, no more than six or seven hit her, but it was enough to do the job. The rest slid into their proper channels with a sickening metal-on-metal grate. The blood channels, built into the table for show, worked just like they were supposed to, draining the red flow away from her body and collecting it in a basin at the foot of the table.

I threw the blanket I was still holding over the whole mess. I got dressed before I retrieved the diamonds from her pants pocket. I had plans for the little beauties.

The blood was overflowing, dripping on the floor. The basin was never really meant to hold anything. I grabbed a rag to sop it up.

The back door opened. Pierre Charon stepped in, cell phone in his hand. "She called me."

"When?" I asked, not looking up.

"Now."

I went to the other side of the table and lifted the blanket. Her eyes were still open, still filled with shock and horror. Her cell phone was in her hand, the connection still open.

"She fingered you from the beginning."

"It had to be one of us."

"You made the right choice."

I stood up and tossed the velvet bag to him. It was caught and pocketed in one motion. I was on my honor they were all there.

"We good?"

He looked from the bag in his hand to the dead body and back again. He had the diamonds and someone to blame for it. "We're good," he said.

"Now what?" I asked.

He tilted his head toward Eastern Boulevard. "Eden Memorial. We've cashed in a few favors."

By the time the hole was filled, the sun was just beginning to rise. Sunrise in Las Vegas is something to behold, the way the rays reflect off the gold and brass of the Strip hotels. With no way to know from which direction the light is really coming, there's no way to set your compass. I lit a cigarette and basked in its directionless glow.

ALL ABOUT BALLS

BY JOSÉ SKINNER

East Las Vegas

P eople in other academic disciplines made fun of American Studies. The joke went: If you check "undecided" one too many times as your major, they put you down for American Studies. Ortiz was in his fifth year as a graduate student in American Studies, and he still hadn't decided on a topic for his master's thesis. He hoped Professor Philippe Talon, the ethnographer, might become his thesis advisor, but he'd have to impress the man in some unusual way to earn this honor.

Dr. Talon, a burly Belgian, was the author of numerous studies of aboriginal peoples throughout the Americas. Talon was fond of debunking other anthropologists' accounts of the innate peacefulness of native peoples—to him, violence was a constant universal, and he was full of tales of aboriginal violence. Rumor had it that he had eaten human flesh with cannibals in the jungles of eastern Peru, that in Venezuela he had been forced to take part in a ritual castration of a Yanomami captive, and that he had fathered a child among a war-loving, Stone Age people in Brazil. Students who had been to his home reported seeing a shrunken head on his mantel. Ortiz had never spoken to him at length, though whenever the redoubtable professor happened to be in his office, and Ortiz happened to pass by, he invariably glanced in to behold the man buried among his papers and journals, his thick, blond-haired fingers stabbing at his keyboard, his neck spattered with the red tattoo of some indigenous ceremony he'd participated in in the Amazon rain forest.

In that fifth year of his graduate program, Ortiz decided to go to the annual convention of the American Culture Association. The ACA conference was the main gathering for the American Studies crowd. Ortiz believed a couple of days listening to panel discussions by eminent figures in his field might inspire him to finally decide on a thesis topic. If he got lucky, some of those people might invite him to a few after-sessions drinks; the thought caused him to nibble the ends of his long hair with excitement.

The conference was being held that year in Las Vegas at a hotel-casino on the Boulder Strip in East Las Vegas called ¡Viva!, a brand-new place with a Latin theme: dealers in sequined matador jackets, waitresses topped with fruit head-dresses à la Carmen Miranda, that sort of thing. Ortiz had to go on his own nickel—his university would only pay for his trip if he were presenting a paper, which he wasn't. But Las Vegas was just half a day's drive from L.A., and he planned to stay at the Lucky Cuss, a cheap motel on the Boulder Strip not far from ¡Viva!

It had stormed in the Mojave that spring, and as he drove up I-15 the flowering desert spread vast and golden before him like the carpet of ¡Viva!'s casino floor, which he'd seen on an Internet virtual tour of the place. The air smelled fresh and washed, very unlike casino air, but he kept the windows of his vintage Mustang closed because his hair tangled easily.

His glossy black hair and high cheekbones occasionally led people to mistake him for an Indian. "Native," he corrected them, and didn't disabuse them of the notion. No doubt he did have Native blood, on his Latino father's side. His mother was

English, but his father's people had been in California since the mission days, and their blood had surely commingled with that of some long-lost tribe. Even better, he might be kin to some still-existing group, one of these tiny tribes with its own casinos and whose members were all millionaires. Maybe he could take a DNA test to prove the connection. That would be something.

He drew his Vegas street map from his satchel—a satchel made of Moroccan leather, yet old and worn enough to be worthy of an academic—and smoothed it over his steering wheel. He liked studying things when he was driving long stretches—maps, articles, even books. He played a sort of game in which he kept his eyes on the text as long as he dared before snapping them back to the road. He found that while the danger often prevented him from immediately comprehending what he was reading, it had the strange effect of stamping the information photographically in his mind, and afterwards he could recall, in what psychologists called *anamnesis*, whole passages verbatim: a nifty trick for impressing colleagues.

The way to ¡Viva! was simple enough: Continue along I-15, then hang a right on Tropicana and keep going east to the Boulder Highway. ¡Viva! stood midway between Sam's Town and the Lucky Cuss. Sam's Town had an Old West theme, complete with something called a Western Emporium and a nightly laser show called the "Sunset Stampede." Vegas! No wonder the American Culture Association loved meeting here.

He followed the directions he'd memorized and headed east on Tropicana, surprised at how run-down some of the neighborhoods became, jumbles of low-slung bungalows and mobile homes faded in the sun. Obviously not everybody in Vegas was a lucky cuss.

Curious about a particularly shabby-looking neighborhood, he hung a right onto a street with a paintball store on one corner and a liquor store on the other. He followed the winding street past some more trailers and a dried-up park. Going slow now—the street was full of potholes—he opened his window. The warm air carried odors of raw sewage, boiling corn, and burning rubbish. Farther along, a truly foul scent hit his nostrils and he saw a dead Chihuahua in the gutter, bloated to the size of a dachshund. He rolled his window up fast.

The street turned gravelly and petered out at a hodgepodge of trailers and cinder-block huts. In one area, the dwellings were arranged around a kind of courtyard, bare earth save for a dusty elm tree. A compact man dressed entirely in white squatted beneath the tree, hewing, with quick strokes of his machete, a length of wood. The blade of the machete was worn to a wicked thinness: It looked like a long dagger. Behind the man, half-hidden in a doorway, stood a young woman in a white dress colorfully embroidered at the square neckline, biting her knuckles, her black eyes following Ortiz. Two other men, also dressed in white, ducked ghostlike into a squalid alley and disappeared.

The squatting man looked up. Ortiz waved hesitantly, and the man raised his machete in an aggressive salute. Ortiz followed the line of the machete to its tip, and there, as if speared by the blade, he beheld ¡Viva!'s red neon sign, its letters curved into the shape of a chili pepper.

There didn't seem to be any direct way through the wretched little neighborhood to the casino, so Ortiz headed back the way he'd come. But somehow he got turned around in the maze of dirt roads, and found himself driving in a circle. Once again he passed by the dusty square, and once again the young woman's eyes followed him, and the man with the machete watched him too, this time without greeting. Ortiz clutched the steering wheel with both hands, and noticed that the hair on his arms had risen on end. The stench of the dead dog, and the heat, and the pounding brightness of the light made him want to puke.

He finally found his way out, and merged with relief into Tropicana's fast traffic. A few minutes later he arrived at ¡Viva!, where the noise and bustle swallowed him up. He followed the ACA signs up the wide staircase to the mezzanine and registered for the conference. A harried fellow graduate student gave him a canvas bag containing a name tag, a pen, a refrigerator magnet in the shape of a horseshoe, and a book-length schedule of presentations and events. The letters of his last name stood impressively large on the name tag. It was the first time he'd ever had a name tag. He pinned it carefully on his guayabera, above his heart.

Professor Talon wasn't listed among the presenters, but this came as no surprise; when Talon left campus, it was to penetrate little-known parts of the world and encounter their peoples, not attend academic conferences. Talon was the real thing: the utterly fearless ethnographer who knew that field-work was everything.

Ortiz headed to a panel on masculinities. Masculinities Studies was hot; there were six masculinities panels at that year's conference. The one about to start was called "All About Balls" and it offered three presentations: "'You're Not a Eunuch, Are You?' *Pirates of the Caribbean*'s Postcolonial Masculinities;" "The Leisured Testes: White Ball-Breaking as Surplus Machismo in *Jackass*"; and "*Huevos* and Balls: The (Fr)agilities of Maleness in Latino/a Discourse."

"All About Balls" was held, fittingly enough, in the Pancho

Villa Salon. The audience was well-represented by what Ortiz had come to identify as the various academic types: the jovial older male professor, silver-bearded and bearlike, comfortable in his tenured professorship; the anxious junior faculty member, needing that next book to clinch tenure, building her CV by sponsoring panels at the conference while realizing that all this conferencing was cutting into her writing time; fellow graduate students dressed in solid black, ironic and cool, prepared to declare the whole scene a fraud if they found they couldn't finish their dissertations. During the presentations, the older male professors laughed a lot, the assistant professors listened intently, and the grad students feigned jadedness. Afterwards, a few people from the audience, including Ortiz, went up to the front to introduce themselves and chat with the speakers, all professors from various institutions.

"That took some balls," Ortiz told the *huevos*-and-balls man. He was a pint-sized Chicano in a sports jacket and tie. Trim mustache. Ortiz had to stoop to meet the humorless gaze behind the man's rimless glasses.

"I'm not sure I follow you," said the professor, eyeing Ortiz's name tag.

There were certain people who took an immediate dislike to Ortiz, and this guy was evidently one of them. They didn't care for Ortiz's lustrous hair or his height or his colorful guayabera shirts or his authentic *huaraches*. They took him for a poser. Ortiz, in turn, pegged the guy for a former Chicano activist turned academic. Those types were always bitter and hyper-critical. They could never take a joke.

"I mean, like, all of it," Ortiz stammered. "The panel."

"Well, it's all about balls, right?" the man said dryly.

There was nothing on Ortiz's name tag to identify him as a lowly graduate student and thereby unworthy of such animosity. The name tags gave only the bearer's name—sans title—and school. The professor hailed from a college Ortiz had never heard of. Perhaps, Ortiz thought, he felt threatened by Ortiz's far more prestigious university.

"What's your work on, Dr. Ortiz? Mr. Ortiz?" said the professor.

"Mr.," Ortiz said. "Oh, different things." It was flattering to be taken as having a doctorate and "working on" something.

"Ah, *different* things."

"I work with Philippe Talon," said Ortiz.

"Never heard of him," said the assistant professor, turning away.

Heat rose on Ortiz's face as his testicles rose to his body. He stalked from the room and tromped down the stairs. That was bullshit! Everyone knew of Dr. Talon.

Down in the gaming area, Ortiz bought a bucket of nickels and played an old-fashioned one-armed bandit, depositing the coins and pulling the lever fiercely, looking up occasionally to observe the dealers at the card tables absurdly done up in spangled matador's jackets. Weren't the players aware of the irony of being dealt to by "bullfighters"? Didn't they know, stupid bovines, that in the end, the matador always wins? Some people just didn't get irony. Wasn't it incredibly ironic that a professor who had just given a talk on the follies of machismo should act so macho?

His coins soon gone, he got up and roamed the depths of the casino. Sure enough, just as pictured on the ¡Viva! website, the waitresses sported ridiculous Carmen Miranda headdresses made of what appeared to be real fruit. The bartenders wore billowing white shirts and wide red sashes around their waists, like the men who ran with the bulls in Pamplona. Mariachi trumpeters blasted away from a corner of the bar.

A display near the hotel check-in desk caught Ortiz's eye. It was a series of life-sized dancing, grinning skeletons carved of wood, the male figures wearing wide sombreros, the females in lacey granny dresses, their bony limbs comically akimbo.

A voice came from behind him. "*Viva la muerte!*"

Ortiz turned and beheld a young bellhop pushing a cart of luggage toward the elevators.

The bellhop brought his load next to Ortiz. "Pretty wild, huh?" he said. "It's like Day of the Dead stuff."

"Yeah. Who makes it?"

"Some kind of Mexicans. Not your regular kind of Mexicans. I mean . . ." The kid's pimples disappeared in his flush, and he looked away. "Here, I think we got some information about them."

Ortiz followed the bellhop to the brochure rack. Not your "regular kind of Mexicans," were they? Well, he was just a kid. Learning how easy it was to fuck up when you talked to people. Ortiz could sympathize.

The bellhop produced a brochure about ¡Viva!'s collection of south-of-the-border folk art and handed it to Ortiz. "Enjoy!" he said, moving his cargo along.

Apparently the hotel-casino had a whole gallery somewhere full of colorful ceramics and squat onyx figurines and more of these dancing skeletons. The skeletons, according to a brief blurb, were carved by an indigenous people from the remote lowlands of the southern Mexican state of Guerrero. The Mictlanos were famous for their wood carving, which they executed entirely with machetes.

Could the odd barrio he'd stumbled across earlier that day be a community of transplanted Mictlanos? Certainly in L.A. it was possible to find neighborhoods of indigenous peoples from specific regions of Mexico or Guatemala. Why not Las Vegas?

The Mictlanos—that wasn't what they called themselves, but the name bestowed upon them by surrounding peoples. Mictlán, in Aztec mythology, was the ninth circle of the underworld, or something like that. Ortiz tried to remember what else Dr. Talon had said about them in his lectures. Weren't they the group Dr. Talon had referred to as having particularly "attractive" but "dangerous" women, a remark that had brought complaints from some of the female students? Ortiz recalled Talon describing with relish some kind of ritual confrontation between two Mictlano men over a woman, something about a midnight machete battle following a stylized exchange of insults, and a grave dug ahead of time for the loser.

Ortiz whipped out his laptop and Googled *Mictlan* and *Las Vegas* and got zero hits. So: If this truly was a group of Las Vegas Mictlanos undiscovered by ethnographers, what a find. What a fucking find! Now that was something he could write about—something that might impress Talon.

Ortiz abandoned the casino to discover that night had already fallen. The darkness hung thick beyond the lights of the Boulder Strip, as if the Mictlanos (if that's what they were) had brought the black jungle night with them. He hesitated. Maybe he'd better wait until the next morning before he ventured back into the barrio. But had Talon ever hesitated to go anywhere on the face of the earth? Of course not. The man had balls. Ortiz had balls. He had to check out his discovery one more time before going to his motel.

The odor of the putrid Chihuahua guided him to the square. His Mustang bounced along the rutted road, its headlights brushing up and down the tree the man had been sitting under earlier in the day, carving his wood. Ortiz came to a stop under the tree and shut off the engine. Silence and darkness rushed in on him.

A man's gruff voice erupted suddenly in the quiet, followed by a slapping sound. Another slap and a woman's cry: "Ay, ay!" A lull; and then another slap, another sharp "Ay!" It was impossible to tell where exactly the commotion was coming from. Ortiz expected to hear weeping or sobbing, but no: Only a stoic silence followed.

Ortiz waited for a moment, drowning in the blackness, before starting his engine and taking off. Whatever was going on in that shack, he told himself, it wasn't his place to interfere. To do so would ruin his research before it even got off the ground. Anyway, there was no telling what was really happening. Rough sex? A ritual driving out of evil spirits? Whatever it was, he had to respect these people's culture and remain neutral.

Just as he suspected, the Lucky Cuss Motel was not for truly lucky cusses, but it wasn't bad, either. Unfortunately, the only room they had left smelled as if a dozen chain smokers had rented it for a week. He peeled the sheets apart and looked for hairs, but the bed seemed clean enough. He lay on it and contemplated what he'd heard: the gruff male voice, the slaps, the woman's cries. But again, there was no need to jump to conclusions. All he knew for sure was that he was one lucky cuss to have that community of transplanted Native Mexicans to do some real fieldwork on.

But his sense of good fortune didn't prevent him from falling into a restless sleep full of snarling dogs and dancing skeletons and screaming women, and the next morning he woke up groggy and headachy. The sun glowed with hellish intensity bright behind the heavy golden curtains. He showered quickly and threw on a fresh guayabera and khaki pants. He grabbed a large coffee at a 7-Eleven and headed once again to what he already dubbed Little Mictlán. The coffee and crystalline desert air cleared his head. By the time he got to the barrio, he felt better.

The dead dog and its stink were gone. The cluster of trailers and cinder-block shacks, bare of any adornments, were hardly cheery, but the morning light had evaporated the previous night's sinister feel. Ortiz pinned his name tag to his shirt and strode to the first hut and knocked.

The young woman he had seen standing there the previous afternoon opened the door. She wore the same kind of white dress, embroidered at the square neckline with strangely elongated animal figures. She was small-boned and pretty, her hair woven in a single long, thick braid—hair lustrous and black as his own. She glanced at his name tag. He was glad he'd thought to put it on—it identified him as in some way official.

"*Hola*," he said. "*Yo soy investigador? Ortiz es mi nombre?*"

His Spanish wasn't great, he knew, but "*investigador*," police-y as it sounded, was Spanish for "researcher," he was sure of that.

"*Investigador?*"

"*Sí.*" No need to complicate matters, just yet, with explanations of what kind of investigator he was. He asked if he could enter.

The woman hesitated, then stepped back. Ortiz ducked inside. The room was unfurnished except for a straw-bottomed rocking chair and a long, rough-hewn—machete-hewn, no doubt—bench running along one wall. Aluminum foil covered the one window; an incandescent bulb burned nakedly in the ceiling.

The woman remained standing near the open door, keeping herself visible to the outside.

"*Ustedes son Mictlanos, no?*" he asked, giving his friendliest smile.

"*Sí*," she said faintly.

Bingo. He had his people.

"*Qué hacen aquí?*" The question—"what are you doing here?"—came out more brusque than he wanted, but his Spanish wasn't good enough for polite subtleties. He kept his smile, the bright smile an ex-girlfriend had once called "innocent," and asked if he could have a seat on the bench. She nodded. He motioned for her to sit as well, and she obeyed, taking a spot at the end of the bench where she could still be seen from the street. The sunlight coiled silver along her braid.

Spanish was clearly not her first language either, but he managed to ascertain that her husband and the rest of the men in the community worked construction jobs as well as carved the comical *calacas*, as she called the skeletons, for ¡Viva! That was where they were at the moment, at their construction jobs—they'd be back later, she said, though she was unable to specify exactly when. It occurred to Ortiz that these men might make better informants, to use the anthropological term—and his was an anthropological investigation, was it not?—than this hesitant young woman.

Ortiz had a weakness for women's legs; the sight of a well-shaped female leg made his own legs literally weak, gave them a heaviness. This woman's brown calves were perfectly shaped, as if turned on a lathe, and her small foot arched nicely in her sandal, a sandal very similar to his *huaraches*. Her toes were small and round. She was certainly no *India patarrajada*, no "split-footed Indian," to use the most common anti-Native epithet in Mexico, the equivalent perhaps of calling an African American "nappy-headed." He flicked his own Native hair behind his shoulders with both hands.

Slowly, discreetly, she bunched her dress in her hand, drawing it up along her leg. He swallowed, and watched. There, beginning about mid-thigh, she revealed to him a gigantic bruise, yellow-tinged on the edges and shading into a deep, mottled purple.

"Jesus!"

She jumped to her feet and smoothed her skirt. "The men will be back later," she repeated. She stepped out of the house. It was clearly time for him to go.

Ortiz made his way back to ¡Viva! and the conference in a kind of daze. He attended another panel presentation, but all he could think about was the young woman, and her bruise, and the way she'd inched her skirt up to reveal it to him. He fantasized tending her injury, applying Native-style poultices made of wild herbs and macerated cactus fruit they'd gather together in the flowering Mojave, and his own legs grew weak again.

He found the gallery of Mexican folk art and contemplated the Mictlano *calacas* there. The skeletons in this display wore formal dress, the females in furs and gowns, the males in tuxedos. One of the male *calacas* was a dapper little guy in glasses who reminded Ortiz of the rude professor from the day before.

Ortiz returned to the barrio around 5, when most of the conference-goers were heading off to their wine-and-cheese receptions for this new program or that new journal. Good for them. He, Ortiz, had fieldwork to do. And the balls to do it.

He found a group of Mictlano men under the elm tree, drinking Bud Lite. Two of them were still dressed in their work clothes—tar-stained jeans, sweaty T-shirts, cement-smeared work boots. The other three had changed into clean *cotones*, which was the term Talon had taught him for the loose white clothing Mexican peasants favored. One of the men dressed in white was the man he'd seen the day before; again he sat wielding his machete against a block of wood, which had taken the wide, lobed shape of a pelvic bone.

Ortiz shook hands all around. Their faces were impassive and their handshakes surprisingly limp for men who work with their hands. They glanced mistrustfully at his name tag. The man from the day before was a full head shorter than Ortiz, but stocky. His face was broad and his eyes small and very red. A dirty cord bound the machete to his wrist. According to Professor Talon, it was customary among men in remote parts of southern Mexico to tie their machete handles to their wrists so they wouldn't misplace them. These folks were the real thing, no doubt about it. Ortiz's research into their ways and how these ways were affected—or not—by their living and working in Las Vegas was going to make a great, great study. Soon enough he himself was going to be tying his satchel to his wrist so as not to lose the invaluable information he gathered.

"*Usted es el investigador,*" the man with the machete said.

"*Sí,*" Ortiz replied. He didn't like the continued looks of apprehension on the men's faces. It was time to be straightforward about what kind of "investigator" he was. That was the only way to get them to be forthcoming about their lives. He certainly didn't want them to think he was with Immigration or something.

"*Soy estudiante,*" Ortiz said. And in a gesture meant to put them further at ease, he unpinned his ACA name tag and tossed it into the clutter of empty beer cans.

"Ah," said the stocky man. "*Estudiante.*"

Ortiz didn't care for the man's slightly mocking tone. Still, everyone seemed to relax at the revelation that he was just a lowly student, and that was good.

Ortiz then made a gesture they found very funny. He drew his thumb and forefinger along his mouth and made a twisting motion, as if locking his lips. Whether they took this to mean that the secret of their existence was safe with him or that he was asking them to be discreet about his visits, he would never know; he himself didn't know what he meant, exactly. Both these things, he supposed. In any case, they guffawed, and popped him a beer.

The men's Spanish was a good deal better than the young woman's—perhaps they weren't *indigenes*, like she, but mixed-blood *mestizos*. Still, he understood only a fraction of what they said, and none of the jokes, though he laughed when they laughed. He made a mental note to bring a tape recorder next time he visited so he could go over everything as many times as it took to decipher it all.

The beer and the talk relaxed him, and every now and then he cast a glance at the hut where he'd found the young woman that morning. He wished she would open the battered door, or at least peel away the tinfoil on the window and peek out, so he could know she knew he was there.

The stocky man, who'd introduced himself as Vicente, continued hewing his wood; now he was working a longer piece, a femur perhaps, striking long slivers from it. He uttered something in a guttural language that was definitely not Spanish. He kicked the wood aside and stalked to the hut, smacking, with the side of his machete, the dog lying in front of it. The dog yelped and scurried away, tail tucked. The man entered the shack and slammed the door.

The other men shifted their feet and sipped their beers quietly. Ortiz could feel their discomfort. He'd blown it somehow. Had Vicente caught him glancing at the shack where the woman—apparently Vicente's woman—lived? In any case, it was time to leave. Darkness was descending, that impenetrable Mictlano darkness that was like a repudiation of the rest of Vegas' gaudy brightness.

He shook hands with the men. When he got to the last one, a tall, gaunt man with deep-set eyes and thin lips, the guy seized his upper arm and said, "*Hay baile el sábado.*"

A dance next Saturday? *Aquí?*

"*Sí, aquí.*" The man moved his hand down and squeezed Ortiz's forearm firmly with his long fingers. Clearly this was an invitation. An invitation to one of their festivities!

"*Cuándo?*" asked Ortiz.

The man raised his bony finger to the growing darkness. "*En la noche.*"

Ortiz skipped the rest of the ACA conference and returned that same night to L.A. He was eager to tell people, especially Dr. Talon, about his discovery, but knew he had to refrain; for now, they had to remain his secret.

Still, he could not keep himself from visiting the professor the day before he was to return to Las Vegas and attend the Mictlano fiesta. That the professor kept his office hours on Friday afternoons was a signal that he didn't really want students dropping in on him, since this was the time of the week when they were least likely to do so. Nevertheless, Ortiz crept down the empty hall to the professor's office and knocked on the door.

"Open!" Talon boomed.

The only decorations on the professor's walls were a spear-thrower and three arrows. He sat entombed in his piles of papers and journals, fixed Ortiz with his glittery blue gaze, and waited for him to state his business.

"I was thinking about writing my thesis on the Mictlanos," Ortiz said.

"Mictlanos, ey? What do you know about the Mictlanos?"

"Not much. That's why—"

"What aspect? What in particular do you want to write about?"

Ortiz hadn't really thought it through. But he'd been thinking about the slaps he'd heard that night in Las Vegas, the woman's cries, the bruise she'd shown him, Vicente's piggish face, and so he said, "Gender relations?"

"Well, that would be fashionable," Talon said. "Easy, too. Gender relations among the Mictlanos basically revolve around the *cinchazo*. Do you know what the *cinchazo* is?"

Ortiz allowed that he did not.

"The *cinchazo* is the blow a man gives to his woman with the flat side of his machete. It pretty much settles everything, at least from the man's point of view. It's very difficult to get the women to talk about it, even to other women. If you intend to do fieldwork on that, you'd best be very, very careful."

Talon drew from one of his piles of papers an article he'd written about the Mictlanos and gave it to Ortiz. Apparently it was a detailed account of the ritual fight between the two Mictlano males that Ortiz had already heard about in Talon's lectures. Ortiz tucked the article in his satchel, thanked the professor, and took his leave.

The next day, Ortiz took off for Las Vegas feeling elated. So the famous Professor Talon had a hard time getting Mictlana women to open up to him. Well, as far as Ortiz was concerned, the young Mictlana woman had already opened up to him by revealing her bruise. She wanted to talk about it. Perhaps that was because he himself was Native, or looked it. Or because he simply inspired trust. Talon was, let's face it, a loud, aggressive European. It was surprising any Native peoples at all had ever confided in him.

Pleased with the thought of someday surpassing Talon as an ethnographer, Ortiz hadn't yet bothered to read the article the professor gave him, but as he drove he plucked it from his satchel and began his reading-on-the road game. As always in this game, the meaning of the text wasn't going to sink in immediately; the fun would come later when the words, carved in his mind by the danger, came back to him verbatim, as if out of nowhere, triggered by some stress.

Ortiz glanced up just in time up to see a deer or an antelope bounding—no, flying—across the hood of his car. Some kind of hoofed thing, anyway: The cloven hoof came down on his exterior rearview, shattering it. Holy fucking shit. Behind him, the creature continued bounding across the desert in great leaps.

Ortiz stuffed the article in his satchel and took the wheel with both trembling hands. Enough foolishness. He kept his eyes on the road the rest of the way to Vegas.

The sun had already set by the time he got to the city. With a frisson of professional satisfaction, he turned his car away from the lights of the Strip and headed into the dark barrio of his study. The only things he could see were what his headlights illuminated: the potholed street, and at the end of it, the elm tree.

The tree had been hideously lopped, its stumped limbs raised in supplication to the heavens. Who would do such a thing to a tree, especially here in the desert, where shade was so needed? But again, it wasn't his place to pass judgment on these people. They needed the wood for their carvings, after all. Or maybe they turned it into charcoal for cooking, as people did all over the Third World.

Speaking of charcoal, the two men digging behind the huts were no doubt preparing a barbeque pit for the fiesta. That meant the food was a long ways from being ready. Maybe this was to be some sort of drawn-out, all-night fiesta; Ortiz regretted not having gotten something to eat on the road.

Nor should he be drinking on an empty stomach, but already the man who had invited him to the *baile* had thrust into his hand a big plastic glass of *chicha*, the traditional Mictlano fermented corn drink. So okay, cool, let the party begin.

The man ushered him to a rickety metal table set up in one corner of the dusty courtyard. Two other men joined them. Another metal table had been set up in the corner opposite. The only illumination came from a dim kerosene lamp suspended from a wire running from the roofs of two of the huts. But it was enough to allow Ortiz to see Vicente's squat body take a seat at that table opposite.

A four-man band emerged from the shadows and struck up vigorous binary rhythms on an accordion and chicken-scratch strings. The men at Ortiz's table urged more milky *chicha* on him. The drink was cool, if a bit acid. Probably quite nourishing. He drank and listened to the homely music and smiled at his friends. The red neon *¡Viva!* sign shone bright in the distance.

Then, as if choreographed, a group of women assembled themselves in the fourth corner of the courtyard, all dressed in colorful skirts and blouses. Among them was the woman with the bruise. She glanced at Ortiz's table, then at Vicente's, then dropped her gaze to the ground.

Men from both tables began taking women to dance, though not before first asking the woman's husband or boyfriend for permission. Ortiz watched the dancers shuffle in the dust, and loved them. He felt deeply connected to them, to these people whose ancestors—and his, on his Native side—had crossed the Bering Strait and made that immense and brave journey down into Mesoamerica, where they had built vast empires. Now they had returned back north, to the great Nevada desert, where he was ever so fortunate to be witness to their ancient rites.

Okay—maybe he didn't love Vicente so much. Vicente remained at his table, sipping his *chicha* morosely and refusing to look in Ortiz's direction. Ortiz supposed he should have gone to his table right off and greeted him and the other men seated there. Well, he could do that now. He would drink with them. He would win them with his smile.

He stood, swaying slightly. The men with him pushed their chairs from the table. The band struck up a fast-tempoed tune. Ortiz made it halfway across the courtyard when someone pressed a machete into his hand.

And that's when, in its exact wording, Talon's text came to him, as if written in the dark air before him:

The disputed woman's husband smashes the lantern with his machete, and the baile is plunged into darkness. The machetes of the two rivals strike each other, ringing in the night. Cries and insults from all sides reach a joyful crescendo. After the clashing of the machetes is over, a brief silence ensues, until a voice shouts, "Get a light over here!"

A new lantern is lit. It illuminates a group of men surrounding a dead man. The dead man's companions carry his body to the freshly dug grave, while others throw dirt on the pool of blood on the dance floor. Regardless of whether the dead man is the disputed woman's husband or his rival, she weeps copiously and goes to her house, accompanied by female friends or relatives. The victorious man goes back to his table and shouts for more chicha all around, and the band strikes up anew.

Soon the men who have buried the dead man emerge from the shadows. They join the victor at his table and for the rest of the evening they celebrate his triumph, and the community is unified once again.

It was funny. If they wanted him to, he could recite it for them right there in the middle of the courtyard, as if he were addressing an audience of academics. The litany of gibberish might amuse them. But already the lantern was smashed, and the scene, just as Professor Talon's article said, was plunged into darkness.

PART III

TALES FROM THE OUTSKIRTS

ATOMIC CITY

BY NORA PIERCE

Test Site

T he bus is plugging across the sterile moonscape, rattling on the pockmarked desert road. From the last
row of bench seats, Marcus reads aloud from his lesson plans: "Operation Doorstep evaluated the effects of a nuclear explosion on a typical American family. An entire town
was constructed for the test, complete with myriad domestic
structures, stocked refrigerators, bridges, and automobiles."
He looks toward the front of the bus, past the bobbleheads of
tourists from somewhere in the Northeast, past five girls with
razored pink hair, past an extremely old couple in matching
track suits, and finally catches the response from his own students: iPod cords worm down their necks, heads roll in sleep:
a silent consensus of aggressive boredom. The only lively one
is Marcus's class clown, Stanley, who is trying to flirt with the
girls from Coalition Pink, activists on the tour to witness for
the peace movement. They're ignoring him, all but one who
lectures him in a Socialist jargon. *Do you know how many ci-
vilian casualties were estimated in Hiroshima? Do you know how
many cancer cases were settled in relation to this site? We demand
justice and compassion. Do you want to take some literature back
to your school?* Stanley finally turns around in his seat and
huffs, "Damn Pinkertons." A little snort of surprise escapes
Marcus. Stanley knows about Pinkertons?

Seven hours into the eight-hour tour, sixty miles from

the next drab stop. The last stop was so boring that a few of Marcus's students didn't even bother to get off the bus. They are indifferent to the sight of the gutted desert, permanently gouged and bloated, though they've spent their whole lives downwind of the place. Every one of them has some cousin, some old aunt somewhere on a nuked dead-end street.

To tune out, Marcus takes off his glasses. He's severely near-sighted, so the life around him blurs and his world shrinks to the small space of the pages on his lap. The photograph on his Henderson Junior High School Learning Outcomes Objectives for Knowledge (LOOK) Field Trip Planner shows impeccably groomed mannequins tossed about in make-believe agony. In a test house set up farther from the explosion, the family is still intact. All but the dad, whose nose is blown off.

Marcus flips through the official Nevada Test Site handbook he downloaded from the Internet. *In the interest of Cultural Preservation*, it reads, *if any worker should come across what he believes to be human remains, he should stop working and immediately contact his supervisor.* Marcus puts his glasses back on and looks up at the two lone Shoshones across the aisle from him. The Indians have a deadpan, skeptical look about them. They introduced themselves back at the security briefing in Vegas as Jimbo and Robert Bitterroot, taking the tour to get a look at old Shoshone land. Marcus can't remember which one is which. He suspects they're really along to verify the remains of some legendary ancestor, to examine some pottery shards or conduct some ancient ceremony. One raises an eyebrow when he catches Marcus staring at him. The other looks out the window and snorts. What the Shoshone sees in the ash and sand-colored landscape is so startling that the pork rinds he's been snacking on come out of his mouth in little crystalline flecks. "Hey," he calls to the driver, handing his brother the snack bag and standing up in the shaky bus. He wipes the pork rind dust from his chin. "You just passed a body, man."

Marcus's students perk up. They lean across the aisles and crane their necks toward the rear of the bus, where feather boas are dangling around the seats of the Pinkertons. There is nothing to be seen in the back of the bus but a restroom, so the students get up—one, then two at a time—and lean over the unoccupied seats to try to get a glimpse.

"They're from JCPenney," Marcus says. "They're just mannequins."

"Please stay in your seats," the driver says. He sounds bored too.

The Shoshone says, "That ain't no doll, man."

Marcus watches the driver adjust his mirrors and look a little closer. He downshifts, leaves the bus idling, and steps out. The Shoshone follows him and tries to push the bus's front door open, but it buckles back. The kids crowd around one of the rear windows, affording Marcus a tiny, triangle-shaped view of the driver outside. He stands a few yards away, talking on a cell phone, shielding his eyes from the afternoon sun.

"He locked us in?" asks one of Marcus's students—not one of the brightest kids.

The elderly couple rearranges the packs and lunch sacks at their feet, readying themselves to get off the bus.

"Shit," Marcus says.

A female student looks at him horrified. "Mr. Marcus!"

The girl sitting next to her—Sandra—pops her Bubbleli-cious with a bandaged finger. "He totally just said that." She does an imitation of his nasally voice, "He said, *Shit!*"

The driver gets back on the bus and the Shoshone, who remained by the door, slips past him. His brother follows.

"Hey," the driver calls, "you two stay on the bus." But the two men wander over to the figure in the brush. The driver grabs the escort badge hanging on a ribbon around his neck and points it at the rest of them. "We're going to wait here for the military police unit." His eyes shimmy. "Everyone must stay on the bus!"

"Turn up the air conditioner," one of Marcus's students says.

Marcus puts on his menacing face. "Pipe down, Jonathan."

"He said, *Pipe down, Jonathan,*" Sandra makes Mr. Marcus eyes: low-lashed, squinty ones, with hairy inverted-comma eyebrows that she mimes by pulling up the skin between her brows and fluttering her fingers. "He was all, *Pipe* down."

The driver locks them back in and goes after the two Shoshones. Marcus watches them through the little triangle. "Get back in your seats," he tells the kids. The driver remains a few feet away from the body, but waves his arms instructively, while the taller of the two brothers leans over the body and turns his ear toward the man's mouth, as if listening to some last confession.

"I think he's still alive!" Sandra says.

Then the tall Shoshone tilts the chin up to open the airway and the afternoon glare catches a bright red blot on the old man's nose, a wet smudge of blood. The driver backs away a little more, while the other brother makes a bellows of the man's chest. They do this for a while and get nowhere. Then they huddle. After a bit, they all look back at the bus at once, and Marcus feels as if he is sitting with his students and the other tourists outside the principal's office, waiting for the parents to be called.

The driver walks back to the bus with an exaggerated casual gait, followed by the brothers.

On the bus, the elderly woman puts a hand out to stop the two Indians. "Was it really a dead body?'

Marcus watches the driver eye the Indians sternly in the rearview mirror. The one who talks, shrugs.

"I bet he ain't just walked all the way out here and died," says Stanley.

"Calm down," Marcus says. He wipes his glasses on his shirt so hard that the frame buckles and he has to force it back into shape.

"But serious-up, Mr. G. Ain't nobody coulda just walked all the way out here. It hadda been someone on the bus. "

"Ooh," Sandra says, "He was all, *It had a been someone* in here."

"That's ridiculous." One of the Pinkertons waves him down.

"Naw, really. Let's take a count, in case someone's missing, like in that Agatha Crispy movie."

"*Christie* movie," Marcus says. "Agatha Christie."

"He was all, *Agatha—*"

"Shut up, Sandra."

The kids rally around Marcus. *What's wrong with Mr. Marcus? Look, he took off his glasses. Leave him alone, he's upset.*

Marcus looks out the window, dusted with desert debris, at a small cabin on the road ahead. A tall, broad-shouldered guard points a machine gun toward him. But when he looks closer, Marcus realizes the figure is two-dimensional, just a cardboard cut-out meant to scare off wandering activists and moon-landing denialists who might manage to make it past the cages and the warning signs and the punishing landscape.

"There is only twenty-six!" Stanley pumps an arm in victory. "Somebody's missing like in the movie!"

"Awesome," someone says.

The students take off their ear buds and look around. Marcus watches as some of them wrap the ear bud cords around their iPods and stroke the sterile white rectangles affectionately, like babies with their blankies. In the rearview mirror, he sees that the driver's eyebrows have lifted. Marcus can tell he is counting. He flips through the clipboard on his lap, does a second count. Then he turns off the ignition and the bus hushes slowly to rest. He walks to the back of the vehicle. All eyes follow him down the aisle, where he stops and knocks on the bathroom door. When there is no answer, he jiggles the handle and finds it locked. "Hey!" He pounds. "Come on out of there, please." There is no answer. He works the handle again and then grips it like a nine iron and jerks it. "All right," he says. "If this is a joke, it won't be tolerated." He looks sternly at Marcus's students, who shift in their seats. He sits down with the Pinkertons and flips through his clipboard again. "When I call your name, I want you to say . . ." He pauses.

"Say *present*," Marcus suggests.

"Okay," the driver begins. "Barry Marcus?"

Marcus raises his hand. "Present."

The driver goes down the list of Marcus's students.

Present, here, over here, they drawl, just as they do in the classroom.

"James and Robert Bitterroot?"

The two Indians don't say present—it's obvious. The driver marks them on his list.

"Mr. and Mrs. Stevenson?"

"We're here."

The driver calls off a group of women's names and all the Pinkertons answer present.

"Mr. Lancet."

The bus is quiet.

"Mr. Lancet?"

The driver flips through his clipboard again. He covers the page with his hands, reading something carefully. His face blanches a little and he looks up at the two Shoshones.

The bus's radio crackles. *"Bird-Dog Operations calling. Your escort's got your twenty. He's coming up on you now."*

A Black Hawk helicopter flies into view, and for a moment Marcus thinks it's coming for them, but it heads toward Bald Mountain. Stanley gives a play-by-play as a jeep rolls across the lakebed and pulls alongside the bus. A soldier hops out and heads toward the figure on the road. Then the doors swing open and another boards the bus. "You are supposed to do a count at every stop," he says on the way up the three little stairs. He walks past the driver, tosses a few pink boas into the laps of the Pinkertons in the rear seats, and yanks hard on the bathroom door. Then he pulls out a complicated-looking tool from one of several pockets on his fatigues, clamps it between the door knob and the frame, and yanks hard, releasing the door. It flaps against one of the young Pinkertons, who was leaning in to see. She rubs her head. A stench fills the bus, chemically treated urine and feces soaking in the heat. Watery bits trail down the ridges of the bus. No one inside.

The soldier makes a whirling motion with one hand. "Turn it around, back to Mercury." He scans the rows as he walks back to the front of the bus. "Everyone remain calm." Then he steps outside for a moment and talks on a primitive-looking CB that hangs from a box. When he gets back on the bus, he says to Bird-Dog, "Cleared and on our way." The driver puts the bus into gear so quickly that the standing students bob around the interior like wobbly bowling pins.

As the bus turns around and drives slowly past, an MP draws yellow tape around the figure and a few gasps bounce around the vehicle. Another MP holds the man's wrist, as if checking for a pulse.

"Maybe he passed out from the heat," one of the Pinkertons says. "He looks old."

"Maybe you Coalition Pinkertons did it!" Stanley stands up and does an elaborate *Boo-ya!* victory dance that ends with Spock fingers and a bird call. The students press their faces against the bus window. *I don't remember him. Wait, was he that guy who brought the water in from the cafeteria? No, stupid, that guy had red hair.*

"Who was he?" Sandra asks Marcus.

"I don't know, Sandy."

A Nalgene water bottle hangs around the body's neck, evidence against heatstroke. The corpse wears comfortable-looking Tevas, but one of the legs is bent inward at an unnatural angle. The soldier collects things from the man's pockets and lays them out on some hospital-blue tissue paper on the ground. There is a roll of Mentos, a bookmarked paperback, and what Marcus recognizes as a desert first-aid kit.

Back at Mercury, the military escort hustles them all off the bus and into the canteen. A group of scientists in a line shovel macaroni-beef and Salisbury steak out of steam trays and onto paper plates. They notice, but don't seem surprised by the tour group.

Two men in weird outfits—not military fatigues, but not quite suits—ask if anyone saw the man acting strange. Did he seem dehydrated; was he talking funny, slurred? Nobody remembers him. So they corral the tourists around two sets of cafeteria tables, and begin to take each of them, individually, into the kitchen. They start with Mr. Stevenson, whose wife has to remind him to adjust his hearing aid.

While he waits, Marcus watches Stanley create a paper football out of a napkin and shoot it through a goal post Sandra makes with her thumbs and pointer fingers.

"Know what?" Stanley says to her, "We *in* that murder movie, baby."

"Stop saying that," she tells him. But he keeps at it. He stands up and points at various people sitting at the tables. "Check it out, everybody's got a motive for killing somebody around here." He points to the girls. "Them Pinkertons are trying to get them to stop testing." He points to the two Indians. "And they was here first, right? They just want their crib back."

"Stop it," Sandra says.

"Naw, serious-up, we from Henderson, right?" He swoops his hand along the tables, referring to Marcus and his students. "We all downwinders."

"I see you've been paying attention to this unit, Mr. Mathews," Marcus says. "Well done. Now, please. Sit down and be quiet."

Stanley whispers to Sandra: "Why's your finger bandaged?"

Sandra looks incredulous. "My tips got infected! See," she shows him her nails, "the rest are acrylic. Anyways, it was like that when I got on the bus."

"In the movie, everybody stabs the guy one time."

"But he wasn't even stabbed."

"I'm just saying, is all." Stanley leans across the table and mimes the *Psycho* shower scene.

"What about those two?" one of the Bitterroots asks Stanley. "They in on it too?" He points to the elderly woman, and his brother laughs.

When the men in the weird outfits take Marcus into the kitchen, they ask him what he saw.

A body.

Why was he on the tour?

Nevada State Lesson Plans.

Did he see the man out on the flats? Was he acting strange?

He can't recall.

Marcus and his students spend another hour sitting around the table before the military escort returns to drive them back to the entrance, where a bus will return them to Vegas. The escort's radio crackles on during the bus ride and he covers it with his hand. This does little to muffle the sound and the word *suicide* shoots like a pinball through the bus.

As soon as the kids file off the bus at the DOE and retrieve their cell phones, prohibited on the trip, they're texting their friends and shouting over each other. *The dead guy was a famous scientist! He worked on all kinds of, like, big nuclear bomb shit! Check it out. Here's his Wiki. Here he is in a picture with Albert Einstein.* The Pinkertons call the media, who arrive before Marcus's scheduled yellow school bus, and they snap their boas in the air. They shout at the cameras that the scientist couldn't wash the blood off his hands. They take off their pink T-shirts and turn them inside out, revealing a single letter printed on each one, so that standing together they spell out *P-E-A-C-E*. But the cameras linger on Stanley. They even get a quick interview in front of the Hard Rock Hotel & Casino before Marcus is able to hustle him onto the school bus. The article that runs later in the *Henderson Times* shows the highlighted passage from the dead man's paperback. It's a simple quote often attributed to Einstein. *If only I had known, I should have become a watchmaker.*

The kids are mostly asleep and the bus is quiet when they finally pull into Henderson. The parents are assembled in the school parking lot, hugging each other, sharing something out of a steaming thermos. They're watching a portable television inside someone's minivan, and Marcus can see the images clearly. Footage of the blasted-out house from Operation Doorstep runs in a loop with images of the Coalition Pink women and a black-and-white picture of the old man leaning over some papers with Albert Einstein. Marcus can even make out Stanley's yearbook photo crossing the screen.

As the students file off the bus and into their parents' arms, Marcus soothes them. He reassures. He jokes good-naturedly with the parents to break the tension. And finally, when the last of them—Sandra and her four little sisters—pile into their father's Hummer and drive out of the parking lot, Marcus makes his way across the lot to his old Ford Escort.

On the drive home, he cranks up the air conditioner to a frigid blast. He often feels transported out of Nevada when he sits in his air-conditioned car. The ice-cold buffer is a time machine that separates him from any of this place's hot frontier past, from the slaughtered Indian land, from the fact that it's a fucking desert, that his time machine's coolant system sucks water out of the air, *water* in the desert. But today it takes him to his childhood: traveling on a hot bus with his mother, the unfamiliar old man meeting them at the Desert Hotel's pool. He hands Marcus a Roy Rogers—though Marcus prefers Shirley Temples—and kisses his mother. Marcus has never seen anyone kiss her. His mother says to call him Uncle Barry. The old man takes them up to the hotel's panoramic viewing patio on the top floor, and Marcus stands in the hot night holding his mother's hand. He puts his finger through the gentle smoke rings that she blows, and it's a kind of hypnosis: the smell of his mother's hairspray, the laughter and singing, the waiters with trays of Atomic Cocktails. He falls asleep in her arms and wakes up at dawn to a bright flash of light and the sound of kazoos and whistles and clinking highballs. He watches the puff of smoke in the distance. A soft poof, like a tiny sneeze, and then a cloud in the shape of a hot-air balloon. The men shake hands, pound Uncle Barry on the back. The women squeal or put their hands to their mouths and suck in their breath.

He wonders if it happened then. He imagines the invisible particles floating gently downwind, like steam released from a shower, waiting above his house for his mother to return, where it will drizzle onto her like desert rain.

In the rearview, the Vegas lights hover on the flat horizon. Marcus could stop right here on the highway. It's late at night and dead. But he pulls onto the shoulder. He leaves his headlights on, goes around to the front of the car, and leans on its hood, the engine hot under him. He's never been one to pop open a can of beer or light a cigarette, so he does the next best thing—he pours inky coffee from his thermos and drinks it down like whiskey. He feels clean when it scalds his throat. Then he takes out his wallet and turns through the credit cards, the plastic flip-book of pictures: his sister's kids, his '57 Willie Mays baseball card, his mother—dead now for fifteen months—until he comes to what he's after, slipped inside the billfold with his third-grade booklet from Townsite Elementary School. Marking the chapter titled "Fallout Can Be Inconvenient" is an old ID badge. It amazes Marcus that a facility with a bunch of people working on something as complex as a nuclear bomb hadn't yet discovered modern lamination. The thick plastic photograph is black-and-white and the shadow across the face of his father is so dark, Marcus can barely make him out. The *Barry Lancet* label was created on a machine so old it has the uneven ink markings, the blotted *e* and leaking *r*'s of the typewriter era. The scanner at the twenty-four-hour gym where he sometimes forces himself to work out has more sophisticated identification security. He should feel more about it, probably, this picture he's been hating since he found it among his mother's things, wrapped inside his own birth certificate, where the space for *Father* was marked *unknown*. But the hatred is gone. He doesn't throw the badge at the distant Strip lights or burn it in the desert. He just drops it. But he does slip his hand inside his parka and finger the mottled, viscous bit of flesh for a moment before tossing it into the sagebrush. Lots of blood for a little nick with nail clippers. Back in the car, he makes sure to reach into the glove box for a scented wipe, and he slips it across each finger before resting his hand on the clutch.

DIRTY BLOOD

BY CELESTE STARR

Pahrump

The back room of the Leghorn Bar was stuffed with leather-and-denim boys. I hadn't been out in weeks. Hairy trolls in leather chaps were just too much and I wanted someone else's hand on my dick for a change, wanted to see what was up, who was who. Been keeping a low profile recently. I thought most of the guys here looked a little on edge—especially after another body was found in the toilet of some bus depot last month. Just dumped there, it seemed. Papers said the guy was gay. Papers also gave his photo. I'd never seen him, but in Vegas you never really know who you've seen. You can't even remember all the things you've done.

The bar reeked of piss and poppers. Has gone to shit much like the rest of the joints around Pahrump. I try to get downtown when I can, where a hotter stable of young studs passes through the bars and back rooms of Vegas' gaudy universe, but that just didn't seem wise at the time. There was no one in back that I wanted to fuck, no one worthy enough to hum on my stuff, ugly fucks who pranced around with earrings in their eyebrows and tats on their biceps thinking they're God's gift to gay boys, when frankly, I wouldn't piss on them if they were on fire.

Leghorn wasn't like it used to be when the college eye candy from UNLV used to come through. Now it's an eyesore with its busted doors and booths out of order. No one gave a shit enough to fix the place up, make it look like something. It's a hot bed for boulevard boys and drunkards who mistake the floor for a urinal.

I hadn't planned on staying long, but I needed to get out, be myself for a while. The best thing about the Leghorn was its anonymity. This was the place dudes came to hide. And I think we were all hiding a little. It felt safe here, safe because we were locals and because we'd all seen each other before.

I was about to head home when *he* walked in. Name was anonymous to me like most of the back room amigos, though I knew him in a way. I'd done him once, years ago. Could still smell his cheap bargain-bin cologne on my clothes. He wore those same snakeskin boots he had made me kiss. That night we took the only booth that was vacant for our back room fornications. Sex seeped like sarsaparilla from every respected stall. Because our booth was busted, cruisers kept trying to get in on our action. Obnoxious fucks. He blew me while I held the door shut from prying eyes.

He stood in the stark dark of the back, nose in the air like he was too good for the rest of us who were scavenging for a good time. I lingered in a corner, holding my composure. He walked my way. I played my game pretending he hadn't been seen, but for the most part, that summer, we were all beyond tricks. All of us here were looking for something foreign yet familiar, which is something you never really find.

"You want to go in a booth?" I leaned in toward him. His cheap dime-store cologne filled my lungs. "A booth," he repeated. "You want to go in?"

I said nothing but gave my answer by leading the way. The booth wasn't busted and able to lock. Slipped my last five bucks into the mouth of the money slot and channeled the TV to a scene of two blond Marines. We reached under shirts and fingered nipples. I didn't bother to remind him who I was. Didn't feel it was important at that point. Gay porn gleamed against our skin. He tried to kiss me.

"Ain't into that," I said. Who knows where those lips have been? I tugged at his jeans, undid the clasps, and unzipped the copper teeth, exposing hot-white underwear. Even though our booth was locked, it didn't stop cruisers from clawing underneath at our feet.

"You wanna go back to my place?" he asked in a way that seemed almost innocent.

In general, I wasn't the type to spend the night, but I didn't like the idea of someone else having his ass other than me.

"Okay," I finally said, reminding myself that I'd been with him before—simple mouth work and clean up, all very standard shit.

The Nevada night was sultry as we walked out of the bar. Judging from the naked streets, it was much later than I thought—that, or Pahrump was more empty than usual.

"You still drive that Volvo?" he asked.

He had me confused with someone else, but I didn't care.

"I drive an Explorer." I pointed to my car parked between a minivan and some piece-of-shit Datsun.

"We can take my car or you can just follow me," he said.

"I'll follow you," I replied, as that was one of my rules.

He drove one of those new Monte Carlos, silver with a $700-a-month car note, which was the same vehicle I remembered him driving. I could barely keep up with him as he barreled down Rosie Avenue.

We came to some house on Burston Ranch that was gated off to keep out motherfuckers like me. My heart started to do cartwheels because this was what my life used to be like—

meeting guys, going places. It felt good. His place smelled of Taiwanese takeout. It was quaint, unlike the roach motel I called home.

"Nice," I said.

I followed him into his bedroom where there were no quarter machines, no dated, mustard-yellow drapes. Carpet felt like a cloud beneath my feet. Bed was king-size, larger than it needed to be. Still, that said something about him. There was an entertainment center with a TV and a dresser strewn with assorted brands of colognes and other miscellaneous confections.

"We're way out here and I don't even know your name."

"Cray," he said. "And yours?" He sat at the end of the bed to take off his boots.

"Henry." I never give out my real name.

"You don't look like a Henry."

"It was my granddaddy's name," I lied.

"You look more like a Marcus or a Michael to me," Cray said. "Where are you from?"

"Georgia," I answered, which was the truth but also so vague it didn't matter.

"I thought I sensed a bit of the South in your voice," he said as he struggled with those rattlesnake shit-kickers. "Here, help me with this one." Cray pressed the second boot into my crotch.

"So you from Vegas?" I asked.

"Thereabouts. I come from a long line of casino floor managers."

Cray talked like he was educated, which also made me feel better about him and about being there. The boot finally gave, causing me to lose my footing. I stumbled into the dresser behind me.

"You okay?" he asked.

"It'll take more than that to do me in," I said.

"You want a drink?"

"Maybe," I said. "What do you got?"

"Just some rum." It sounded girly, but so what? Booze is booze.

"Make yourself comfortable," Cray said.

It always starts that way. *Make yourself comfortable. Make yourself at home.* Or at least that's the way it used to start.

I pulled off my shirt and pushed off my sneaks, which brought on something I hadn't felt in months: the insecurity of being naked in some dude's place. I don't have the most cut body due to the Southern delicacies of fried chicken and macaroni and cheese. In a strange way, it was nice feeling like this again. I looked in Cray's mirror at my love handles and stretch marks that ran across man tits. I sat on the edge of his bed and took a whiff of the crisp air-conditioned room. Pleasant, I thought. Then I walked around studying his possessions.

We talked as he made the girly drinks in the kitchen.

"So how did you end up in Vegas?" he asked.

I almost gave him one of my stories, then stopped myself and told him the truth. Or at least as much of the truth as I told anyone. "I was offered a job up here working at a magazine. Packed my shit and came up with only two hundred bucks in my pocket," I explained, studying dated issues of *Men's Fitness* on his desk. "I hoped that it would turn into an editor's position, but as it turns out, I'm still stringing. I took a job writing press releases for the city to make ends meet."

"Is that where you're working now?" Cray asked, handing me a glass of rum. "Sorry, don't mean to be nosey."

"No, it's cool. I've been there for about six months now."

Cray leaned on the dresser as we got acquainted. "So, what? You want to be a novelist or something?"

"Something like that," I said in such a way that he decided not to pursue the topic.

"I'm about to take a shower. You can pull back those covers and get into bed if you want. The rum's on the kitchen counter."

I heard the pelting of shower water. With the booze I devoured back at the Leghorn, and the rum, I was starting to catch a buzz. I liked this feeling—getting a little sloppy and looking forward to the sex. Sometimes I liked the anticipation more than the sex. The sad part, you never felt any anticipation in a place like the Leghorn. But I felt it here, in this room.

I opened one of Cray's dresser drawers to find underwear and socks of the argyle type folded and placed neatly in retentive rows. I perused another drawer that was filled with boxers, all white, neatly folded and squared. But beside them was a shiny dildo. I picked it up and it was heavier than I had expected. I held it briefly before I saw what else lay in the drawer: a pair of cuffs and a leather belt.

Strange, really, as I didn't take him for a dude with toys. I looked at them, those metal cuffs, and they didn't strike me as the type you could buy in a sex shop. They were more substantial, thicker and heavier. I felt their weight in my right hand, before I noticed something on the chain—something rusty and scablike. Like dirty blood. Or what I thought was dirty blood. I picked at it and it flaked off, revealing a patch of metal shinier than the surrounding area.

I put them back in the drawer, those cuffs. The calm horniness was disappearing now. I set my rum on the dresser, careful even then to place the glass on top of a magazine. I knew that this was probably nothing—just another guy who dug some kinky shit in private—but I always told myself I'd leave a place if things ever got a little strange.

Clay was still in the shower, the bathroom door open a crack, steam ribboning out into the hallway. I walked past slowly, feeling a little less drunk now, but also feeling odd, not myself really. I figure, what the fuck, I wouldn't be the first guy to bail on a one-night thing before any action took place.

I was in his kitchen, noticing the rum bottle on the counter, when I heard him twist the water off. "Henry," he called, "why don't you fix us a couple more drinks? I'm just starting to get in the mood." But his voice was different, a shade deeper, more direct, though even then I felt I was reading something into it, that I was letting an unreasonable suspicion get the best of me.

Clay was as queer as me. Of that much I was sure.

"Really," he called, "pour us a couple more drinks. The bottle is on the counter. I could use one now."

"Sure thing," I said, moving quietly through the kitchen. His knife rack, I saw now, was missing all of its blades.

"Make mine extra strong."

As I passed his front window, I could see my car three stories below, a maroon Explorer with the sunroof open just a crack. I fingered the keys in my pocket, making sure they were there. I was anxious now, anxious yet sleepy, worn out. In the dim light I focused on the front door, its locks and handle, though I felt I was looking at it through a thick piece of glass.

By then I couldn't see so well, all objects having a softness to them. At first I thought I was seeing his door wrong, but then when I was closer I understood: The deadbolt was a keyed entry, both in and out. No knob. Only a thin groove to accept a key.

I touched the lock briefly, still not believing in full, but then it came to me. I looked around: two windows, the kitchen, the hallway leading back to Clay. It was a cage. I searched for something—a lamp, a hard metal sculpture, a piece of wood set aside for the fireplace—but the room was only sofas and pillows, nothing that could be a weapon.

"Henry," he called, "you pouring those drinks?"

"I'm making them now," I said.

"Good," he said. "Make mine extra strong."

"I will."

I heard what sounded like a cord snapping tight, pieces of leather quickly lashed together.

"Now don't go anywhere," he said, "cause I'm going to be ready in just a minute. Then we can have a little fun."

GUNS DON'T KILL PEOPLE

BY BLISS ESPOSITO
Centennial Hills

My dad taught me all the parts of a gun before I turned five. He showed me with oil-smudged fingertips and a joint hanging out of his lips. "Teresa," he said, "always hold it down, even if it's not loaded. Never point at someone unless you intend to kill."

I smiled and nodded, kicking my bare feet under the table.

He clicked the clip into place. "You can always trust me," he said. "I'll always protect you."

I believed him and, before even learning the alphabet, I knew he made me invincible.

Two days ago, I repeated those words to my son. He laughed through the blood dripping over his teeth.

I stirred a teaspoon of parsley into the pot of sauce while I watched the small flat-screen TV embedded in the door of our refrigerator. The news anchor stood in front of Gilcrease Orchard announcing the continued growth of Centennial Hills.

"Did you hear that, Casey?" I called. "They're finally breaking ground on that new shopping center on the other side of Gilcrease." I dropped a few extra cloves of garlic into the boiling sauce. "That's good for us, right?"

Casey called out something from his office, but it was stifled by the sound of the front door opening and slamming. I heard James's strangled cry. "Mom!" he yelped.

"Honey? What's wrong?" I said. I dropped the wooden spoon on the counter, splattering drops of tomato sauce like blood across the cream-colored tile. Thoughts of the burgeoning housing market were gone, and I was running to him in an instant.

James stood at the front door, his hands to his mouth. Blood came through his fingers in sheets. It streamed down his shirt, onto the carpet. There was so much. A jackpot. He tried to catch the drops, smearing clotted hands across his shirt to displace all the fluid. The metallic smells of blood and perspiration curdled the air. They overpowered even the pungency of the sauce on the stove.

"Jesus Christ," I said. I grabbed the throw off the couch and put it to his mouth. "Tilt your head back. Was it Kevin?"

He reached up to pull some hair from his eyes. "Uh-huh," he mumbled. Warm wet soaked through the blanket. My fingers turned red and sticky.

"Hold this to your mouth," I said. "Lay down on the couch."

"I'm fine here." He pressed the blanket to his face.

I ran to the kitchen and grabbed an ice pack out of the freezer. Casey came in from his office. "What happened?"

"Kevin," I said. I ran the ice pack under the faucet.

"Not again." He sighed and pulled a dish towel from the drawer.

James was in the chair with his head back. Blood dripped down the sides of his face into his ears. It was starting to dry to his skin.

"Here, baby," I said. "Hold this on it." I kneeled in front of him.

He laid the pack over his face. He groaned.

"I told you to stay away from that kid," Casey said. He handed me the dish towel.

"He's outside all the time!" James yelled. His eyes were enraged, the purple mushrooming around them.

"Then you need to stay inside more often," Casey said.

"*Casey.*" I shook my head: *Not now.*

"I can't stay inside forever," James muttered. He slumped into the chair.

"Let me see." I pulled back the ice pack. His skin was raw. His eyes were swelling and turning purple. His nose leaked a trickle of blood. I ran the washcloth over his face. His cheeks were mottled: red, pink, and white with streaks of blood smeared across them. Casey stood behind me. He put his hand on my shoulder and squeezed.

I wanted to protect James, like my dad protected me, but I didn't know what to do to stop the boy who'd been picking on him. I wanted to beat the kid bloody into the dirt. I wanted to press my thumbs into his throat until bright red bruises splashed across his skin. I wanted to kill him, if I had my way.

I learned early on it was the men who fought. What power did I have? A rub on the arm, a doe-eyed blink? I couldn't flirt the kid into submission. It infuriated me that I couldn't just reach out and take control, that I had to coerce and manipulate. When I was younger and used to take my little sister out in her stroller, I'd stuff my pockets with pepper spray, a safety whistle, Dad's buck knife, and a billy club. I would have gladly traded my breasts for muscles so I could be sure to protect her then. I'd do the same now so I could intimidate this Kevin like he was intimidating my son. I watched James spit a mouthful of blood into the towel. I swallowed the impotence burning in my throat.

That night I changed into my pajamas while Casey lay reading *Forbes.* I could hear James getting ready to go to bed in the bathroom at the end of the hall. I sat down facing Casey. He peaked over the edge of the magazine.

"We've gotta do something," I said.

"He needs to stay away from the kid." He turned the page.

"He shouldn't have to be scared to leave the house."

"We can arrange to speak with his parents again. If you think it will help."

"His parents are schmucks. He runs the joint over there."

Casey set the magazine down. "This is what boys do. This is an important lesson for James. He needs to learn not to tangle with the wrong guy. Better now than later."

I stared at the back of the paper, stumped. I couldn't believe he was being so dismissive. But what could he do, really? I'd already talked to Kevin's mom and dad, the teachers, and the principal. They assured me everything would be okay, that Kevin would stop. Even though I'd glared at Kevin from across the street, I was still a parent, an adult. I didn't even make the little jerk's radar. The truth was, you can't stop a mustached teenager who moves onto your street, who has a moped and a vengeance against your son. Not without fear. That was one tool I didn't have.

I stuck my tongue out at Casey from behind the magazine. He didn't look up again as I left the room, closing the door behind me. I walked down the hall to the closet. If my dad was in Casey's place, he would have fixed it. Somehow. Without words. A wop displaced to the desert; just a look and he was intimidating. Casey would probably try to reason with the kid if we ever got ahold of him. When we were younger, I was completely taken with Casey's approach to conflict. He talked steady and calm. Looked directly into the eyes of those who challenged him. Legitimized arguments. Shook hands afterwards. I thought he was the smartest man I'd ever met, and I was in love with him immediately. Before Casey, everything in my life had been bristled with a slight sense of danger: where we lived, who we knew, even my dad himself. Casey's composure was a hell of an aphrodisiac.

As we got older, though, his resolutions began to drive me nuts. Casey's civility dragged problems out forever, fraying them one strand at a time, while I wanted to scream, to yell, to tear and bite. I didn't want to "come to an understanding" with the pizza delivery boy. I wanted him to go back and give me my fucking pizza the way I ordered it. I wanted action and response. Especially now.

I pulled the heavy metal lock box from the top shelf of closet. Dust shivered and clung to it. James was still in the bathroom brushing his teeth. I stepped over a wet towel, which lay in a heap, to get through the doorway. He glanced at me and spit in the sink. Pink. Black crescents with purple edges ringed his eyes at the bridge of his swollen nose. I pointed to the edge of the tub. "Sit," I said.

"What?" He ruffled his hair, misting the mirror as he sat, then touched a finger to his split lip. He winced.

I sat next to him, the box on my lap. "I want to show you something." I leaned across the sink to tighten the faucet.

"Is that Grandpa's—?"

"Yup."

"I thought Dad made you—"

"Nope."

I clicked the code in the box. It opened with a snap. James leaned forward. I edged the top up. I could smell the oil. It made me remember sitting with my dad, at the kitchen table, oiling and cleaning his guns. "It was Grandpa's favorite." I said. "He wanted you to have it."

I picked up the .44. It was heavier than I remembered. The white butt was worn and yellowing. The metal was flawless, though, shining like a new car. "I wasn't strong enough to shoot it by myself. Still not," I said. "I had to lean against Grandpa. You'll be able to handle it on your own one day."

"You want me to shoot Kevin?" He sounded irritated.

"No," I said solemnly. "This isn't about Kevin." I shrugged. "Not exactly." I shifted. I wanted James to experience a spark of power, to hold the gun, understand its potential. Even if he never shot it in his life, I wanted to embed the symbol in his mind, the knowledge, the concept, so he would never feel helpless. "I'm only going to teach you because I trust you. You're too smart to ever do anything stupid." I paused. "But men need to know how to use one." I narrowed my eyes at him. "Just in case."

He nodded grimly and leaned against me. I felt his skinny frame against my arm.

"This is your first lesson," I said. "Take it by the butt. Don't put you're finger on the trigger. Press this release to check for bullets." I modeled for him and swung the wheel open. I let the bullets fall into my hand. "Always make sure it isn't loaded before you aim." I held it out for him. "Here, take it."

He traced a finger across the mirrored metal. "I'm tired, Mom."

I shrank back down, the gun going limp in my hands. I sighed. "If that little prick touches you, ball up your fist and hit him as hard as you can. Then run."

"Mom. He's an *eighth* grader." He said it like eighth graders swung batons and guarded mini-marts after hours. He raised his eyebrows, then his battered face crumpled. He sucked in two shallow breaths.

I rested the gun on the sink. I wrapped my arms around

him. He felt heavier, a lump of flesh. "We'll fix this, honey. Your dad and I will fix it. I promise."

After a moment he pulled away and stood up with a small stumble. "Don't worry about it," he said with a sniff. "I'm getting a lot of exercise running." He smacked his belly. "Finally getting rid of some of that holiday weight." He grinned.

I rolled my eyes. "Don't tell your dad about the gun."

He made a knowing face and held up his hands. "I don't want to hear about it either."

I grabbed him for a quick hug, then listened to him go into his room. The bathroom was a mess. His bloody clothes in a heap in the corner. Dirty handprints on the tile. I wiped up some toothpaste and looked in the mirror. I pulled the skin under my eyes. When I was a kid, I would have taken any opportunity to examine a gun, practice my aim. Still, I couldn't help but feel a little impressed. I chuckled. Making jokes, damn kid. I put the gun back in the box and went to James's room to tuck him in.

I was born in '68, six years after the Test Site's last nuclear detonation but still a few decades before the mega-resorts would come to really alter the look of southern Nevada. Back then, Vegas really was the Wild West, with tumbleweeds blowing down the teenaged Strip. My parents both worked in the casinos. Dad bounced around a lot. Usually because he couldn't stay at any one job too long without punching someone out.

Vegas was more visceral in those days. Now all the sharp edges have been worn down, sanded to a dull impression to make the town's tables more accessible. Then there was no glossy exterior, nothing to hide us from the fact that we lived in the middle of a desert, miles away from judgment. Guys got murdered for counting cards. Locals could get a comp to the buffet anytime, day or night. There was no charade like there is now. No casino nannies or carnival games, no street attractions. No, in those days, Vegas was here for one thing: sin.

We lived five minutes from the Strip in a trailer park, before we finally got a house, before my little sister was born. The trailer park was the last thing between the town and open desert. Dad loved it because we just had to walk to the end of the property to shoot our guns. "I couldn't do this back in Brooklyn," he'd always say, his accent flaring for a moment in the dry wind. In the summertime, I'd trail behind him, my bare feet crunching the parched dirt, the rocks biting them like piranhas, the stickers hooking themselves between my toes. By fall, my feet would get so tough that I could walk across glass. The sun would scorch my neck well into October. At night, my mom would lay cold towels across it so I could sleep.

My parents traded shifts so someone could always be with me when I was young. Mom doing cocktails days and Dad dealing nights. We were lucky. Dad and I spent a lot of time watching reruns and cleaning his guns, talking and making snacks. Once, when the July heat kept us from venturing too far, Dad had given up for the couch. I stuck outside to play with some neighborhood kids. I was ten or eleven. A teenaged boy I vaguely knew coaxed me behind the dumpsters.

"Show me your panties," he said. He was wearing blue jeans and no shirt.

"No," I said. I dug my bare toes into the powdery dirt.

"C'mon, just show me." He pinched me hard on the arm.

"No. Leave me alone." I turned to go.

"If you leave, I'll chase after you and hit you in the face."

"You'd have to catch me," I sneered.

"I'd catch you easy. I'm bigger. Show me your panties and I'll let you leave."

I turned around and took off running as fast as I could. I heard my heart beating loud in my ears, but it didn't cover up the stomping of his sneakers inches behind me. Get to the steps, I thought. I ran as fast as I could through the parking lot and the patch of desert between the dumpsters and our trailer. Inside, my stomach flipped with the idea that I had provoked this. I'd given the boy reason to think he could look at my panties. I wanted to stop and stand up for myself, but I was too scared. He was bigger than me. Then my stomach flipped again, thinking about Dad. I wouldn't tell him if I could just make it home. I would be in trouble for going behind the dumpster with this boy who Dad had never liked and had specifically told me to stay away from. As soon as I hit the grass at the base of our slot, the boy's slapping footsteps died away. I kept running, hopping over the tomato plants and hitting the aluminum door with all my weight. I'm sure I shook the entire trailer.

"What happened?" Dad asked. He was still lying on the couch, smoking a cigarette. His pink bowl was on the floor filled with potato chips and pretzels. M*A*S*H played on TV. I panted against the door. It didn't matter what I said, I realized. There was no use lying. Dad could always read my mind.

"What happened?" he repeated. He sat up, already angry. I caught a sob in my throat thinking I was in trouble.

"You were playing with that boy, weren't you?"

My face got hot. I gulped a nod.

"What did he do?"

"He, he . . ." I stammered and coughed. "He told me to show him my panties!"

Dad's eyes clouded red. His fists clenched. He grew as big as the room. The walls rippled. I closed my eyes anticipating his roar. Even the TV laughter shrank away.

"But Daddy, I didn't show him. I told him no, and he said he'd punch me!"

"*Motherfucker!*" he growled. He was outside before I could control my sobs. I followed, squatting to watch from behind the slats of our picket fence.

Kids dotted the street. Dad moved so determinedly that summer seemed to freeze. He walked like a soldier into combat across the pavement, barefoot in his dusty jeans. The boy was sitting on the steps of his trailer. He turned to go inside when he saw Dad coming for him.

"You stay right there, you little cocksucker," Dad said.

The boy froze. Dad stomped up to him and wrapped an enormous hand around his skinny shoulder. He dragged him off the steps. The boy moaned like a dying cat.

"You listen to me," Dad snarled, inches from the boy's pained face. I could barely hear him, but I knew what he said. "If you ever come near my daughter again, I will rip your fucking balls off and shove them down your throat."

The boy's mother ran down the steps, screaming, "Let him go! He didn't do anything! Let him go!" She cried into her hands, unable to release her son from Dad's grip. "Let him go!" she wailed.

"You understand me, you little prick?" Dad said, shaking the boy back and forth.

The boy groaned, but managed to nod his head. His face burned bright pink.

Dad let go. The boy stumbled back. His mother engulfed him. She cried into his shoulder. Dad walked back toward our trailer as quickly as he had left. I felt a mingled sensation of pity for the boy and personal triumph. Dad picked me up when he returned. He asked me if I was okay.

"Yes," I mumbled, still in shock.

"You know, boys do stupid things," he said carrying me into the living room. "You're getting older now and you'll have to watch out for them." As quickly as he had gone into the rage, he was back, Dad again. Even his thick mane had settled down to his normal messy hair. He set me on the couch. "But the lucky thing is, you are too smart for them and you'll never let someone tell you what to do. You're tough." He brushed some sticky hair away from my face. "I'm proud of you for sticking up for yourself."

I felt like crying all over again, but I wasn't sure why. I often felt like that when Dad told me something important. I wanted his trust and his approval more than anything. I'd seen him angry, and I'd seen him rip guys apart. I loved that he was on my side, always.

I never respected a man so much until Casey came along, completely the opposite, but still a man in his own way. Casey was kind of a big deal in town, doing energy consultations with the casinos, helping the buildings to follow FCC guidelines and save money on energy at the same time. It was the kind of job that wasn't around ten years earlier. The days of covering its troubles with lightbulbs and neon were over. Vegas had to grow up, and the town struggled just like I did to fit into mainstream society. Casey was helping us both.

The next morning, Casey pulled back into the driveway after dropping James off at school. He didn't have any appointments until later that afternoon. I'd been pacing the kitchen, wanting to talk to him before I left for work. I was standing at the door when he opened it.

"Jesus!" he said, startled.

"We haven't prepared James for the real world," I said. "We've made everything too safe."

"Honey. This is what boys do." He set down his keys. He grabbed an apple from the fridge. He kissed me on the cheek, then stuck the fruit in his mouth.

I followed him. "Think about it. We live in this house with an alarm system. We have air bags in the car." I folded my arms tight in front of me.

"You didn't want the Lexus because of the airbags." He smiled and winked at me. He walked toward his office.

I rolled my eyes. "We're not *prepared* for anything," I said. I was at his heels.

"We have every kind of insurance you can imagine." He pulled up the blinds.

"But look at James. The shit has hit and he has no idea how to handle himself. He's too insecure to stick up for himself. He's terrified." I sat on the edge of the couch.

"He should be terrified," Casey replied, sitting behind his desk. "Have you seen that boy yet? He's a moose."

"James should feel invincible." I paused. "He should be feeling out his . . ." I grappled with my hands, trying to pull the words out of the air. ". . . his machismo. I don't know." I threw my hands up.

"We didn't raise him like that."

"That's the problem."

"What do you want to do, Teresa?" He dropped his hands on the desk. "You can't follow him to school. You can't spank the other kid." He picked up a stack of papers and straightened them. "The boy doesn't like James for whatever reason. James can't help that. He needs to stay out of the kid's way."

I crossed my legs and stared at Casey. "I want to take James shooting."

"What? No way."

"It will give him self-confidence. So he isn't so scared."

"You're being incredibly impractical." He turned toward the computer and punched in some data. "I think it's a terrible idea. It won't solve anything. There's nothing good that can come from it." He was done talking. It infuriated me.

"You know, Casey, sometimes it's nice to be the toughest guy in the room."

"Yeah, *honey*," he said derisively, "but it's better to be the smartest."

I slammed the door as I walked out. Then I slammed the garage door and the door to my car. There was a part of me that knew Casey was right. A little nagging, weak part that I wanted to hit with a brick. I took a deep breath, a trick he'd taught me. I stretched against the leather of the car seat. I put my keys in the ignition and started the engine. I did love the Lexus, but I still questioned my decisions when Casey let someone cut in line at the grocery store or talk too loudly during a movie. He may have the power of debate and banter, but his presence never kept anyone from getting in our way.

En route to work, I stopped my car in front of Kevin's house, the engine running. It was nice house, like ours. Little assholes like him didn't belong in these neighborhoods. Centennial Hills was designed to give a sense of community. Parks in the center of the developments with benches and swings, where boys should be able to run around safely. Homeowner associations to prod us about maintaining our yards and replacing the bulbs in our porch lights, to keep everything uniform and clean. But it was bullshit. There couldn't be community without someone to protect the streets, to weed out the jerkoffs like we did the dandelions. I wanted to walk into Kevin's house and strangle him, maybe his mom and dad too. I knew my small frame wouldn't make the impact. No, I would have to do more; I would have to make a much larger statement to get the kid to back off. I revved my engine. I pulled off our street.

I was a complete waste at work that day. I kept checking my watch, wondering if James was in class or at his locker. If maybe we got lucky and Kevin stayed home. I owed Janet, my boss, a short script for a commercial that would be shot soon, but I couldn't bring myself to do it. I sat in front of my computer, slumped over. I drew a sketch of the .44. Casey would never let me take James shooting. He'd make me listen to statistics about gun violence. He'd quote studies on children raised with guns in the home. I'd hear about it for days. By the end of it, he'd have me thinking it was time to buy James a tutu. Guns never did me any harm. I etched in the front sights on my picture and wrote *BANG!* down the side of the paper.

I remembered when Dad gave the .44 to Casey at dinner a few months after we were married. Dad was streamlining his collection and couldn't imagine another man wouldn't want a shiny .44 like Dirty Harry owned. I'd shot the gun a few times growing up, always with my back to Dad's brick-wall chest to absorb the shock. I knew the gesture was something special—his way of welcoming Casey into the family, man to man. I could tell Casey had no clue what the act meant. He told me later he thought it was some kind of *omertà*, as though my dad had handed him a dead fish wrapped in a newspaper. *You take-a my daughter, I take-a you life.*

"Wow," Casey said. A plate of spaghetti sat on the table in front of him. "Thanks."

"I like knowing you can protect my daughter. And that gun can kill a wild boar."

"Boar attacks are up this year," Casey said, turning the guns in his hands. "Thanks, Tom. I'll keep it in a safe place."

Dad grinned and grabbed Casey's free hand. Then he became serious, staring into my husband's eyes and gripping his shoulder. "If it ever comes down to you and someone else," he said, "it has to be you who stays standing. You're in charge of her now." After a long moment, in which Casey and I both shifted with unease, Dad smiled again. He smacked Casey on the back of the neck. "You may not be an Italian, but you're a good kid anyway."

Later that night, Casey laughed about the absurdity of needing a gun. He put it in the closet. Then he tried to pull off my panties.

"Why don't you want it in the nightstand?" I gripped my underwear.

"It's too big." He worked on my bra.

"It makes me feel safe," I said. "My dad told you to protect me."

"Stop worrying." He kissed my neck and worked his fingers up my leg. "You're safe. You're safe with me," he whispered. "You're safe."

In the end, I trusted him and let him lock the gun away. Casey did what he said. He provided, protected. He worked long hours and gave us a stable home. I was safe by his side; I was safe in his arms. There was comfort in lying next to him at night, while the wind tossed the curtains around, knowing that I was important enough for him to love. I'd feel the muscles in his chest flex against my back as he moved into sleep. I'd smile. He gave me more security than I ever expected.

Casey was just so damn smart. Everything he did was gilded with wisdom and success. Even our neighborhood; he moved us out here right before the boom. There was nothing for miles then, but we paid so little for our home. If we tried to buy it now, we couldn't afford it. I'd be an idiot not to do what he said.

But new Vegas suited Casey. He had almost no connection to what it used to be, where I had come from. There was no grit to him and no way to adapt. Instead, he was making the town adapt to him, taking apart one casino at a time. Stripping their primitive wires and bringing them up to speed. There was something nice about the old ways, the plumes of smoke that hung over the slots, the burnt-out haze of electric lights on Las Vegas Boulevard. The fact that I could walk barefoot down the Strip. The fact that my dad could bust a guy in the head and still find another job. I always wished a little that some old-time aggression would find Casey. That he'd go blind with emotion, let something muss his hair, even if it meant we'd have some hard times. With Kevin harassing James, I wanted something to snap in Casey worse than ever. But when that bug of insanity hit, it wasn't Casey it got, like I'd vaguely hoped. It was James.

I'd been taking a stab at the copy in front of me when my line rang. It was the clerk at James's school. He'd done something, gotten in trouble. I needed to pick him up.

"Janet," I said, grabbing my coat, "I gotta pick James up from school. I gotta go."

"Is he sick?"

"No, he's in trouble."

"James?"

"I *know!*"

"You're worthless today anyway."

James had never been in trouble at school before. He charmed his teachers and got A's on all his tests. His homework was always neat. He enjoyed presenting projects to the class. I wondered if there had been a mistake.

At the school, the secretary ushered me into the dean's office. The dean was a tall man, balding. "Your son has something to tell you," he said, leaning back in his chair. I felt almost as scared as James sitting in the light-blue office in front of the big oak desk.

James's head drooped. "I peed on Kevin's ball."

"On the playground," the dean said.

"You peed on his ball?" I asked, confused.

"It was a soccer ball," James replied.

I leaned back in the chair. Stumped. Then I imagined my son, fed up with the pushing around, whipping out his little pecker in a show of machismo, screaming at the bigger kid, *I ain't scared of you, asshole!*

"We're going to suspend James for three days," the dean said. "We have a no-tolerance policy for things as inappropriate as what your son did." He stared at me as though I'd been there to unzip James's pants. "I trust it won't happen again."

"He hit me at recess," James said. He looked at me. "In the stomach."

"Now, son, you need to take responsibility," the dean said. "Regardless of what Kevin did, it's you who violated his property. If you're going to become a good young man, you need to not make excuses for your actions."

"Bullshit," I said. They both stared at me. I grabbed my purse. "Do you see my son's face? That's from Kevin. And he's sitting in math class right now with no repercussions." I looked at James, threateningly, then back at the dean. "It won't happen again. But do me a favor and make sure that other kid keeps his hands off my son at recess or we *are* going to have a problem."

I had to sign something. James needed his backpack. Soon

we were outside again, James at my heels, making our way to the car.

"That guy's a schmuck," I said as I started the engine.

James didn't say anything.

"I'm not mad at you," I said.

"You're not?"

"Nope. Actually, I'm a little proud of you," I smiled. We pulled onto the street.

"Why?" he asked. He pushed hair out of his face.

"Because you stood up for yourself."

"But all I did was pee on his ball."

I shrugged. "You didn't let him push you around."

"So I'm not in trouble?"

"When I was little, my dad always told me that no matter what I did, he would stick up for me, even if I was wrong. He'd always be on my side. And he always was."

"Really?"

"Yeah, even when I didn't always do the best stuff."

"Like what?"

"Like when I threw a container of coleslaw at a boy because he was picking on me. Or when I punched a guy in the stomach because he called my friend Pimple Puss."

"You did that?"

"Yeah. Don't think I want you to go around picking fights, but I want you to feel like you can stick up for yourself if you have to. Whatever happens, good or bad, I'll be on your side."

He smiled down at his knees. I finally felt like I had gotten through to my son. "You up for ice cream?" I asked.

At home, James was quiet. Lights were off, books were closed. Drapes were drawn. We kept looking at each other and shrugging. Neither one of us knew what to do in the wake of his offense. James had never been in trouble before; I'd never been more proud. Casey would be pissed, though. He was going to blame me for this and probably want to ground James for a month. I just couldn't let him.

When Casey finally got home, the sky already turning purple like the fading marks around James's eyes, he stared at us suspiciously. "What's wrong?" he asked. He sat on the couch.

"Everything's okay," I said. "But James has to tell you something."

James looked at me. I nodded. "It was P.E. and we were playing soccer," he said. He sat up straighter. "I ended up on Kevin's team, but he kept pushing me away from the ball. Then he said that it was his ball so I couldn't play."

"That little asshole," I said. I couldn't help feel triumphant. I bounced in my seat.

"Keep going," Casey said to James. He looked confused.

"So I started to walk away. He took the ball and threw it right at me, and it hit me on my ear. Then he came to get the ball and punched me in the stomach too."

"What a fuck this kid is."

"Teresa! Let him finish!"

"I went up to the nurse's office," James continued. "And I must've not heard the bell, cause I went back outside after they gave me the ice pack and everyone was gone."

"Wait," I said. "So when did you pee on the ball?"

"He did *what?*" Casey asked, then shook his head. "You peed on Kevin's ball?"

James shifted nervously. "I thought about what Mom said. About me sticking up for myself, so I peed on it. The P.E. teacher saw me."

"But Kevin didn't see?" I asked.

"No, he was in class."

"So he doesn't even know you did it?" I asked.

"No," he repeated, "he was in class."

I fell back into my chair, deflated.

"Well, that's not so bad," Casey said. "I can understand wanting a little revenge."

"Are you crazy?" I hollered at Casey. "*That's* okay to you?"

"You seemed thrilled a minute ago," he said, shocked.

"That's when I thought he did it in front of everyone." I looked at James. He seemed terrified. "That's just sneaky," I said, and I walked upstairs.

When I was a kid, I'd stay barefoot until November, about the time my mom started wrapping me in jackets. The walks my dad and I took across the desert would continue all year. Dad always with the .44 on his hip, me carrying my BB gun, then a .22 as I got older. Once, we were about a mile from home checking out a nearly dried-up spring. I was young, carrying a salami sandwich in one hand and choosing rocks to put on my windowsill with the other.

"Look, Teresa," Dad said. "A dust devil."

In the distance, a funnel cloud twirled and spun dust into the air. We watched it hop and bend, twisting itself like an exotic dancer. The wind around us picked up. Wrappers from our sandwiches lifted into the air. Dad kneeled next to me. Bullet casings rattled on the ground. The dirt devil continued twisting toward us. My jacket and my hair pulled away with the wind. I dropped my sandwich in the dirt.

"Daddy?" I said. I wanted to ask what would happen if it came straight at us. We were too far to run back to the trailer. There wasn't anything to hide under. The dirt devil moved closer, like it was coming to shake our hands. Everything around us jumped and clattered. Our clothes flapped against us like loose tarps. My hair covered my face. My heart pounded. I wanted to run.

"Just stay next to me," Dad said calmly. The devil tore toward us, whistling and leaving rivets in the dirt. It was bigger now, as tall as a house. I looked up just as it was about to engulf us. Then it was gone. I was wrapped tightly in my dad's jacket, crushed to him in a comfy nest of chest hair and warm skin. I'd been plucked from the world and sheltered. Even though the earth rattled around us, I was safe and still.

I lay in bed thinking about the dirt devil the night James peed on Kevin's ball. I stared up at the high ceiling, the fan turning slowly. If it had been me and James in that wind, I wouldn't have been able to protect him. The thing was, though, I hadn't seen a dust devil in years. Maybe the town was too built up now. There was no room. Maybe Las Vegas had grown out of its tantrums of youth. And maybe I was trying to fit James into a mold that was no longer necessary.

Casey cracked the door, slipped into the room, and shut it silently. I watched the strip of light from the hall widen and disappear. I didn't move. I listened as he put his watch on the table, put his shoes in the closet, and emptied his change onto the dresser. Then he went into the bathroom and turned the water on in the bathtub. The bath was for me; he knew I'd still be awake. I peeked over the covers and watched him shuffling though my bottles of scented bubble baths, choosing something special for me. He put one down and picked another. He poured some into the water. He dimmed the lights, lit candles. Then he came into bed and lay down next to me.

I rolled over and rested against him. "I'm sorry," I said.

"Me too," he whispered.

I moved my leg over his and rubbed his chest. "You didn't do anything wrong." I put my lips against his ear. "You're right," I said softly. "James needs to learn the right way to handle these situations." I kissed the line of his jaw. I wanted to feel him submit. I needed him to forgive me.

He leaned closer. "I just don't want him to get into more trouble than he has to."

"I know." I ran my finger under his boxers. I smelled lavender from the bath.

"He's a smart kid," Casey said.

"I know." I lifted myself on top of him and bit the corner of his lip. I felt his arms move around me. "I want to take him shooting, though."

"Teresa," he said. He unhooked his arms.

"So he knows what to do if he finds a gun or if someone breaks in." I kissed his chin.

"It'll never happen."

"Just once. Then I'll lay off." I sat up straight and pulled my T-shirt off. "I promise."

I leaned forward. Casey gave in. I didn't like doing it this way, but it was all I had.

The next morning James was sitting at the table reading a book. I could hear kids out on the street shouting and playing. "Put it away," I said.

He snapped to attention and threw the book aside, like it was porn.

I dropped the box on the table. I clicked the code into place. The .44 shone before us.

"Pick it up," I said.

James reached for the gun. He took it by the butt, careful not to touch the trigger.

"Do you remember how to check if it's loaded?"

He pressed the release. The wheel snapped open. Five bullets. The first chamber always empty, like I was taught.

"Pull them out. Careful."

He slowly plucked each bullet out and laid them in my hand. I dropped them into my pocket. "Safe?"

He nodded.

"Put the wheel back. James, I want you to know that I love you very much. I would do anything for you."

His wrist bent awkwardly as he tried to support the weight of the gun.

"I'm sorry I haven't been able to stop Kevin from picking on you." I touched his shoulder. "And I'm sorry I was mean to you last night."

"That's okay, Mom."

"It's not. But I realized something. Your dad was right. You shouldn't have to fight if you're smart enough. There's always going to be a bully around, so you have to figure out how to deal with guys like Kevin. You need to be smart. You need to be confident in yourself." I gave him a small smile. I felt awful for how I had acted. All this time, I had wanted James to trust and respect me. I screwed up. "Pick up the gun," I said. "This is how you aim."

I showed him the front and rear sights and how to center them. I told him to aim at the TV, the plant by the window, the fireplace.

"A gun is a very powerful weapon," I said. "Whenever you feel scared or vulnerable, I want you to remember that you know how to use a gun. That makes you a little more powerful. If you feel powerful, it's gonna come out your pores and everyone else will feel it too. I guarantee you that guys like Kevin will take a powder. And if it ever got more serious—probably never will—but if it did, you'll be the one left standing. I promise."

"Okay," he said in a small voice.

"In the meantime, stay out of Kevin's way."

He nodded and smiled.

"Now go get some sneakers on and go find your dad. We're going shooting."

He jumped up and ran toward the garage.

I picked up the shiny gun lying on the table. It was heavy like a brick. I loaded the bullets into the chamber with soft clinks. Today we would kick up rocks and look for snake holes. We'd eat salami sandwiches while sitting on boulders. Then I'd lean against the car and fire the gun, even though it might blow my arm out of joint. Casey would be able to shoot it on his own. James would have to wait. I couldn't support him the way my dad supported me. He'd be able to do it himself one day.

I walked out to the porch to check the sky. Blue. No clouds. Birds flapped between the trees. Just like in the commercials advertising the new housing developments. I held the gun behind me. Kids shouted up and down the street so I was careful not to let the shiny metal catch their attention. I leaned against the wall, the gun still at my back, my finger dusting the trigger. A boy playing in the street scooted in front of our house. He was throwing a football to some friends I couldn't see, but I could hear their shouts. He was a big kid with a hell of an arm.

"*Motherfucker,*" I mumbled. It was Kevin.

I watched him move, swagger. Not a care. I pulled the gun in front of me. I held it in my palms, adjusting it to catch the light of the sun. I bounced a few rays into Kevin's eyes. He glanced over, involuntarily. But the glance became a stare. I watched the recognition change his face, ebb his pride. He turned away and threw the football again. I shot another beam of light into his eyes. He struggled to catch the football. He looked nervously toward me. I held the gun up, so my message was clear. I nodded my head. I pointed my finger at the gun, then back to him. He swallowed. His friends shouted for him to throw the ball. He looked away and tossed it. If he looked back again, I was already gone.

MURDER IS ACADEMIC

BY FELICIA CAMPBELL

Mount Charleston

illicent Margrave, known affectionately to her students as M, an Associate Professor of Political Science, is sitting in Bagel Nosh on Maryland Parkway, a half-block from the university, reading the paper and licking the cream cheese off her pumpernickel bagel. It's 1984 and a serial killer stalks Las Vegas. So far, six women, ranging from their mid-thirties to late their late-forties, all writers and teachers, have been targeted. All have been smothered in black plastic bags. Each has had the thumb and first two fingers of her writing hand severed. The middle finger is placed in the victim's mouth, which is sewn shut around it, while the thumb and index finger are thrust up the vagina. They are otherwise not sexually molested. The last detail has not been made public. The little city of some 600,000 persons is in an uproar.

She is chilled by the account of the most recent murder, fully aware that she fits the profile of the victims, as she is well known for her high-profile, ultra-liberal writing. While her colleagues who want to pretend they are in the Ivy rather than the Cactus League look askance at her work as not traditional enough, her student following is as varied as the city's population, including, among others, mobster's kids, a couple of very savvy hookers looking more like Midwestern college girls than the campus's traditional coeds who delight in looking like hookers, and an assortment of ex-cons, with a sprinkling of current con men.

She acquired the ex-cons when the university in its infinite wisdom briefly decided that all ex-cons should report to a specific advisor who would keep tabs on them, and she had volunteered, angry that they should be singled out after they had paid their debt to society and fearful that some asshole who would make their lives miserable would be appointed. She is particularly fond of a couple of them who know her troubles with her dean, and pleaded to be allowed to teach him a lesson in the parking lot. "We won't hurt him. We'll just teach him to respect you." She refused, of course, but finds it neat that someone wants to look out for her. She's pleased when she looks up to see them approaching her table. Somehow they always seem to know where she is. The two Es, Ed and Earl, sit down in the empty chairs across from her and proceed to lecture her on her personal safety, particularly insistent that Moose, her giant mastiff, is not enough protection, and that she needs to buy a gun, a street sweeper preferably, which has so much fire power she can't miss and will turn whatever marauder is foolish enough to invade her space into hamburger. As ex-felons, they can't buy it for her, but they can help her pick it out. She promises to think about it.

The veteran of three marriages, one to a fellow political scientist, one to a casino pit boss, and one to a black activist, she is the mother of three grown children, one by each husband. Although her body has begun to thicken and she is no longer beautiful in the traditional sense, she is still striking and has lost none of her charisma.

"We're serious, Dr. M. We worry about you. You trust too many people," says Ed as he leaves. "We'll do our best to keep checking on you." She assures them that she will be careful and smiles as she waves for the waitress, thinking how sweet they are and how much more she likes them than her administrators.

Millicent Margrave thinks of herself as M and prefers to be called such. "Just call me M," she will say with a toss of her head. "That's the letter M, not Em as in Emily." She takes a certain delicious pleasure in identifying herself with James Bond's runner M. She loves the Bond novels, but thinks him something of a fuck-up.

She is an avid reader, too intelligent to ever subscribe to dialectic of any sort. She is in fact far too intellectually curious to do well in an insecure provincial university. That she is there at all is the result of circumstance. Chet, her first husband, finished his degree while she was pregnant and hadn't yet finished hers, and he managed to get hired at what was then semi-affectionately called Tumbleweed Tech.

The young campus was legendary for its faculty suicides. The acting dean who hired her ex in the '60s after a telephone interview had driven around and around the campus, then five buildings in the middle of the desert, for weeks, psychologically unable to get out of the car, eventually shooting himself in it in front of Grant Hall the week before their arrival. Chet's contract rather bizarrely noted that he was a replacement for Mary Ledger. Mary had finished herself off with sleeping pills and booze the previous semester. A new hire, a Shakespeare scholar, killed himself before arriving on campus, which she and Chet giggled was very efficient of him.

Before the first year was out, Chet had fled academe for the neon lights and run off with a change girl from the Silver Slipper, leaving M behind to cope. Desperate, the Political Science department offered to let her fill out his contract. Equally desperate, she agreed. Marco, named after Marco

Polo, was born and she settled into a routine of classes, diapers, and finishing her dissertation. As soon as she finished her doctorate, the department offered her a contract at eighty percent of what Chet had been making. She took it, and she's been there ever since.

Marco was two when M met Les Margrave, the pit boss. He seemed rather Humphrey Bogarty—she'd always liked Bogart, who always seemed to know what he was doing, *Casablanca* and all that—and two months later married him. Much to the surprise of what she called the M watchers, the marriage, both years of it, was a success. That she retained his name is a mark of that. Little Humphrey was born two months prematurely out of shock when Les was the innocent victim of a shooting in a convenience store robbery.

Grover, the black activist, was her next husband. Their marriage might have worked, she often thought, if he hadn't attempted to step into Les's shoes. They tried to make a go of it for three years. Lena was born, a beauty from her first breath, and M and Grover decided to call it quits before their fights ruined the children.

This succession of marriages served to alienate the self-righteous among her colleagues, who certainly outnumbered her friends. "They're afraid you are having a good time," Galen used to tell her.

An angular Canadian with a sharp wit and a vast store of knowledge, Galen had been her mainstay after she and Grover split. Her colleagues had been horrified when she married someone from the gaming profession. "She might as well have married a black," they whispered, the '50s not far behind them. But she was socially finished when she married Grover, their professed liberalism not extending to their peers. She'd have been finished at the university, too, if she hadn't pushed for tenure when Les was killed. Galen had shamed them into it. It cost him the chair when the vultures gathered after she married Grover, but he had never reproached her.

Galen was gay and, of necessity, in the closet, so the two of them entered happily into a conspiracy in which they pretended to be lovers, a conspiracy which protected both. Her kids liked him and the affair gave the vultures something to be liberal about. Truth be told, it would have been difficult for anyone observing their intimate laughter to tell that they were friends not lovers.

Leaving Bagel Nosh, M heads for her detested office. On the ground floor facing the quad, its huge windows make her feel vulnerable. Outside her door lurks Danny, the new kid in the department. She doesn't much like him. He moves oddly, halfway between a slither and a skulk, head tilted to one side. He seems to exist in black-and-white rather than in color. His students bitch about his classes and she thinks he probably isn't very bright.

"I hope you're being careful, you know, because of the murders," he half whispers confidentially.

"Don't tell me you think I'm in danger."

"Well, you do fit the pattern. I mean, you are a middle-aged woman and you are pretty well-known for your writing," he throws out, sidling to the door. She wonders if he's trying to freak her out or if maybe he's the murderer. After he leaves, she heads toward the mailroom.

"M, my dear." It's Raph, the drunken poet and one of her favorite cohorts on campus, calling from the depths of his cluttered office. He looks like the corrupt cherub that he is, dark curls falling around a baby face just beginning to blur from his excesses.

"What brings you this bright morning to this pustule on the ass of academe? This carbuncle on the posterior of education?" In rare form this morning, his voice rises, "This horripulation on the butt of phrontistery. This ingrown hair in the fanny of the athenaeum. This excoriation in the seat of learning," he ends with a flourish.

She drops a kiss on his curls. "You're cute. What's phrontistry?"

"A disparaging synonym for the educational establishment," he responds, the laughter leaving his face.

"What's wrong, Raph?"

"The Little Colonel has stabbed me with his julep stick, hoisted me with his own petard, a chicken bone I believe. In other words, my darling M, he has put me on notice that my performance is unsatisfactory, that I should have published at least another chapbook by now, and I am on my way out." Raph, née Raphael Waters, looks ready to cry.

"Why that miserable little fucker!"

The Little Colonel is their nickname for their mutual dean, Ned Chauven. Ferret-faced, stubby, arrogant, ignorant, and bigoted, he got his job through Vegas juice, the liquid that greases this city and elevates those who have it to positions for which they are unfit. He married the sister of a regent, and, to no one's surprise, was lifted from relative obscurity to the deanship after the death of good old Dean Longacre. He has been a worse tyrant than anyone could have imagined, applying a brutal form of publish-or-perish to those he dislikes. Truth be told, while Raph is a popular teacher, he has written very little in the past few years, maintaining that grading freshmen essays depleted his creativity and he shouldn't be required to publish.

"It's okay, Raph, We'll fight. He can't get away with it." For a moment, her fighting spirit emerges. "Why did he do it?"

"Do you want the real reason or the good one?"

"Both."

"Darla Port."

"Darla Port! The blond twit who used to be the Colonel's bimbo? No!" she gasped.

"Believe it, my dear M. She's finished an MFA in creative writing somewhere and had a book of poems published in some obscure place. It's called *ImPort*, would you believe, with all the revolting connotations that conjures up; ergo, he's letting me go for affirmative-action reasons. I'm being replaced by an ugly blonde! She's the only ugly bimbo I ever knew."

M grits her teeth over his sexism, but simply says, "Ah, good old affirmative action, the process by which the administration insures that there will be no equity for anyone. Remember how we fought to get an Affirmative Action Officer, then they hired that poor semi-literate ex–football player who sat around and looked terrified while they told him what to do?"

Realizing that she's late, she bids Raph goodbye and rushes to class.

Later that evening, she is sleeping fitfully, dreaming that she is negotiating her way down a narrow several-hundred-foot-high stairway with no handrails, leading to what looks like a food court on a beach, when she's blasted into heart-pounding wakefulness by the telephone. She'd fed Raph dinner earlier and they'd both drunk too much wine. Raph was reeling when he left, but she was too far gone to take his keys, so she let him go. She is losing her capacity to handle alcohol and she feels rotten.

"It's me," Raph is saying. "I'm in jail. You have to get me out right now!"

She fumbles for the light. "What's up—drunk driving?" A cascade of books from the nightstand hits the floor and her toe while she scrabbles for a pen.

"No, old traffic warrants, but there might be more," he wails. "Get me out of here!"

"Are you in City or County?" Awake now, her faculties working, she tells him to hang loose while she arranges bail.

"M," he whines, "they were really nasty, making noises like now that they had me, they might even look at me for the murders. I think they hate poets. Get me out of here!"

"Listen, Raph. They always hassle people. They're just messing with you. Don't answer any questions. This is crazy! I'll be there as soon as I can."

"M, I have to hang up. A bunch of guys are pushing me. They want the phone. You've got to help me!"

For a moment, she looks stupidly at the phone, now buzzing a dial tone, then drops it into its cradle. Cursing under her breath, not bothering to comb her hair, she drags on a pair of soiled khakis from the laundry basket, adds a Greenpeace T-shirt and sandals, checks in her purse for credit cards, and heads out the door for Main Street and Fast Freddie's Bail Bonds. She is really sick of taking care of people who can't seem to take care of themselves.

Fast Freddie, who she met in the days of her activism, is in the nature of an old friend and likes to deal with the *pahfessor*, as he calls her. He'll be able to find out what's going on and recommend a good lawyer. He's a Vegas character of the type mentioned before who always seems to be there when she needs one. From convicts to con men, they all love M and love to take care of her, all the while lecturing that she should never trust anyone like them, especially them, and should get rid of the losers who seem to surround her and want her to take care of them.

Like a Hopper painting, Main Street is deserted, a few neon signs illuminating the dark street. At first she thinks that she's missed Fast Freddie's, then realizes that an alien name is on the doorway. *Jennie Ledbetter, Bail Bonds.* Jennie is every inch a bondswoman.

About forty-five and heavily made up, clouds of metallic frosted big hair surround her suspicious face. She sports a pair of handcuffs painted on one fake thumbnail and a key on the other. She peers at M over her bejeweled half-glasses. "What can I do for you?" she sneers.

"I'm looking for Fast Freddie," M answers, and realizes that she must look like a bag lady in her unkempt clothes.

"Fast Freddie ain't here anymore. Maybe I can help."

"I used to know him. I liked him. I have a friend in trouble. I need his help."

Deciding M isn't worth her time, Jennie tells her that Freddie got in some trouble and sold her this place, but that he has a new one, Jack Be Nimble, further down on Main.

"There's a neon sign with a guy jumping over a candlestick out front. I don't get it, but you can't miss it. Tell the guy at the desk you're looking for Freddie. He'll know where he is."

Moments later, M drives past the Jack Be Nimble sign and has to make a U-turn to get back. Entering, she sees a heavy, bald black man sitting at the desk. He looks up. "Hey, it's Professor M," he says, smiling and rising.

It takes her a moment to rake Tommy's name from the bottom of her memory and adjust it from the elegant young man who used to escort her to get her spouse out of jail where he'd landed for civil rights protesting to this middle-aged stranger. Suddenly, the world comes into focus and she's grinning.

"It's great to see you, Tommy. A friend of mine is in trouble and I came to find Freddie."

"What kind of trouble?"

"He was picked up for traffic warrants tonight and told me they said something about hassling him for the murders. He's wimpy, and they were probably just rattling his cage. He's flipping out."

"Whoa, that's heavy. Any chance he's the killer?"

"Come on, Tommy, you know me better than that. What's up with Freddie?"

"He started drinking again and screwed up the accounts, so they stood on his hands for a while. He's okay now, but doesn't usually come in until about 9."

"I can't wait. This poor guy doesn't have a macho bone in his body. He's terrified"

"Is he a fag?"

"Not unless it's happened in the last two hours."

Tommy tells her to grab a cup of coffee from the pot in the corner while he checks on things. Staring out the window at the flickering shadows of Jack Be Nimble jumping on the pavement, she can't hear what he is saying, but his expression seems grim. She contemplates taking up smoking again, the seedy atmosphere seeming to require it, but changes her mind as Tommy says, "You're in luck, lady." She turns to hear, "The computer's down again, which means we may be able to spring him before they know what's happening, then you can get a lawyer to buy him some time. I don't know what they've got on him, but for some reason they screwed up and took him to City instead of County."

"Who shall I get?"

"Does he have any money?"

"You've got to be kidding. He's another professor. Just

got fired by the Little Colonel. Oscar Goodman is not in his league."

"So that Colonel shit is still around?"

"Some things never change, Tommy."

"I'll close up and we'll see what I can do with the boys in the lockup." He puts a *Back in twenty minutes* sign on the door and slides into the passenger seat of M's ancient Toyota.

"It seems like old times. What do you hear from Grover?"

"Not much. He writes at Christmas and sends a really weird present, like six months of the Fruit of the Month Club. He's crazy about Lena, who is absolutely gorgeous and in grad school in Tulsa, so he goes to see her a few times a year and helps with her expenses."

Tommy reaches over and pats her hand, white-knuckled on the steering wheel. "We're getting old, kid."

"Not only that, but we are here," she says, gunning the car up the parking ramp. They walk through the tunnel-like area from the parking garage, across the atrium with the dirty fountains that seem to spit old candy wrappers rather than water, through the doors on the other side, to the desk where the officer in charge looks at her like she is shit. She is momentarily startled until she remembers how she is dressed. A few words from Tommy and the cop quickly changes his expression to one of helpful concern.

For a moment, her old self surfaces and she wants to scream—but first spit in the bastard's face. Tommy's foot grinding into her instep reminds her to smile back.

"If you will just have a seat over there," the cop says, pointing her to the orange plastic chairs, "I'll have him for you as soon as I can."

Escorting her to the chairs, Tommy says, "I got to get back to the office. Bring him right to me. I'll try to have Freddie there when you arrive." He makes a fist and punches her gently on the arm, "Hang in, kid."

An endless hour later, Raph emerges looking like a wet chicken. She wants to kick him for being such a wimp. They must just have been harassing him with the serial killer bit. She forces a smile. "Hey, Raph, you can write an epic poem about this."

"Take me home, M."

"Not until we go to Jack Be Nimble's and straighten out your bail bond."

"Not now," he whines.

"Yes, now." Her voice drops and she speaks evenly, trying to hold back her annoyance. "You, sir, are in a shitload of trouble and you'd better pull up your socks and get ready to defend yourself. If you act like a victim, I guarantee you will become one. I will do what I can, but you have to care enough to help yourself. Now shape up!"

"But you don't know what it was like."

She can't believe that he is whining for sympathy. She is tired and sorry that she's come. His puffy face now reminds her of the young Peter Lorre in the old movie M.

"Bullshit!" she snarls. "Either grow up or I am going to send you back to deal with this yourself."

He puts on a hurt look, then opts for seriousness.

Seeing the expressions moving over his face, she has a moment of cold uncertainty. "Raph, did you do it?"

"Jesus, M, don't joke."

"I wasn't being funny. Why were they trying to finger you?" She pulls into a parking space in front of Jack Be Nimble's.

It is light now, and already hot. Incredibly tired, she wants only for this to be over. Raph and his problems are too much.

She's too old to be involved with the system like this. She doesn't want to play anymore.

Tommy is sitting at the desk. Freddie hasn't shown up yet and isn't answering his phone. Raph signs the appropriate papers. Naturally, he has no money, forcing M to drag her Visa out of her purse and sign for the thousand dollars bail, the ten percent that the bondsman gets up front. Ten thousand seems like a hell of a lot for traffic warrants. Her lips tighten as she thinks of the vacation she won't have. Her salary is a lousy $23,000 a year and she knows Raph will never pay her back. She tells herself that he's an innocent friend, that he's just inept and she shouldn't be so impatient.

Telling Raph to get in the car, she turns to Tommy. Catching him off guard, she is touched by the look of concern on his face.

"Let it go, lady," he says, "You don't need this."

"I know, Tommy, I know. And thanks."

Resisting Raph's pleadings that he is unnerved and wants to stay at her house, she dumps him at his dingy apartment. She hates his apartment. It's long and narrow, the only window a sliding glass door to the balcony at the far end that seems to let in no light. The Navajo white walls feel dirty even though they probably aren't.

She's dimly aware of the method to his madness. The apartment is an appropriate backdrop for the suffering romantic image that he wants to convey. His few friends hate the place, so he gets to go out a lot without reciprocating. Of course, the thin-thighed young women in his classes find him irresistible and the dinginess becomes a turn-on, which they describe endlessly to their more sophisticated friends, who don't envy their sitting on his floor listening to his poetry and drinking bad red wine.

She drives home unaware that he's beginning to see her as a defector. She's been smarter than to sleep with him, keeping their relationship on a strictly friendship basis, not trusting him the way she does her ex-cons and con men with whom she doesn't sleep either. She's never had any illusions about him, but has always liked him anyway. He makes her laugh and there aren't too many people around who can do that. She doesn't really see him as one of her stray pups, although outsiders might.

She tries to wrap her mind around the possibility that he might have committed the murders, but can't do so. The cops must have been just harassing him.

She doesn't know that as soon as she is gone, he leaves the apartment without showering, shaving, or changing clothes.

Neither does she know that, a couple of hours later, Martha Jones will open the door to her Paradise Valley condo and half skip to her Honda, grateful once more for her covered parking space. She's just signed a contract for her second novel and Continuing Ed has asked her to teach a creative writing course in the fall. The *Review-Journal* is going to do a story on her and all's right with the world. She's on her way to pick M's brains for an exotic locale for her next book and has no way of knowing that M is sleeping, having completely forgotten their appointment.

M's never paid any attention to Martha's looks. She is a hell of a neat person, smart, funny, and loyal, and great to be with, and M has always wondered why some man isn't smart enough to see what a great companion Martha would be. While she yearns for romance, she is truly an innocent, never having had a serious affair. It's not surprising then that her face lights up when she spots the man leaning on the pole next to her parking space, holding a picnic cooler. Everything else is going well. Maybe her luck in love will change too.

"Want to play hooky?" he grins.

For once Martha decides to follow a whim. This is a good day. M will just have to understand.

"What's in the cooler?" she asks.

"Goodies for you. You'll never in this world guess, so just wait until we get to Mount Charleston," he answers, getting into the passenger side of her car. "My wheels are in the shop. I had Findlay drop me here." He reaches over and turns on the radio, dropping his hand to stroke her knee. She gulps, but doesn't protest.

Once on the mountain, they have hiked almost to Cathedral Rock when he suggests a detour. There, in a secluded spot, he tenderly asks her to close her eyes for the surprise.

She leans against a tree and squints them shut, listening to him fumble with the cooler. Then she asks, "Can I open them yet?"

"Not quite."

The last thing she sees is his face distorted by passion as he forces her back, pulling the black plastic bag over her head. "Die, ugly bitch, die," he intones. Quickly performing the mutilations, he returns the bag and knives to the cooler, placing them under the sandwiches and plates, and takes the main trail down to the lodge where he has left his car earlier.

He enters the lodge, drinks a beer, eats some nachos, and then dumps the murder paraphernalia from the cooler into the trash.

Smiling, he makes the uneventful drive home to sleep.

It's 3:30.

At the same time back in Las Vegas, M wakes up from her nap realizing that Martha hasn't appeared. They were to meet here before deciding where to go for lunch.

Thinking she might not have heard the doorbell, M checks

outside for a note or some sign that Martha might have been there.

A shudder runs through her. Something must have come up. Even Martha can have something come up, she tells herself, pressing her face against the cool glass of the sliding door that separates her from the inferno outside.

By 4, after telephoning all over town, she is frantic about Martha but keeps telling herself to chill, that Martha is an adult after all. Finally, to take her mind off Martha, she reluctantly dials Raph's number to see how he is faring. There is no answer.

At 6, the doorbell rings. She opens it to Raph leaning jauntily against the porch pillar, holding a bunch of supermarket flowers and a bottle of cheap red wine. "Friends," he says, holding both out to her.

She stands aside for him to enter, more than a little annoyed at his boyish assumption that eight dollars worth of flowers and wine are recompense for what he has put her through in the last twenty-four hours.

As she makes no move to accept his offerings, he goes past her to the kitchen where he scrounges up a vase for the flowers, then reappears asking if she wants him to open the wine or if she wants something else.

"You're an ass, Raph," she says, unsmiling.

"Don't do this, M," he says, suddenly panic-stricken. "You are my best friend, my only real friend. I can't face this without you. I need your help."

"Where were you this afternoon, Raph?"

"I couldn't stand the apartment, so I drove to the lake, then I came back to see you."

"Why didn't you sleep? We were up all night." She can't understand how he looks so invigorated with no sleep at all.

"Come on, comb your hair and I'll take you to Chapala's for dinner."

Realizing that she is hungry, and feeling rather ashamed for treating a good friend this way, she shakes her head and smiles an acceptance. "I guess I'm too old for this sort of thing. In the old days, it would have made me wired like you. Hang on while I get ready."

From the bedroom, she calls, "It's been a weird day. Martha stood me up and I can't get her on the phone and no one's seen her. I'm worried about her." She emerges, purse in hand. "Did you hear what I said?"

"Oh, what could happen to old mud-fence Martha, the ugliest woman I've ever met?"

"You know, sometimes I really hate you," she says, locking the door after her.

He doesn't answer, but opens the passenger door of his Bronco, heaving the cooler into the backseat before she can get in. They drive the two miles in silence.

Seeing them arrive, Rosie, their favorite waitress, ushers them to their usual booth. They order margaritas before they realize how empty the usually buzzing restaurant is.

"Where is everybody?" asks M.

"It's the murders," answers Rosie. "Everybody is scared. I was afraid to stay at home so I came to work."

"Oh, come on," Raph says. "Who'd want to hurt a pretty lady like you? Nobody is hurting pretty ladies."

Rosie sashays off, unimpressed.

They drink one margarita each, then order another round, plus nachos. M goes to wash her hands, giving Raph a chance to slip some white powder into her fresh glass.

"Are you going to break down and get me a lawyer, pretty lady?" asks Raph when she returns, turning on all of his charm.

His hand hovers near her glass where he can accidentally spill it if she answers correctly.

"Raph, I can't. They don't really think you did it or I wouldn't have been able to get you out. I think you can do with a public defender. Some of them are quite good. We used to work with them a lot in the old days. Besides, I don't have the money. You're already into me for the thousand dollars bail, which I doubt I will ever see. Besides, it's time for you to grow up and take some responsibility."

"So that's all our friendship means to you, is it?"

"This is friendship. I'm neither your mother, nor your girl-friend. I have to take care of myself. You need to stand on your own feet, not mine."

"Then we will drink to friendship," he says, raising his glass in a toast.

She raises hers, takes a big sip, makes a face, and puts the glass down. "This doesn't taste right. Maybe I'll order a beer." She turns, looking for Rosie, and he quickly switches glasses.

"Mine's fine. Take another taste."

She does and it tastes fine. Thirsty, she drinks it too fast. She doesn't seem to notice that he isn't drinking. He signals for another round; making the switch back will be easy.

Rosie brings the drinks, but looks worried. She's never seen M overindulge and asks if she'd like some coffee. M blinks and nods. The drinks seem to have hit her and she feels very odd. She takes another sip of the original drink, which is now in front of her, and tells Raph that she thinks she should leave. She's had too little sleep and too much alcohol.

He partially supports her as they leave the chilled restau-rant for the inferno outside. With some difficulty she manages to get into the Bronco.

"I think you need a little walk," he says, heading across

Eastern Avenue into Sunset Park, ill lit and deserted at this time of night.

"I just want to go home," she moans, barely holding onto consciousness, but growing dimly aware that her survival depends on it.

"You told me to think for myself and I am. You know, you really aren't very pretty anymore. In fact, you're almost as ugly as old mud-fence Martha was." He drives to the center of the park. "Now, get out." He opens her door and she spills onto the ground, dead weight, feigning unconsciousness. He swears and drags her into the hidden area in the mesquite trees where some kids have built a fort. "I liked you once, but you leave me no choice," he mutters before going after the murder kit.

Placing the kit down next to him, he kneels over her inert form, unaware that they have been followed and that two figures are making their stealthy way toward him. He wonders if he should try to bring her back to consciousness, because it would be so much more fun if she were awake. He wants her to know just who she's been messing with.

"*Ding, dong, the bitch is dead,*" he sings under his breath and reaches for the plastic bag, when he feels the gun barrel on the back of his neck. Tommy clicks the safety off.

"You filthy, ungrateful little fucker. I ought to kill you right now, but you aren't worth going to jail for, so I'll just keep you here for the cops, who'll be here any second. On your face, hands behind your head! If you've hurt her, your time in jail will be very unpleasant."

The cops come and Tommy and Fast Freddie, two unlikely guardian angels, hand over their prisoner and take M home. When they arrive, Ed and Earl, are waiting outside the house and all troop inside.

"It's a good thing you've got this fan club," Tommy tells

her. "Ed and Earl have been tailing you since yesterday morning at Bagel Nosh. They followed you to Fast Freddie's and called after you left. They can't pack heat, so we agreed to come in if things got sticky, so here we are."

"God, I love you guys," she says tearfully, giving each a hug and peck on the cheek as they leave.

Later in bed, feeling like Dorothy in Oz, she whispers to Moose, "There's no place like home."

THE ROAD TO RACHEL

BY JANET BERLINER

Area 51

The mirror crack'd from side to side;
"The curse has come upon me," cried
The Lady of Shalott.
—Alfred Lord Tennyson

In Las Vegas, greed is king, the culture of anonymity is God, and ritual rules them both—except in the case of my friend Alex "Legs" Cleveland. Though a full-blooded Piute, he had refused to seek his spirit guide, declaring it to be nonsense. He carried no totems to the gambling tables, liked black cats, and walked defiantly under ladders. Upon the few occasions a minor doubt crept in, he pushed it aside as if it had a bodily presence and reminded himself that luck was what you made it.

Like today, he thought, leaning against the mirrored pillar that separated the elevator from the picture windows on the twelfth—thirteenth, really—floor of his high-rise apartment building. Today, luck would be making a few bucks on the ponies, enough to delight his latest chorine.

It was not for nothing that they called him Legs.

He watched the shuttle to Area 51's Groom Lake circle and head toward the Janet Airlines terminal. The morning sun caught its wings and highlighted the snow at the top of

Mount Charleston and the elevator dinged behind him. The doors opened and he saw a shadow reflected briefly in the mirrored column at his side.

Stepping toward the elevator, he turned to let the other passenger in, but there was no one there. Strange, he thought, lifting his leg to step inside. He stopped in midair like a dog at a fire hydrant and stared at the large, unconscious, bleeding man who lay awkwardly against the opposite wall.

Gagging, Legs pressed the emergency button. He called down to security and went back to his apartment. The man lived in the apartment above his, so it stood to reason that the cops questioned him closely. They said the man, who had bled out, was a research nut who kept a telescope trained in the direction of Groom Lake. Legs said, "Too bad," but said nothing about the shadow that had passed behind him in the foyer. He felt no need to get involved.

No longer in the mood to go downtown, he lay on the sofa he'd placed over the stain left by the suicide of the last tenant. The suicide itself didn't bother him, nor the fact that Vegas was the suicide capital of the world. But the dead man in the elevator was something else. He thought seriously about moving out of the Towers, but decided against it for the moment, at least until after Martin Scorsese came to town to make *Casino*. The director intended to use the entrance to the building in a key scene. As a self-styled talent scout and a resident of the building, Legs would have access. The opportunity to meet De Niro and Woods and stand near Sharon Stone's long limbs was irresistible.

Meanwhile, his last client had been a major flop. He owed money to his shyster attorney in Los Angeles, among others, and right now his only income was derived from making collections for his great-uncle Willie, the loan shark.

He looked at his watch. It was 4 o'clock.

Willie would be waiting.

"Way-Out" Willie Cleveland, whose given Piute name was Nattee-Tohaquetta, had hit town in the early '30s to play him some poker with the big boys. He played in small cardrooms until Wilbur Clark's Desert Inn went up, thanks to the Cleveland mob led by Moe Dalitz. On and off, he worked for Moe, and took to playing poker at the Desert Inn. On the day the poker room closed, as a private joke between them, he took on the name Will Cleveland and returned to playing downtown, where his poker career had begun.

On this day, November 16, 1999, Willie spread a winning hand and reached for the biggest pot of the day.

The players were not happy. "Not you again, Willie." "Gonna take it with you when you go, Willie?" "Gonna give it back to the Indians?"

The dealer tapped the top of his hand. "Uh-uh. I'll push 'em," he said, as if Willie didn't know the rules.

Willie grinned and started to stack his chips. He threw a handful at the dealer, who looked stunned. One chip, maybe two at the end of the day, but a handful?

"That's it for me," Willie said. "Deal me out."

The dealer called for empty racks. "See you tomorrow then."

"Nope. I'm done." Willie looked over at the chip runner, who took the three filled racks off the table, flashed on the first time he'd called her Monica, and did it again for old times' sake. "What's your moniker, girl?" he said.

"Moniker?"

"Hokay, Monica. One rack's for you. Cash me out and get Legs."

Legs, who'd brought his great-uncle downtown in good time to cash in his dinner comp from the day before, was in his "office" at the back of the sports book. He had collected the day's money and noted it in Willie's black book—loan sharking being his uncle's avocation. He was no ordinary shark. Sometimes he gave loans and washed them away; other times he had bones broken. It was all, he said, good clean fun.

Legs ambled into the cardroom, maneuvered his great-uncle and his wheelchair out onto Fremont Street, and looked down with some affection at old Way-Out Willie, who was possibly the shrewdest, most outrageously inventive player in town. He claimed to be 150 years old and his greatest pride was that he still had a good number of his own teeth.

Wondering if any of that was close to the truth, Legs took a cab to Willie's place later that day. It was a budget motel catty corner from the Las Vegas Convention Center and across the street from Country Club Towers. They ate what was left of Willie's deli sandwich in silence. When they were done, Willie belched and cleaned his teeth with his fingers.

"They'll be here for me at midnight," he said. "You won't be seeing me again."

"What the hell . . . ?"

"Quiet down and listen."

Legs made as if to zipper his lips as, for what indeed turned out to be the last time, Willie told him the story of his life.

Right before his thirteenth birthday, Willie was commanded by his father to leave home and search for his spirit guide. Handing him a carved pipe and a bag containing dried fruit of the peyote cactus, his father said, "Follow the dreams this brings you. They will lead you to your spirit guide. Do not return until you have found each other."

Willie looked closely at the pipe, ran his fingers over the

carvings, put the mouthpiece in his lips, and sucked. He heard a tiny whistle of air, a melody almost. Alone in the darkness, he filled the pipe, lit it, and took one short toke. He inhaled and waited for something to happen. It did nothing at all for him, so the following morning he packed a small bag with a few eggs and other provisions and bade his mother, his father, his sisters, and his uncle farewell. Happy to be getting away from his father's control, he headed through Paradise Valley in the direction of Walker Lake.

That night, the pipe warmed him and caused him to dream of walking with the Piute Nation from the Humboldt to the Carson. When he awoke, his feet took him first to Cottonwood Station and then to Carson Lake. Finally, when he reached Walker Lake, he made camp in a sheltered place where he could find easy fodder in the small weirs and damns, which diverted the fish from the main lake. Nearby, he found an edible grass containing a seed that was pleasant to chew and, when dried and smoked, induced new and different dreams.

Soon, he ran low on peyote and provisions and high on confusion. He felt lost and lonely and thought longingly of his family. The peyote had also increased his hunger. Thinking to allay his hunger with fish, he made camp behind one of the large scrub bushes that dotted the shores of the lake. He chose to sleep first and fish later. Perhaps, he thought, his spirit guide would come to him and he could head for home with the dawn.

His wish was granted, if only in part, when his dreams were interrupted by the poking head of so strange and hideous an animal that he was sure he had gone mad. What he saw looked like a giant sage hen, with its legs and neck devoid of plumage and incredibly distended so that it stood well over six feet. The feathers that covered its enormous body were an odd grayish-brown color. The good part was the gigantic egg, which he could see within his peripheral vision; the bad was that he could never go home again. He didn't dare lie to his father, nor could he tell him that this bizarre-looking creature was his spirit guide.

He pushed at the bird, such being what he presumed it to be. It skittered to one side, but made no attempt to fly. He would have understood if he'd known anything about ostriches. However, he did not, yet.

Thus began a lifetime of adventure for Nattee-Tohaquetta, who walked to Austin with his ostrich—the infinitely stupid beast having decided that he was her master.

Then came a stroke of good fortune. The boy met a lovely young woman by the name of Dora who took him into her heart and unto her bosom, settling him at her place of employment—the larger of Austin's two whorehouses.

The years passed quite happily for Willie, or Natty, as the girls called him in those days. He became for them a mascot of sorts, mostly because of his diminutive size. He did not threaten them, nor they him, and on his sixteenth birthday they took it upon themselves to initiate him into manhood in the pleasantest of fashions.

Dora, in particular, pleased him. To his delight she felt the same way and they became a couple. She, of course, continued plying her trade, but she pleasured him on the side and, in what free time she had, taught him the skill of reading. One of the first books he chose to read was on the subject of ostriches.

His newly gained knowledge led him to his first and possibly most unique money-making idea. He would buy more ostriches and breed them for their skins, their feathers, and their meat. Thus, Willie's Ostrich Farm and Whorehouse was born.

Legs motioned to show that he had a question.

"Go ahead," Willie said. "Make it fast."

"Were those ostriches mean, Uncle Willie?"

Willie laughed. "Mean and stupid. Kick a man to death right easy for no given reason."

Legs zippered his mouth and Willie continued. He was happy, he said, until one gloomy day his ostrich conspired to lead her fellows away from Willie's Farm and Whorehouse and onto the road that led from Austin to Belmont. Like some kind of revolutionary army, sixty-three strong, the ostriches crouched down upon the road and took occupation, leaving Willie no longer the owner of an Ostrich farm.

"It made no never mind to me," Willie said. "I was tired of them stupid critters and wasn't worried none about them being turned into steaks. Them buggers sure could run. Forty miles an hour sometimes. I knew they'd be okay. Knew my guide would keep an eye on me, anyhow."

Willie proposed to Dora that she go with him to Las Vegas. When she showed no interest, he split the money from the sale and suggested she buy a house where she could ply her trade or not, as she pleased. They said a tearful farewell. When he reached Las Vegas, he settled into the life of a gambler as if he had been born to it.

He stopped to catch his breath and asked Legs for something to drink. Legs poured one for each of them. He was awed by Willie's stamina. Though physically frail and confined to a wheelchair, the old man remained a guy to be reckoned with. He had become someone to whom knowing was everything, yet he felt no need to share his knowledge.

He played poker every day, in ostrich-leather boots, a cowboy hat with an ostrich feather in the band, and a huge turquoise bolo around his neck. Mostly, he enjoyed the camaraderie and the inherent respect he was given as the oldest local at any table.

He enjoyed winning, but those other things, like the knowing, were even more pleasing to him. Having driven for the mob, he knew where the bodies were buried. Hell, he'd even helped bury some of them. He knew the answer to the mystery of Union General John C. Fremont's lost cannon, left behind somewhere around Walker River, and knew the secret of Tahoe Tessie, the monster in the waters of Lake Tahoe.

Best of all, he boasted to Legs, he knew for a fact about some of the mysteries of Area 51. He told no details, named no names, except to warn Legs cryptically to stay off the road to Rachel.

"Time to close the circle," Willie said to Legs that night. "Time to push the money to the pigeon at the table so they'll have sommit to push to me." He tapped his bulging wallet. "This here plus what's in your mattress is half yours. Fifty big ones for you, fifty for our people."

He reached for the hat he had placed on the floor next to his chair, rubbed the hatband as if for luck, and handed it to Legs.

"Put on the hat," he commanded, "and give me my black book."

Legs did as he was told. Willie ripped the notebook into small pieces. Legs felt like crying; Willie held outstanding markers from God, Satan, and half of the population of Las Vegas.

"Any questions before I go?" Willie asked.

"Go where?" Legs asked.

"They're coming to get me."

"They who?"

"You don't need to know. Take me outside. Wheel me to the 7-Eleven and leave me there."

There were times Legs wasn't any too fond of the old man, but this was inhuman. "All you need is a nap," he said.

"The man upstairs and I had a chat, and it's time for the big dirt nap."

"What about your spirit guide? You gonna take him with you?"

"Don't mock him," Willie said. "He'll do what he does. Probably stick with you, I imagine."

Legs laughed.

"You don't disrespect him, now." Willie sounded dead serious. "You make him mad, he'll do you." He leaned back and closed his eyes. "You give our people their money, you hear?"

"What if I keep the cash?" Legs asked, parking Willie's chair outside the 7-Eleven.

"You'll be knee deep in shit," Willie said. "Ostrich shit."

Sure, Legs thought. He would run right over to the reservation and hand over fifty K. Not. Sitting at the slot machine closest to the door of the convenience store, he watched a white Jeep Cherokee pull up to Willie. A tall, slender woman in camouflage coveralls got out and wheeled the old man up to the back of the truck. Someone inside must have opened it up and let down a ramp. Willie was wheeled onto it and lifted into the vehicle. The door shut behind him. As the Cherokee pulled away, Legs caught a glimpse of a small decal of an ostrich on the corner of the rear window.

And Willie was gone.

Legs missed the old man, but his sense of loss was easily salved by having money to burn. He paid off some of his debts, bought a car and a new wardrobe, dated high-maintenance women, and ate only in the best of restaurants.

He also gambled. Badly.

A week before the movie company was due to film at the Towers, he was down to the second fifty thousand and rethinking his position on luck. Driven to do something, he visited a guy best known as the Chinaman to ask his advice about how to change his luck. He had to pay up front.

After much careful thought, the Chinaman told him he had to rid himself of the evil spirit of a big ugly animal, which was in close pursuit. "You see him, you smash his soul," the Chinaman said.

"I do that how?" Legs asked.

The Chinaman's advice was simple. Legs had to cover every surface of his home with mirrors. In that way, he could smash the image of the hovering spirit in the mirror and thus destroy its soul. "One, two, you crack mirror and creature turn into nothingness."

Legs lost a thousand dollars that night. Deciding that he could do worse than take the Chinaman's advice, he hired a workman to do the job.

"Done." The workman laid down his tools and took out a pack of cigarettes. He held them up, as if asking permission to light one.

Legs nodded and poured a drink with a none-too-steady hand. "Inspection time," he said.

They walked around his Country Club Towers apartment, with Legs intent on examining every surface. Mirrors now covered each one, including the refrigerator handle, the faucets, the toilets in both bathrooms. Satisfied, he opened a fireproof box full of cash and paid the rest of his tab.

When the workman left, he stood for a moment and surveyed his territory. He'd long since cleaned what he could of the old blood hidden under the sofa where the poor prior tenant had offed himself; what remained of the last fifty grand from Willie was in the fireproof box.

Everything was copasetic.

"There's no way that vindictive son-of-a-bitching ostrich guide is going to get me now," Legs said out loud.

By now, the filming of *Casino* was drawing to a close. Legs had managed to finagle an invitation to the wrap party and was admiring himself in the new living room mirror when he saw a large shadow behind him. Without missing a beat, he picked up one of the bricks he'd lined up in readiness and threw it at the image.

The mirror fractured into a thousand pieces.

"Got you," he said, figuring he now owed the Chinaman another stack.

He called the man who had installed the mirrors and offered to pay him double if he fixed the damage right away. After he had let the guy in, he put on his late Uncle Willie's cowboy hat and went downstairs to join the crew and whoever else showed up. One of the cameramen recognized him and offered him a drink. As he reached out for it, fire alarms ripped through the early evening and the party was over. It was a small fire, on his floor.

A cop tapped him on the shoulder. He turned around and saw that it was the same one who had interviewed him about the body in the elevator.

"I remember you. It's Cleveland, right?"

Legs nodded. "Where's the fire?"

"Fire's out." He pointed upward. "That your apartment? Number 1201?"

Legs nodded again. "Can I go up there?"

"I'll take you. Gotta question you anyhow."

The apartment was gutted, but the fireproof box filled with

cash was intact. The mirror man lay on the floor facedown.

"Smoke inhalation," the cop said. "We're waiting for the coroner. Know anything about him?"

"He installed my mirrors."

"Was he a smoker?"

"Yeah," Legs said.

The cop turned to greet the coroner, who examined the body, then turned it over. There was blood underneath and two odd-shaped holes in the man's stomach.

"Looks like he was kicked by some big-ass mule," the cop said.

"Can I go now?" Legs asked. "I don't have a mule."

"For now." The cop looked at him as if he were examining a roach. "But don't leave town. Where can I find you?"

"Horseshoe," Legs said. "I'll get a room."

He'd been playing on the Strip since Willie had left. This time, he picked up his box of money and rode a bus downtown. His plan was to put his money in the cashier's cage at the Horseshoe, play a little hold 'em, eat a late-night steak at the coffee shop, and get a player's rate for a room. His warm welcome in the poker room was followed by repeated questions about his Uncle Willie.

"How's old Willie?" "Where's old Willie?" Even the waitress at the coffee shop asked, "Where's the old boy?"

Tired of the questions, Legs said brusquely, "How should I know? He's dead."

Lying on his bed in the small hotel room, Legs tried to figure out why his life was overflowing with dead bodies. He stared at his uncle's hat perched on top of the television set. "It's your fault, you old bastard," he said.

Too tired to get himself a woman and disinterested in watching TV, he thought back to Nattee-Tohaquetta—alias

Willie Cleveland—and his last night in Las Vegas. He didn't sleep any too well but he did wake up with a plan, something to clear his head. He would rent a convertible and drive out into the desert where the last of *Independence Day* was being filmed. The location was in Rachel, a small town in the middle of nowhere, five or ten miles from Area 51. Willie had warned him to stay away from there, but what the hell. Maybe he'd meet someone interesting, maybe not, but at least there wouldn't be any bodies with strange holes in them or cops who thought he was a killer. Tomorrow he'd get back to business, start looking for new clients, maybe even make a plan to take what was left of Willie's fifty K to the reservation.

One thing he knew for sure: He'd had enough of Country Club Towers. He should have known it would be a place of bizarre happenings, with its strange architecture—off-kilter walls, a swimming pool that got no sun, and a tennis court that got no shade. The owner was old and very rich. His trophy wife was a tough broad from south Texas who ruled the place like an army sergeant. Despite being one of only four high-rises in Vegas, there were always empty apartments. The trophy wife moved tenants around until she had emptied the whole penthouse floor, which had its own elevator and locked entry. The entire floor was given over to pimps and prostitutes.

Not that Legs had anything against them. It was the dead bodies he could do without.

Top down, radio on full blast, he dug out the rest of a joint he'd hidden at the bottom of his wallet. He followed it with a candy bar he'd picked up on his way out of the Horseshoe. The sun was shining, the top was down, and he felt good until he glanced in the rearview mirror and saw what looked like an unmarked cop car. He pulled over to let it pass, but it pulled over with him.

Careful to maintain the speed limit, he veered onto Highway 375, which would take him to Groom Lake Road. The street was gravel but not unpleasant to drive on. After about twelve miles, with the cop still behind him, he swerved to the right down a narrow unmarked road. The car behind him made a U-turn, but Legs kept driving. A mile or so down, he saw what looked like a very large animal lying across the road. He started to circle around it, then planted his foot on the brake as a white Jeep Cherokee like the one that had taken Willie came hurtling toward him.

There was nothing he could do but watch.

The Jeep screeched to a halt. The same tall woman stepped from the passenger side, holding a gun in her hand. A man, also dressed in camouflage, stepped out of the driver's side, walked over to the animal, and kicked it. Legs didn't know much about weapons, but the pistol in the woman's hand looked real enough. Too late, Legs realized that these people were Camo Dudes who patrolled Area 51. He didn't have a camera, so most likely they would simply ream him out and hand him over to the Lincoln County Sheriff's Department.

"Ostrich is dead," the man said. "Told you he wouldn't make it to the road, not after what I shot into him." He looked at Legs. "Dead as you'll be if you don't do what you're told."

"Move over," the woman said, getting behind the wheel of Legs's car.

"I . . . uh . . . uh . . ."

"We know who you are, Mr. Cleveland."

"How . . . ?"

"We figured your uncle might have told you a little too much about our business. Know what I mean?" Her laugh was harsh.

The man roped together the legs of the dead ostrich and looped it around the bumper of the van.

"Hope you're into ostriches, Mr. Cleveland," the woman said. "Dumb creatures. With Willie gone, someone's got to take care of them."

Twenty minutes down the road, the van pulled up in front of a huge barn, barricaded by a wide iron bar. The man removed the bar and Legs was shepherded inside. Corralled in the middle was a large flock of ostriches.

Legs closed his eyes, prayed for the cop who had been following him, and promised God that if he got out of this, he'd give Willie's money to the Piutes right away. He'd never gamble again, never drink, never—

"Okay, Mr. Cleveland," the woman said. "In you go. Our soldiers have been restless. Your job is to calm them down so that they do what we need them to do. Maybe later, if they don't kill you, we'll show you some of our other brigades. Noah knew what he was doing when he saved the animals."

She handed him a key to the paddock.

"See you later, if there's anything left of you to see," the man said, and he and the woman walked out of the barn.

Legs heard the bar falling into place and felt the warm trickle of urine down his legs.

Moving to the far corner, he hunkered down and tried to control his fear. The ostriches looked calm enough to him. Most of them had their heads buried in the sand. The rest milled around in an almost listless manner, nudging each other occasionally. They were huge creatures, with small heads, long thin legs, and bodies that must have weighed three hundred pounds. Telling his story, Willie had said that his ostriches had marched away like a revolutionary army but never attacked unless provoked and that their brains were smaller than their eyes, which were none too large.

Maybe, Legs thought, he could find a way to free them,

but what was the point if they killed whoever they'd been trained to kill? Or if they killed him.

Either way, it seemed to him, he was a dead man.

He was still staring at the birds when the barn door re-opened. The man stood back while the woman, who had changed into a pair of short-shorts, came toward him. She held a large syringe in her right hand. Praying it wasn't meant for him, he said, "You got some pair of legs. Get me out of here and I'll make you a star." He squinted at the name tag attached to the collar of her shirt. "Ava. Perfect. Why would you want to be here when you could be a headliner?"

"You're a funny man, Mr. Cleveland." She came closer.

"Legs," he said. "Call me Legs."

"All right, Legs. Let's talk. What did Willie tell you about his work here?"

"Nothing."

"Nothing? That's hard to believe."

"Believe it."

For a moment the woman was silent. Legs figured he had nothing to lose by asking what was it they were doing to the ostriches to turn them into killing machines and why they were doing it. He was as good as dead anyway. Might as well know what he was dying for.

"Willie told you nothing?"

"Nothing."

"Tell me something, Mr. Cleveland. Legs. Do you also have an ostrich spirit guide?"

Legs shook his head. "I don't believe in that stuff."

She looked at the syringe in her hand. "He did. It kept him safe in there."

Legs could feel the sweat running down his neck. "What did he do here?" he asked again.

"He worked with the ostriches. Taught us about them."

"Why?"

She held up the syringe. "He wanted to live to be old and keep his own teeth. There was a price to pay and he paid it."

It was all Legs could do not to reach out and knock the syringe out of her hand. "I don't mind false teeth," he said.

She laughed.

"Those dead men at the apartment . . ." Legs began.

The woman waved at the ostriches. "Our first real experiment."

"But why frame me, and how did you get the beasts out of there?"

"No harm in telling you, I suppose. They disintegrate when the job is done. As for why you, why *not* you? There's always got to be a mark. If we let you go back, you'll be up for murder."

"I'll tell them—"

"What? That we're training an army of killer ostriches? You've got to be kidding. It's called a rock and a hard place, Mr. Cleveland. Work for us the way Willie did and we'll cover for you. Don't, and we'll let you pick between those animals in there and the Las Vegas Metropolitan Police."

"How much time would I have to spend here?"

"As much as we say."

In his mind, Legs heard old Willie telling him to stay off the road to Rachel.

Now that he had disobeyed, he saw only one realistic possibility open to him: He would work on Ava, which wouldn't be the worst punishment in the world. She did have great legs, and who knew, maybe she could sing.

ABOUT THE CONTRIBUTORS

PRESTON L. ALLEN is a recipient of a State of Florida Individual Artist Fellowship in Literature and the Sonja H. Stone Prize in Fiction. He is the author of the Miami-based thriller *Hoochie Mama* and the award-winning short story collection *Churchboys and Other Sinners*. His latest novel is *All or Nothing* (Akashic Books, 2007). He lived in North Las Vegas, near Nellis Air Force Base for a brief period of time in the '90s.

Robert Fleck

JANET BERLINER is the Bram Stoker Award–winning author of six novels, including *The Madagascar Manifesto* trilogy with George Guthridge. She is the editor of six anthologies, including two with illusionist David Copperfield, and one with Joyce Carol Oates. In more than thirty years in publishing, Berliner has also worked as an editor, agent, ghostwriter, teacher, and lecturer. Born in South Africa, she now lives in Las Vegas while she plans her escape to the Caribbean.

Anna Reid-Taylor

FELICIA CAMPBELL has trodden the mean streets of both Las Vegas and UNLV for more years than she cares to admit. A professor at UNLV, she has gained international attention for her pioneering work on the positive aspects of gambling and risk taking. As a book critic, she gave weekly reviews on KNPR for over twelve years. Currently, she is executive director of the Far West Popular and American Culture Associations. She is also editor of the *Popular Culture Review*.

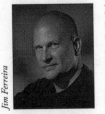

Jim Ferreira

DAVID CORBETT is a former private investigator with considerable case experience in Las Vegas. He is also the author of three critically acclaimed novels: *The Devil's Redhead,* a finalist for Anthony and Barry awards; *Done for a Dime,* a *New York Times* Notable Book and a Macavity Award finalist; and *Blood of Paradise,* named one of the top ten mysteries and thrillers of 2007 by the *Washington Post* and a *San Francisco Chronicle* Notable Book. For more information, visit www.davidcorbett.com.

Chamutta Tanchanpongs

BLISS ESPOSITO was born and raised in Las Vegas, where she learned the intricacies of the gaming world. She writes about the hidden side of the city, the details below the glitzy surface. She recently earned an MFA from UNLV in creative writing.

Wendy Duren

TOD GOLDBERG is the author of two novels and the story collection *Simplify,* winner of the Other Voices Short Story Collection Prize. His long-running column in the *Las Vegas Mercury,* "Cheap Wisdom," garnered three Nevada Press Association Awards and his writing appears regularly in *Las Vegas City Life,* the *Los Angeles Times Book Review, Jewcy,* and *E!* He teaches creative writing at the UCLA Extension Writers' Program and in the MFA program at UC-Riverside.

Harry T. Moran III

JAQ GREENSPON lives in Las Vegas and has been writing professionally for over twenty years. He has been read widely on several continents and has had the pleasure of seeing his words mangled by professional actors on a number of TV shows and film sets. In Lithuania he is like a god.

Billy Logan

JARRET KEENE is the author of two poetry collections, *Monster Fashion* and *A Boy's Guide to Arson,* as well as the unauthorized rock-band bio *The Killers: Destiny Is Calling Me.* He has edited several books, including *The Underground Guide to Las Vegas.* His primitive post-apocalyptic black-metal band Dead Neon promises to crush your soul.

Charlotte Mausolf

LORI KOZLOWSKI was born and raised in Las Vegas. A journalist and a published poet, she is a graduate of the University of Southern California's Master of Fine Arts Writing Program. Her first book is about the Mafia. For more information, visit www.lorikozlowski.com.

Keith Kaplan

CHRISTINE MCKELLAR is a resident of Las Vegas and a freelance writer. She is the author of three novels: *A Port of No Return, The Shadows of the Sea,* and *The Devil's Valet.*

Piquera

PABLO MEDINA was born in Havana, Cuba. He is the award-winning author of ten books of poetry and prose, most recently *The Cigar Roller: A Novel* and *Points of Balance/Puntos de Apoyo*, a bilingual poetry collection. He is the recipient of fellowships and grants from numerous organizations, including the Rockefeller Foundation, the National Endowment for the Arts, the Lila Wallace–*Reader's Digest* Fund, and the Cintas Foundation. He teaches at the University of Nevada, Las Vegas.

Erin O'Brien

JOHN O'BRIEN was born in Oxford, Ohio in 1960 and graduated from Lakewood High School in 1978. He had several jobs, including busboy, file clerk, and coffee roaster, but writing was his true career. He began in 1987 and wrote up until his death on April 10, 1994. O'Brien committed suicide by gunshot two weeks after learning that his novel, *Leaving Las Vegas*, was to be made into a movie. Two more of his novels were published posthumously: *The Assault on Tony's* and *Stripper Lessons*.

Anne Yard

SCOTT PHILLIPS is the author of three of the most highly acclaimed crime novels of recent years. His debut novel, *The Ice Harvest*, was a *New York Times* Notable Book of the Year and won a California Book Award. Its follow-up, *The Walkaway*, continued his success, with the *New York Times* calling it "wicked fun." His third novel, *Cottonwood*, was published by Ballantine. Phillips has spent enough time at the poker tables in Las Vegas to know what works and what doesn't.

Ibarionex Perello

NORA PIERCE is the author of the critically-acclaimed novel *The Insufficiency of Maps*, a selection of the Barnes & Noble "Discover Great New Writers" program. She is currently in residence at the Cité Internationale des Arts in Paris, and at work on a new novel. She teaches writing at Stanford University, where she was formerly a Wallace Stegner fellow. She has a love/hate relationship with the Nevada desert, and was once millimeters (millimeters!) away from a million-dollar jackpot.

Kerry Davies

TODD JAMES PIERCE is the author of three books, including the novel *A Woman of Stone* and the short story collection *Newsworld*, which won the 2006 Drue Heinz Literature Prize. He is an assistant professor of English at Cal Poly State University in San Luis Obispo, California.

Melynda Nass

JOSÉ SKINNER'S *Flight and Other Stories* was a finalist for the Western States Book Award for Fiction. He worked as an English/Spanish translator and interpreter in the criminal courts of New Mexico before earning his MFA at the Iowa Writers' Workshop. His fiction has appeared in *Boulevard, Colorado Review, Witness, Bilingual Review,* and the anthology *In the Shadow of the Strip: Las Vegas Stories.* He currently teaches creative writing at the University of Texas–Pan American.

CELESTE STARR is a male-to-female transgendered escort based in Pahrump, Nevada. "Dirty Blood" is her first published story.

Cody Boor

VU TRAN was born in Saigon and grew up in Tulsa, Oklahoma. He is a graduate of the Iowa Writers' Workshop and was a Glenn Schaeffer Fellow at the University of Nevada, Las Vegas, where he currently teaches creative writing and literature. His stories have appeared in *The O. Henry Prize Stories,* the *Southern Review, Glimmer Train, Harvard Review,* and many other publications.

Also available from the Akashic Books Noir Series

BROOKLYN NOIR
edited by Tim McLoughlin
350 pages, trade paperback original, $15.95
*Winner of Shamus Award, Anthony Award, Robert L. Fish Memorial Award; finalist for Edgar Award, Pushcart Prize

Brand new stories by: Pete Hamill, Arthur Nersesian, Maggie Estep, Nelson George, Neal Pollack, Sidney Offit, Ken Bruen, and others.

"*Brooklyn Noir* is such a stunningly perfect combination that you can't believe you haven't read an anthology like this before. But trust me—you haven't. Story after story is a revelation, filled with the requisite sense of place, but also the perfect twists that crime stories demand. The writing is flat-out superb, filled with lines that will sing in your head for a long time to come."
—Laura Lippman, winner of the Edgar, Agatha, and Shamus awards

LOS ANGELES NOIR
edited by Denise Hamilton
360 pages, trade paperback original, $15.95
*A *Los Angeles Times* Best-seller

Brand new stories by: Michael Connelly, Janet Fitch, Susan Straight, Héctor Tobar, Patt Morrison, Robert Ferrigno, Neal Pollack, Gary Phillips, Christopher Rice, Naomi Hirahara, Jim Pascoe, and others.

"Akashic is making an argument about the universality of noir; it's sort of flattering, really, and *Los Angeles Noir,* arriving at last, is a kaleidoscopic collection filled with the ethos of noir pioneers Raymond Chandler and James M. Cain."
—*Los Angeles Times Book Review*

NEW ORLEANS NOIR
edited by Julie Smith
298 pages, trade paperback original, $14.95

Brand new stories by: Ace Atkins, Laura Lippman, Patty Friedmann, Barbara Hambly, Tim McLoughlin, Olympia Vernon, Kalamu ya Salaam, Thomas Adcock, Christine Wiltz, Greg Herren, and others.

"The excellent twelfth entry in Akashic's noir series illustrates the diversity of the chosen locale with eighteen previously unpublished short stories from authors both well known and emerging."
—*Publishers Weekly*

D.C. NOIR
edited by George Pelecanos
384 pages, trade paperback original, $14.95

Brand new stories by: George Pelecanos, Laura Lippman, James Grady, Kenji Jasper, Jim Beane, Ruben Castaneda, Robert Wisdom, James Patton, Norman Kelley, Jennifer Howard, Jim Fusilli, and others.

"[T]he tome offers a startling glimpse into the cityscape's darkest corners . . . fans of the genre will find solid writing, palpable tension, and surprise endings."
—*Washington Post*

MANHATTAN NOIR
edited by Lawrence Block
257 pages, trade paperback original, $14.95
*Two stories selected as finalists for EDGAR AWARDS

Brand new stories by: S.J. Rozan, Jeffery Deaver, Lawrence Block, Charles Ardai, Carol Lea Benjamin, Thomas H. Cook, Jim Fusilli, John Lutz, Liz Martínez, Maan Meyers, Martin Meyers, and others.

"A pleasing variety of Manhattan neighborhoods come to life in Block's solid anthology . . . the writing is of a high order and a nice mix of styles."
—*Publishers Weekly*

BALTIMORE NOIR
edited by Laura Lippman
294 pages, trade paperback original, $14.95

Brand new stories by: David Simon, Laura Lippman, Tim Cockey, Rob Hiaasen, Robert Ward, Sujata Massey, Jack Bludis, Dan Fesperman, Marcia Talley, Ben Neihart, Jim Fusilli, Rafael Alvarez, and others.

"Baltimore is a diverse city, and the stories reflect everything from its old row houses and suburban mansions to its beloved Orioles and harbor areas. Mystery fans should relish this taste of its seamier side."
—*Publishers Weekly*